HARD SUN

ALSO BY J. B. TURNER

Jon Reznick Series

Hard Road

Hard Kill

Hard Wired

Hard Way

Hard Fall

Hard Hit

Hard Shot

Hard Target

Hard Vengeance

Hard Fire

Hard Exit

Hard Power

Hard Duty

Hard Lights

American Ghost Series

Rogue

Reckoning

Requiem

Jack McNeal Series

No Way Back

Long Way Home

J.B. TURNER

HARD SUN

A JON REZNICK THRILLER

This is a work of fiction. Names, characters, organizations, places, events, and incidents are either products of the author's imagination or used fictitiously. Any resemblance to actual persons, living or dead, or actual events is purely coincidental.

Published by Thomas & Mercer, Seattle

www.apub.com

EU product safety contact:
Amazon Publishing, Amazon Media EU S.à r.l.
38, avenue John F. Kennedy, L-1855 Luxembourg
amazonpublishing-gpsr@amazon.com

ISBN-13: 9781662527395
eISBN: 9781662527388

Cover design by @blacksheep-uk.com
Cover image: © Collaboration JS / Arcangel Images; © Jan Miko / Shutterstock

Printed in the United States of America

To my wife, Susan

Port de Sóller, Mallorca

Three minutes to midnight. Target en route.

Frederick Hicks chewed nicotine gum and peered through the eyepiece of the night vision scope attached to the Siyavash sniper rifle. The rifle rested on a sturdy tripod, Hicks's finger on the trigger. Window wide open, he looked out over a stretch of water, down to the secure naval base opposite. Six hundred and thirty-three yards away. Perfect line of sight.

He was watching and waiting in the dark, stifling attic at the top of an abandoned cliffside house. His position was set back in the room, hidden from sight.

Hicks searched the intended target area. The base was mostly used as vacation accommodation for members of the Spanish military. His weapon, a clone of the M40, was fully loaded with a five-round magazine.

He checked that the fine lines of the reticle's crosshairs were in sharp, algae-green focus. A uniformed man in the naval base's gatehouse was smoking a cigarette, checking his watch.

Hicks felt his T-shirt sticking to his sweaty skin. He had done his homework. He had already zeroed the sights. He had calibrated his rifle scope. But since his position in the attic was marginally steeper than expected, looking down on the target, the adjustment had been slightly less than the previously calculated firing solution.

A multitude of factors, also including the bullet's trajectory and windage, had to be taken into account.

His preparation had begun three days earlier. In near-identical nighttime conditions, at isolated cliffs on the north side of the island, he'd practiced shooting through a Garmin Pro Chronograph. The device had given the ballistics calculations for the muzzle velocity. Over and over again, he'd shot, with the same Siyavash rifle, six hundred and thirty-three yards, from an elevation of five degrees down to the target area.

Hicks did one final check of the ballistics meter. It gave real-time atmospheric readings. Humidity ninety-two percent, temperature of seventy-seven degrees Fahrenheit, and a wind speed that had dropped to only four miles per hour left to right.

Hicks, like any experienced long-range shooter, knew the importance of having the correct dope; shooter shorthand for "data on previous engagements." He obsessed about attention to detail. It was vital to understand all this information to determine how much drag would be on the bullet. The ballistics meter also calculated the bullet drop over the distance and the estimated wind correction. The technical portion of every shot was making a correct wind call. But to compound matters, getting an accurate wind reading inside a room, and at night, increased the difficulty.

When Hicks had slipped into the abandoned house the previous night, he had ascended to the attic and begun to do the final readings. He'd rechecked the data each and every hour until zero hour.

Hicks chewed the gum hard. He was ready. The line of sight was perfect. His earpiece buzzed into life.

"Target approaching. Two minutes ETA."

"Copy that."

Hicks saw lights approach outside the base, adjacent to the marina. He tracked three SUVs as they slowly approached the gates. The convoy came to a stop. A few moments later the gates slowly opened. The cars drove through onto a deserted parade ground.

He studied the first SUV as two plainclothes Civil Guards climbed out. Then the third SUV, bringing up the rear. Finally, he focused on the back door of the second SUV. *The target vehicle.*

The door opened.

A thickset, silver-haired, elderly man, Luis Muroz, climbed out wearing glasses and a short-sleeved white shirt and jeans. He was smiling. Hicks recognized the face from the surveillance photographs taken three days earlier. He held his breath, finger on the trigger. The target was in the crosshairs.

Hicks squeezed the trigger, and the recoil jolted hard. The noise in the enclosed space, even with the suppressor, temporarily deafened him. He watched as the old man fell to the ground, as if in slow motion, blood gushing from the gaping wound in the center of his chest. Security men rushed toward him, panicked, looking around to find out where the shot had come from. The target was not moving.

One shot, one kill.

Hicks collapsed the tripod and placed it in the large backpack at his side, along with the rifle. He carefully picked up the shell casing, dropping it into the bag. Zipped it up. He walked through the abandoned house, leaving through a side door. He climbed on his bike, strapped on the backpack, and began pedaling down the steep hill toward the port.

He turned into a narrow side street and cycled for a couple hundred yards along a dimly lit, narrow road, not far from Repic Beach.

Hicks braked beside a white van parked on scrubland. He got off the bike, took out a key, and opened the back doors of the van. He lifted the bike into the rear, shut the doors, locking them tight, before climbing into the driver's seat.

Hicks took off the backpack, leaned over, and pulled back the passenger seat, exposing a hidden compartment. He carefully placed the backpack into the space before slamming the seat into an upright position.

Then he started up the van and pulled away slowly. He steered away from the port, heading out of town, on through the illuminated Sóller tunnel, the adrenaline of the assassination finally kicking in.

One

Rockland, Maine

The silhouetted figure strode along the breakwater toward him.

Jon Reznick watched as the beam from the lighthouse picked out the spectral shadow. The man walked carefully, deliberately, along the granite slabs as the cold waters crashed against the breakwater. Standing on the shore, watching them, were two other figures, one with binoculars pointing right at Reznick.

Reznick's senses were alert as the man approached. He was packing his Beretta. The man got closer. A paunchy, middle-aged white guy, dragging hard on a cigarette. It took a few moments for Reznick to recognize him. A man he had met only a couple of times before.

The man was Daniel Black, and he worked for the Agency.

Black threw his cigarette in the water. "It's been a while, Jon."

It was nearly a year since Reznick had last seen Black. The senior CIA clandestine officer had helped him out in Los Angeles. A Mexican cartel boss and Hezbollah money-launderer had been brought down, in no small part, by Reznick's efforts. Black had pulled some strings, ensuring the LAPD hadn't taken things further, despite Reznick leaving a trail of bodies in his wake.

"I hope I'm not disturbing you," Black offered.

Reznick smiled. "Just a little."

The CIA man turned and looked out over the dark waters of Penobscot Bay. "Before you ask, I know I wasn't invited here."

Reznick stared at him.

"Hope you don't mind me dropping in unannounced. First time I've been up here. I like it. Better air than LA, that's for sure."

"What do you want?"

"I'd like to talk."

Reznick valued the peace and serenity of his late-night walks along the breakwater. A time to reflect. A time to clear his head. "So talk."

"I've got a proposition."

"I don't know . . . I've got a few things on."

"You need to hear me out."

"I'm kinda busy."

"You don't look busy to me."

Reznick closed his eyes and breathed in the fresh, salty air. He enjoyed his downtime. The chance to unwind and get away from it all. But Daniel Black's arrival signaled that all that might be about to change. "What's really on your mind, Daniel?"

Black got out a pack of cigarettes. He carefully took one out and slipped it into the corner of his mouth. He lit up, inhaling hard. "I was talking to Martha Meyerstein yesterday," he said, putting the packet and lighter back in his jacket pocket. "I believe you knew her during her FBI days."

Reznick knew her very well. He had worked on numerous classified operations with Meyerstein over a number of years, called in to assist on highly sensitive investigations. "How is she?"

"Martha? She's good."

"She's no longer with the FBI, Daniel."

"That's right. I met her in DC. She's giving lectures in Washington on national security, geopolitical issues, domestic terrorism, radicalization. She's taken to her new life like a duck to water. Doing talks for students, NGOs, government intelligence agencies. Very highly thought of. She sends her regards."

"Daniel, I'm not a big fan of small talk. Why are you here?"

"I wanted to speak to you face-to-face."

"Why?"

"We've got a little problem in Europe. It's a thorny issue."

"What kind of issue are we talking about?"

"National security, what else? It's what we're all about, right?"

"And you want me to do what exactly?"

Black dragged hard on the cigarette, staring off across the dark waters. "You know how it is."

"No, I don't know how it is. But I'm guessing it's not good."

"Basically, yeah. Here's the thing. We've got a serious problem. There's an issue that needs to be fixed. And quick. We're talking something that could be exploited by foreign powers. But also, it's an issue that might prove embarrassing for any number of people in this country and abroad. If that's not enough, the CIA is in the dark."

"That's all very vague."

Black chuckled. "I can tell you more. What do you say?"

Reznick felt conflicted. He desperately wanted to take a vacation. He had imagined a week down in the Lower Keys, assuming no hurricanes were blowing through. Maybe a week or two over in Italy. Maybe a month island-hopping in the Mediterranean. He had even contemplated heading to Jakarta to visit his daughter. "I don't know."

"We need you. This is not up for discussion. That's what I've been told."

Reznick twisted his mouth. "Why is it not up for discussion?"

"It's time-critical. We need your skills. Level of experience. But it means we need you on the ground in less than forty-eight hours. You either do it or we're out of here."

"Isn't there anyone else?"

"There is."

"But?"

"But we want you. *I* want you. I recommended you."

Reznick turned and looked out over Penobscot Bay, the silhouetted birds in flight, swooping low over the water. "I need to know more. A helluva lot more."

Black glanced back down the breakwater toward the two guys still watching them.

Reznick asked under his breath, "They work for you, Daniel?"

"Yeah, they're good."

"If they're good, why not send them?"

"Jon, we need people who've been around the block. I need results. And that's why I came all this way."

"I don't know."

"Listen, can we talk somewhere else?"

"No one around to hear us, Daniel."

"Just one-on-one. Private. How 'bout a drink?"

Reznick sat in the back of the SUV beside Daniel Black on the short journey to his house on the outskirts of Rockland. He wondered what exactly Black wanted him to do in Europe. What was the urgency? He expected this was to do with Mexican cartels opening up new channels in Western Europe.

Black kept his eyes focused ahead. "I believe your daughter is working for us in Jakarta."

Reznick glared at Black. "I don't talk about my daughter or her work. Ever. That's a red line. Do you understand?"

"I understand. I have a daughter. She's a major-league pain in the ass."

"Why's that?"

"I split up with her mother eighteen months ago."

"Sorry to hear that."

Black shrugged. "Nature of the job. Away ten months of the year. Not conducive to a home life."

"What's your daughter doing, if you don't mind me asking?"

"I don't know."

"You don't know? What does that mean?"

"It means I don't know. She doesn't tell me. Last I heard she was in Paris, shacked up with an Albanian jazz musician. You believe that shit?"

"Jesus."

Black sighed. "He's a self-declared Maoist."

"He sounds like a barrel of laughs."

The SUV rambled down the rutted, bumpy dirt road that led to Reznick's home, built by his father when he had returned from Vietnam. The vehicle pulled up sharply outside the house, leaving clouds of dust in its wake.

Reznick got out first, followed by Black. He turned around. "Your two pals want to join us?"

"Just me and you, Jon. If that's alright."

"They want coffee?"

"They're fine."

Reznick unlocked his front door and turned on the lamps.

"Nice place," Black said.

"It's quiet. I like quiet."

Reznick walked out the back door to the rear deck, overlooking Penobscot Bay. Lightning bugs buzzed around in the humid night air. Waves crashed onto the rocks below.

Black surveyed the scene. "I like it here. I could get used to this."

"You still hanging around LA?"

"Mostly Europe now."

"You like Scotch?"

"Are you kidding? Damn right I like Scotch."

Reznick went inside, picked out a bottle of Laphroaig single malt from his drinks cabinet, and a couple of cut-glass tumblers. He went outside and pulled up a seat at the wooden table on the porch. He poured a healthy measure for each of them and handed a glass to Black, who was already sitting.

Black pressed his nose into the top of the glass to catch the peaty aroma of the amber liquor. "Now we're talking." He raised his glass and clinked it against Reznick's. "Good health, my friend."

Reznick took a swig of the Scotch. "What's on your mind? And where exactly are you based these days?"

"My territory is Europe. Southern Europe. My focus is on Spain."

"You're pretty far from home then."

"Last time we met you were in LA, right?"

"That was crazy."

Reznick's mind flashed back to the previous year, when an ex-Delta pal, Angel Ramos, had been murdered by a drug cartel. "It was challenging. But we got the bad guys."

"*You* got the bad guys. I saw what you did. I saw it play out in real time. And remembering that got me thinking."

"Got you thinking about what?"

"Who would be a good fit for a complex operation in Europe? What you did in LA was why I thought of you."

Reznick sipped his Scotch, the liquor warming his belly. "I'm listening."

"I reread your file. It said you were in Mallorca a few years back. That interested me even more."

"Why?"

"You got a feel for the terrain. You were in Cala San Vicente, right? And you were hooked up with Mac, the former SAS operative."

Reznick nodded. "Correct."

"I know that operation was hushed up, obviously. You hunted down a renegade American special ops medic who nearly killed Martha Meyerstein."

The memories flooded back. The explosion on the boat that Martha Meyerstein had been a guest on. A meticulously planned operation by a deranged former US Army special ops medic with a grudge against Reznick, who had several years earlier foiled a bid by the same crazy to kill the President. "Tell me what you want. And I'll tell you if I can help you."

"We've got a real problem, Jon. The analysis points to state-level actors pulling the strings."

"Daniel, spit it out."

"Three days ago, a man, a retired Spanish intelligence operative, was assassinated. He had operated at the highest level in Madrid, based for several years at NATO headquarters in Brussels. He was also the former head of the secret police under Franco."

"That's quite a résumé."

"His name was Luis Muroz. And he was assassinated, if you can believe it, when he was within a Spanish naval base on the island. But the shooter is believed to have hit him long-range."

"So he should have been safe inside the base?"

"Correct. The barracks are used, these days, mostly for accommodation for naval or army personnel enjoying a cheap vacation. The base's full name is the Military Residence of the Navy Tramuntana."

"So they thought Muroz would be secure until he was transferred, I'm guessing?"

"No question."

"How was he killed?"

"Sniper took him out."

Reznick sipped his single malt, listening intently.

"It hasn't been reported in the press. It hasn't been reported anywhere."

"That's interesting. So a media blackout?"

"Correct."

"What else?"

"The naval base is located in a small, sleepy town in the northwest of the island. Port de Sóller. Only a few people knew he was being moved there."

"Which probably tells us that the shooter had access to some degree of inside knowledge."

"We don't know for sure. It's too early to say. But that's the working assumption. It's a fucking mess, Jon. I won't lie to you. Whoever did this may have penetrated encrypted communications within Spain's intelligence community. Maybe even within NATO itself."

"Why was he taken to the base in the first place?"

"There was internet chatter about leftists wanting to kill him for still being free after all these years. He was a Falangist. Nationalist. Authoritarian—some might argue fascist. He was linked to tortures and disappearances. And he was on social media and podcasts for years, calling for a return to those days. Vehemently anti-immigration. So Spanish intelligence moved him before he could be harmed. They wanted to interrogate him. Find out exactly what he knew."

"So, there's chatter about leftists . . . do we know who else might be in the frame?"

"We can't rule out Basque separatists. Perhaps ETA. But they put down their weapons years ago."

Reznick nodded.

"Besides, their MO is car bombs. Shootings at close range from motorcycles. That kind of thing. What happened to Muroz looks like a carefully planned, carefully calibrated operation."

"Which leaves?"

Black sipped his whisky and looked off into the distance. "Honestly? We just don't know. And that's the problem."

"Wait. Are you seriously telling me the CIA doesn't have a clue who did this?"

"Swear to God. We're working with the NSA and the Spanish Civil Guard and their intelligence agencies, and they seem to be at a loss as well."

"I'm not buying it."

"You're not buying what?"

"Your answer. I don't believe you don't know who it is. Maybe you don't know for sure, but you must have an inkling."

Black stared off into the darkness for a few moments. "I wish we did. That's why we need your help."

Reznick knocked back his Scotch as Black did the same. Then he poured them both another large glass and handed Black his drink.

"Thank you."

"It's all very interesting, Daniel. But how could I possibly help? My skill set is tracking down and neutralizing a target. You don't have a target. You need to give me something. Anything. Tell me more about the man who was killed."

"Muroz? He held many state secrets. And that's what's causing so much concern inside the Agency and the Pentagon."

"He held many state secrets? For what purpose?"

"Perhaps for leverage. Blackmail. What we believe is that Muroz may have been killed for the simple reason that he held many classified secrets on powerful people. Spanish politicians, the Spanish royal family, European industrialists. Covert sex tapes. Hundreds, maybe thousands, of hours of recordings of bugged calls, bugged apartments, bugged restaurants. Video footage. It's mind-boggling."

"You think someone powerful wanted him out of the way?"

"We can't rule it out. But my best analysts don't believe it. Only a handful of people knew the tapes even existed. We didn't hear about them until recently."

"So, was he a control freak?"

"Muroz? No question. We have reason to believe he recorded every meeting he'd had since the mid-sixties."

"I'm guessing someone would pay a lot of money to get their hands on those tapes."

"You would get a treasure trove of state secrets. Any nation state would kill for that. And I mean that."

Reznick sipped his drink, catching a faint buzz from the liquor. "You like this stuff?"

"Love it." Black eyed the lights of some fishing boats out on the water. "What are you thinking? Any reservations?"

"Here're my thoughts. There's more to these secret recordings than European businessmen and Spanish intelligence intrigue, right?"

"Correct."

"What are we talking about? You need to tell me straight. American state secrets?"

Black shifted in his seat but held his tongue.

"Your silence is very telling, Daniel. That won't cut it for me. I need to know what you know or you can count me out. Are there American interests here? And if so, precisely what are they?"

Black still stared out over the water. "This can't go any further."

"I know the drill."

"Covert recordings of American politicians, some very well known in the 1960s and 1970s, three vice-presidents, and four former directors of the CIA. Some of it very damning, I believe."

"That changes the equation somewhat. How are you only hearing about this now?"

"The NSA intercepted an encrypted message sent from a Civil Guard intelligence officer to his boss in Madrid. He mentioned that Muroz was dead. But the officer also said that a source had heard rumors that Muroz had boasted about the covert recordings. And there were names."

"American names?"

"Well, the name David Rockefeller was mentioned. He was tight with the CIA at the time. Also mentioned were former CIA directors Richard Helms and William Colby."

Reznick whistled as he heard the names of the most powerful American intelligence operatives since the Second World War. "And what was so sensitive that we need to get our hands on the recordings?"

"I believe there were discussions in the CIA and some foreign intelligence circles pertaining to concerns about anti-American Falangists taking over after Franco died. That was a recurring concern in the 1970s. And even into the 1980s."

"So American secrets over decades. Cold War stuff, right?"

"It's got the potential to be a nightmare if it falls into the wrong hands. It will expose duplicitous American foreign policy across Europe. There were military and economic threats against friendly nations if they didn't crack down on student protests, believing they were fronts for Russia. Widespread surveillance on American citizens living and working in Franco's Spain. But there are other things that need to remain secret, even after all this time. Bottom line? We need to get our hands on whatever this guy recorded. All of it. And that includes, we believe, recordings of Russian foreign ministers within their embassy in Madrid, restaurants in Barcelona, and on walks in parks. Decades of them."

"Where are all these tapes and footage stashed?"

"That's the thing, we don't know."

Reznick threw his head back. "Come on. What the hell is this bullshit, Daniel? What the hell does that mean?"

"Muroz's home was raided, pulled apart. They weren't there. There was nothing."

"Buried somewhere?"

"Maybe. But someone got to him before the Spanish could interrogate him."

Reznick peered out over the dark waters beyond. "Which appears to suggest that Madrid's intelligence has been compromised. Maybe by a state actor. Maybe a spy. Maybe a sleeper cell working for a foreign government."

"It's something we've considered."

"Is there anything else you're not telling me, Daniel?"

"The intercepted message we have from Madrid indicates that information pertaining to a former director of the CIA, who became a politician, might be among the recordings."

Reznick knew exactly who he was talking about. "That's very cryptic."

"We're the CIA."

"Let me ask you something. Is this just a way for the CIA to clean house?"

Black said nothing.

"It is, isn't it?"

"Maybe."

"Do you think it is?"

"It doesn't matter what I think."

"I need a name."

"If I had to hazard a guess, I would say that the name might be related to the Warren Commission and around that timeframe."

Reznick knew that the Warren Commission had been set up to investigate the assassination of JFK way back in 1963. "Someone who was on the Warren Commission? Are they mentioned in the tapes?"

"Most certainly."

"Allen Dulles? Former director of the CIA? Pal of Rockefeller, right?"

Black took another sip of Scotch, then peered into the glass.

"Bottom line, Jon, we're concerned these recordings will fall into the wrong hands. By that I mean Russian, Iranian, or Chinese intelligence agencies could learn about the spy networks we laid down decades ago. Assets we put in place. That are still in place. We can't have that."

"Why can't the Spanish just find out where the tapes and recordings are?"

"That's why they pulled in Muroz in the first place."

"Are you seriously telling me the Spanish don't know where the tapes are?"

"Correct. They had heard some mention of these illicit recordings."

"And now the CIA doesn't know where the tapes are either?"

Black winced.

"How in God's name will I be able to find them if the Central Intelligence Agency can't? You're not giving me anything. And I don't know who targeted Muroz, so I don't know who to target."

Reznick shook his head. "How the hell will I be able to find a haul of covert recordings no one knows the whereabouts of? Are you kidding me?"

"I think you can do this."

"How?"

"You need to figure it out. Someone got to a retired intelligence agent. A foreign power is our best bet. That's where you come in."

"That doesn't explain why this guy Muroz was neutralized."

"Maybe for what he said. He was a hate figure for immigrants from North Africa in particular. Maybe some foreign intelligence service was concerned that this guy was in possession of these secret tapes and didn't want them released. We really don't know for sure. Maybe he was going to sell them to the highest bidder."

Reznick struggled to process what was being asked of him. "I still don't get it. What exactly is the real purpose of this mission?"

Black shifted in his seat. His voice was nearly a whisper. "It's twofold. First, we want you to find and safely retrieve the secret recordings."

"That's not what I do, Dan."

"I know. But that's part of our request."

"I don't fucking do requests."

"You can figure this out."

"But we don't know where the hell they are! Why not get your defense attaché in Madrid to do it? Try and get him to figure it out. Why not get an extraction team put in?"

"Extraction team? No. We don't want the Civil Guard or anyone knowing we're aware of the recordings."

"Spain is in NATO, right?"

"Yes."

"We already share intelligence with them, right?"

"To an extent."

Reznick closed his eyes for a moment. "I don't think I'm the right person."

"Jon, with respect, I disagree. This is not about our personal feelings, man."

"I don't have any personal feelings about this guy or his beliefs. Not interested."

"This is also not about one dead former intelligence operative. It's not about a guy involved in kidnappings, killings, and disappearances. It's about our country. The United States. National security is at stake! That's what this is about."

Reznick glared off into the distance.

"These are American secrets that, if they fall into the wrong hands, could be devastating. Sowing seeds for our enemies at home and abroad."

"Devastating for the CIA?"

"Maybe. We need those tapes."

"So what about the defense attaché?"

"I don't know if I should tell you this."

"Tell me what?"

"Two days ago, our defense attaché was on his way to the island. Intel suggested the tapes were buried under Muroz's patio."

"And were they?"

"No. A Civil Guard technical team scanned the concrete using ultrasonic pulse echo. It came back negative. No anomalies."

"So is the defense attaché still on the island?"

Black shook his head. "He arrived in Palma on a private jet, checked in to a hotel in the city's Old Town. But almost immediately he sensed he was being followed."

"There was a tail?"

"A woman and two men. We believe the attaché has been compromised in some way. Someone had advance notice of his movements and plans. Tracked since he left the embassy in Madrid."

"Spanish intelligence?"

"Correct. They're desperate to get the recordings. Former presidents, members of their royal family, it's all on those tapes. They thought that by bringing their retired spy into safe custody they could simply interrogate him and find out where he put this trove."

"So what about the defense attaché's replacement?"

"It's all politics, Jon."

"What the hell does that mean?"

"The State Department thinks the replacement is too young. They have liaised with the Agency on this matter in the last twenty-four hours. The talks have taken place at the highest levels within the State Department and the Agency."

"And what was the outcome?"

"They want you. *I* want you."

"Why?"

"Plausible deniability—why do you think? You don't work for the Agency. You don't work for anyone."

Reznick groaned. "Daniel, gimme a break. What the hell is this crap?"

"Jon, I wouldn't be here if I didn't think you were the right person for the job."

"You want me to be a bag carrier, is that what you're saying? Find some tapes and haul them out of the country?"

"I believe the way you operate, what you know, how you deal with threats—aligned with the technical expertise of Trevelle Williams—is a perfect fit for this operation. You're the best there is. You were the guy that tracked down the former CIA intelligence officer selling secrets to the Russians. You found him and neutralized him."

Reznick nodded.

"Besides, you come highly recommended."

"By who?"

"Former Assistant Director Meyerstein. With you and Trevelle on this, I believe both of you can figure this out."

"Figure this out? It's not a jigsaw puzzle."

"You know what I mean."

"The question is, why do you want someone with my skill set? The NSA and CIA should be able to get in, get out. The CIA station in Madrid should be more than capable."

"It's politics, Jon. Spain is a friendly country. We don't want to go in with a full team and show contempt. That would be . . . diplomatically speaking . . . problematic. We need all the friends we can get in Europe right now. As it stands, there are two military bases in Spain where there is an American military presence. We don't want to jeopardize that in any way. Besides, if we thought it was straightforward and we knew where those recordings were, we would have gotten them by now."

Reznick felt his shoulders tensing up, a familiar feeling. "So we don't know where the tapes are. We don't know who this assassin is. Anything else I'm missing?"

"I need an answer from you first, before I go further. Will you do it?"

"I think you're holding out on me. Spill it!"

"Very well. I want you to know the main reason I'm here. I want you to find out who did it."

"You said that."

"Then you kill him."

"How the hell am I supposed to neutralize the target if I don't know who or where he is? You guys usually provide at least that basic level of intel."

"We don't have that."

"This is bullshit, Daniel. How am I going to track that guy down if you can't? It's a mess."

"I'm not arguing. But we have our reasons."

"Tell me this . . . you're one hundred percent sure this is a national security issue?"

"Absolutely. No question about it."

Reznick closed his eyes for a few moments.

"I need to know one way or the other," said Black.

"When do you need an answer?"

"Now."

Reznick searched for Black's entourage. He found them mostly hidden about fifty yards away. They were good; but he was better.

"Do you have other plans?" Black asked.

"Me? No, but I was thinking about a vacation to Europe."

"So what's it going to be? I need to get back to the Deputy Director of Operations within the hour."

"You want me to neutralize the shooter?"

"Essential. Think of your country. You in?"

"Fuck it. I'm in."

Two

The following evening, Reznick caught the red-eye United flight from JFK to Palma de Mallorca Airport. He had a row to himself in business class. He enjoyed a glass of champagne, knocked back a couple of Dexedrine, and put on his noise-canceling headphones. He opened his iPad and listened to an audio file of a hastily compiled CIA dossier on the assassinated retired Spanish intelligence agent Luis Muroz.

Muroz, he learned, had been an eighty-eight-year-old veteran of the Social Investigation Brigade—Franco's secret police. A man feared in left-wing circles for his brutal interrogation and torture methods, including savage beatings with batons, mock hangings, waterboarding, cigarette burns, and cuts and slashes from razor blades. His reputation for protecting the brutal reign of Franco was unsurpassed. His victims had included journalists, writers, philosophers, university professors, workers, students, union organizers. Also leftists, communists, homosexuals, Marxists, anarchists, Jews, Catalan nationalists, and immigrants. Muroz was notorious for the political repression of and torture of any opposition to Franco. All had either been jailed, beaten, kidnapped, or just disappeared.

This had happened during the multiple states of emergencies from the 1960s to Franco's death in 1975. Muroz had also led the scheme in the early 1970s where up to three hundred thousand babies, born to poor working-class mothers, or born out of wedlock, were kidnapped from hospitals across Spain and given to devout Catholic mothers. Their biological mothers were told that the children had died, when in fact they had been taken away by nuns.

Reznick read on, horrified. Muroz was not surprisingly known to have been on the hit list of various left-wing terrorist groups in the 1970s, including the Red Brigades, but also the Baader–Meinhof Group in West Germany. He had also been a top target of ETA, the Basque separatists, who had killed one of Muroz's closest aides within the Social Investigation Brigade in the late 1960s.

Reznick shut down the iPad and took off his headphones when he was served his dinner and a second glass of champagne. After he had finished eating, he continued his research. He learned that Muroz had narrowly escaped death when his colleague, who had borrowed Muroz's car while his boss was undergoing cataract surgery, was blown up. Even after he retired in 2001, as Black had mentioned, Muroz had remained a controversial and hugely divisive figure in Spain. He had been given a million-euro advance to write his memoirs, and moved to a sprawling villa in Port de Sóller, on Mallorca's rugged northwest coast, overlooking the Mediterranean. His book, when it was published, revealed much of his role in Franco's secret police and across the intelligence community. But nowhere in his memoir did he mention that he had also been covertly taping VIPs, politicians, industrialists, CIA directors, Russian intelligence operatives, even European royalty, for decades. He had filmed interrogations of political opponents, too. A rumor about the stash of covert audio tapes and surveillance video footage had first emerged when an old friend of Muroz, dying of lung cancer, told his son about the treasure trove of intelligence

Muroz had acquired over the decades. He wondered if Muroz had intended to sell it to the highest bidder.

A few years back, Muroz had been signed by a celebrity speaking agency in Madrid. He was paid ten thousand euros to give a thirty-minute talk on geopolitical security risks to senior managers in tech. The move had sparked outrage across Spain.

Reznick finished listening to the dossier when the flight was halfway across the Atlantic. He asked himself who could have organized the assassination. The list of groups who had grudges or nursed long-held grievances and wanted vengeance for Muroz's crimes was long. He imagined myriad political terror groups who were still active; Islamists, and even foreign states, would have liked to neutralize Muroz too. He finished his champagne and felt himself falling into a deep sleep.

When Reznick was awoken for breakfast, light streamed into the cabin as they entered Portuguese airspace. He opted for freshly squeezed orange juice, black coffee, and a bacon sandwich. It was nearly two hours later when the plane touched down on the island of Mallorca.

The doors of the plane were opened, and a blast of boiling hot air, like an industrial hairdryer, filled the cabin. He put on his sunglasses and ambled down the steps into a vortex of heat.

Reznick and the rest of the passengers were escorted through a security door at Palma airport. Inside, it felt marginally less oppressive but was still way too hot, as if the air-conditioning wasn't working properly, his T-shirt already sticking to his back.

Reznick slunk through security with his fake passport under the name William Nader. He took off his sunglasses so his face could be biometrically analyzed. He had been told by Daniel Black that the NSA and CIA had already tweaked the US-designed software of Spain's border security so he could walk through, his real identity undetected.

Then he headed out of the sweltering terminal and into the fierce heat outside, waiting in line for a cab. A few minutes later, a taxi pulled up. He sat up front beside the driver, backpack at his feet, grateful for the cool air-conditioning blasting in the cab.

Reznick gave the driver an address.

"Not a problem," he said. "You from America?"

Reznick nodded.

"I would love to go to America," the driver said excitedly. "I want to go to New York."

"It's a tough city. What's wrong with Mallorca?"

"Mallorca is wonderful. But there is not enough work. I only work for five good months of the year if I'm lucky. May to September for the tourists. But I need to work all year round. It's not enough."

"Best of luck with New York. Make sure you have plenty of money before you head over there. It ain't cheap."

The driver nodded. "I guess so. Thank you for that advice."

It was a thirty-five-minute journey to the port town on the rugged northwest coast of Mallorca.

Trevelle Williams had booked Reznick into an Airbnb apartment overlooking Port de Sóller's main promenade and beach, directly above an artisan coffee shop. Reznick knew Muroz had lived on the outskirts of the town, in an exclusive area above the traditional enclave of Santa Catalina, previously the fishermen's part of town.

The cab pulled up, and Reznick handed the driver a hundred-euro note. "That's too much, American."

"Keep it."

"Very kind, thank you."

"If you make it to New York, you'll need every cent you can get."

Reznick got out of the cab with his backpack and suitcase. He walked up to the apartment building's front door, which was next to a tiny bar. He entered a four-digit code into the security keypad. The door clicked open, and he climbed an airless stairwell, hauling his suitcase and backpack.

He entered the same code on a keypad outside the apartment. Inside, the space was flooded with natural light, with fabulous views out over the beautiful cobalt water of the bay, yachts bobbing on the water. He felt grubby after the long flight. He quickly showered and changed into fresh clothes. A white linen shirt, jeans, and black Asics sneakers, as well as a Barcelona soccer hat he had bought at JFK.

He picked up his backpack and put in his iPad, military-grade binoculars, and headphones, along with two small bottles of water from the refrigerator, then his fake passport in a zipped side pocket.

Reznick felt another blast of heat as he stepped outside. He wanted to get his bearings in the small town and have a look around. He turned right down the promenade and strolled past a boutique, a gift shop, a coffee shop, and a couple of nice hotels. In the distance, he saw a sign for the naval base, which was located behind a high fence at the far end of the port. Reznick wanted to get up close and see the exterior of the base for himself.

He heard an old, trundling, orange-painted tram jolting along the tracks as it passed by on the seafront on its journey from the inland town of Sóller. The tram was crammed with tourists, taking photos, selfies, leaning out of the open windows. After they disembarked at the port, the tourists spread out along the promenade and many crowded toward the marina, gift shops, bars, and coffee shops.

Reznick walked on past souvenir shops, another upscale boutique, a cool-looking café, a bank, an art gallery, a couple of restaurants, and several bars with tables full of old Mallorcan men sitting, watching the world go by, smoking, drinking beer or coffee.

He continued on past the marina, past yachts with flags fluttering for the European country they were registered in. He counted Germany, Britain, France, Holland, Denmark, Portugal, and, of course, Spain. More smart restaurants fringed the far side of the marina.

Finally, he reached the unremarkable gatehouse of the naval base, which was set behind a low wall with a chain-link fence on top. Cameras high up inside the base were checking the comings and goings through the main gate.

Reznick explored the entrance, noting the gate that Muroz had been driven through only a few nights earlier. He assumed reconnaissance had been carried out in the area around the base—either the sniper or another operative, as he'd surely been working as part of a team. The shooter must have had technical backup in order to know the precise movements of Muroz.

Reznick suspected the computer systems of the Civil Guard had been compromised. Muroz might have been under surveillance for weeks by the assassin and his team.

Reznick climbed a nearby set of concrete steps as it afforded him a view over the inside of the base. Low-rise barracks, mostly now residential for vacations and breaks for Spanish military. A parade ground, too. He walked up more steps, away from the base, past some refurbished fishermen's cottages that had been modernized and turned into nice townhouses used as rentals for European tourists, primarily in the summer months.

He hiked down a winding hill and past a tapas bar, patrons enjoying the al fresco dining, then returned to the fringes of the promenade.

Reznick stopped off at a small coffee shop with tables outside. He ordered a black coffee and croissant and sat down. He looked across the harbor to the houses perched high up on cliffs on the other side of the water. Then he took out his binoculars, surveying the beautiful properties. He quickly realized that the location on the west side of the harbor, with the advantage of elevation, might very well give a perfect, uninterrupted line of sight into the base.

He felt excitement as he examined the exteriors of the beautiful villas, some highly modern, with floor-to-ceiling glass behind huge terraces. He figured the terraces and balconies of any of these houses would have a highly advantageous view of the base. He theorized that the shooter, after scouting the location—and having inside knowledge that Muroz was going to be moved to the naval base—had chosen a location high up on the cliffs for the operation.

He studied the road that snaked its way from the promenade where he was sitting, around the horseshoe-shaped bay, past apartments and restaurants, and up the hill on the other side of the bay to the villas on the cliffside. He figured if the shooter had hunkered down there, chances were he had escaped down that road.

Reznick placed his binoculars on the table. His gut feeling, even at this early stage, was that the houses on the cliffs opposite had been the sniper's location. Forensics had estimated it was a "long-range shot."

He sipped his coffee. The caffeine jolt to his system felt good, reviving his jetlagged body. A couple more Dexedrine swallowed.

A few minutes later, he felt more alive. Alert. Wired.

Reznick ate his croissant, finished the scalding coffee, and ordered another. The sun was hot on his skin. Before it had been oppressive, but now it felt good. A sign above a nearby pharmacy indicated it was already thirty-three degrees Celsius. Reznick calculated that as ninety-one degrees Fahrenheit. Another tram screeched into view, and came to a stop across from the café. Throngs of tourists disembarked, a couple of groups being escorted toward boat excursions.

He felt sweat sticking to his linen shirt. He pulled down his baseball cap to shield his eyes from the sun's glare.

Reznick checked the report from a Spanish intelligence forensics expert, which speculated that the gunman might have fired from a car parked on an overlook, close to a house on the opposite side of the water from the base, given the elevation and angle of impact of the bullet. But the report also revealed that the houses on the cliffside had been searched by local police. All eighteen occupants—British, Scandinavian, and German tourists—had been interviewed, but nothing had seemed amiss. Their identities had all checked out. No one had heard a shot.

The expert also speculated that the gunman might have fired from in or around the lighthouse that overlooked the naval base from the other side of the bay.

Reznick picked up his binoculars again. He looked up toward the lighthouse, located on a promontory at the western entrance to the port, and surveyed what looked to him like the highest elevation point. He wondered whether the shooter could have gained access to the lighthouse itself, climbed to the top, and fired from the external balcony used for maintenance. But he assumed there were surveillance cameras in and around the lighthouse.

He put away the binoculars, zipping up his backpack, and left a twenty-euro bill underneath his coffee cup. Then he picked up his backpack, slung it over his shoulder, and made his way back to the apartment. He sat on the balcony overlooking the promenade and picked up his iPad, rereading the forensics report, not wanting to miss any details.

Reznick speculated on the motivation for the assassination. He understood there were numerous groups or individuals who had wanted Muroz dead. In recent years the retired spook had been outspoken against rising immigration into Spain and Mallorca from countries in North Africa, including Morocco. He'd talked openly about “Islamists in our midst” in provocative posts on social media and on his podcasts. It could easily have been a left-wing group with a long-held grudge against Muroz—or maybe even a disgruntled relative of Muroz’s victims during the Franco era—who had assassinated him. But then again, perhaps this was indeed the work of ETA. The problem with that theory was that the Basque separatist group had renounced violence. Or that was the official line at least.

What intrigued Reznick was the tens of thousands of hours of covert recordings Muroz was believed to have had. Tapes of meetings. Footage of interrogations and torture. He needed to find them. That was his brief. But where? Talk about a needle in a haystack.

Maybe the trove of covert recordings had already been recovered by Spanish intelligence, and they’d killed him. Or maybe he’d blackmailed the wrong powerful figure.

Reznick was also intrigued about what Daniel Black had said about US involvement. Conversations of former CIA directors who had visited Spain, over multiple decades, had been covertly recorded. Maybe the tapes revealed secret deals offered to the Spanish government. Illegal agreements, smoothing over concerns in the 1960s and 1970s regarding the American military presence in Spain.

So where would Muroz have kept such a priceless intelligence treasure trove? Reznick was starting to wonder why the hell he had ever agreed to this crazy mission, if indeed it was a mission. It felt as if a team of FBI investigators would be far better suited to examine the evidence and get what they needed. But like Reznick always did, he began to work the problem and try to figure it out.

He knew Muroz had lived in a luxury villa on the outskirts of town. He hadn’t been informed of any other properties the man had owned. The Civil Guard had gotten a warrant to search the home after the assassination. But despite an exhaustive search—ripping up floorboards, knocking through walls, looking for hidden compartments, digging up the garden, scanning the concrete patio for the cache of recordings—nothing had been found. At least, that was the official story.

Reznick took out his binoculars again and considered the terraces of the nearby properties. A man wearing cargo shorts and a polo shirt was sitting on a balcony, laughing as he talked into a cell phone. He turned his binoculars toward Repic Beach, currently packed with sunbathers. Behind it was a pedestrianized zone at the far end of the port. In the water, children and adults paddled and swam—just another summer day under the hot Mallorcan sun.

He put down the binoculars as another packed tram rumbled by. The temperature felt as if it was rising.

Reznick felt rather exposed on the open balcony. He had a great line of sight over the town. The problem was that the balcony also allowed others—whether walking on the promenade or using binoculars from a balcony—to observe him.

He went inside. He texted Trevelle, explaining he needed another place nearby. Ideally with a terrace or balcony facing away from the promenade.

A few moments later he was given the name of a boutique hotel a couple of hundred yards away, only a block from the promenade. *Ask for a mountain view room.* He packed his things and made his way over.

The hotel was set up perfectly. He asked for the mountain view room as Trevelle had told him. The receptionist handed him a card for a fourth-floor room, situated at the rear of the property. The balcony opened out to astonishing views of the Tramuntana mountain range. Most importantly, he was out of sight and not able to be observed. The way he liked it.

Reznick opened up the room's safe and put his passport and keys inside, carefully locking it. He showered and put on a fresh polo shirt, jeans, and sneakers, and got ready to go back into town. He picked up his backpack, slung it over his shoulder, and strolled out, past Hotel Eden and down to the promenade, until he reached a bar overlooking the marina.

He sat in the early-evening sun for an hour, watching kids splashing in the water with their mothers and fathers as the molten sun went down. It was an idyllic scene. It was shocking to think an assassination had been carried out in such a delightful, peaceful place. A busker was playing Spanish guitar while kids kicked a soccer ball around on the beach.

Reznick's gaze was drawn up again toward the villas perched high up on the cliffs on the western edge of the town. It was as if his focus was being pulled inexorably toward them.

The more he obsessed about that particular area as the location where the shooter had taken up position, the more he saw it was the only credible long-range position that afforded the line of sight. And it also would have given the shooter an escape route away from the main promenade, and allowed him the precious time needed to get away.

Reznick scoured the bay between the bottom of the cliffs and the naval base. He looked for trails or paths down the cliffside to the water, allowing access or escape. A group of local boys were swimming out to a diving platform a hundred yards away, out on the water.

Reznick again considered that privileged enclave high up on the cliffs. His problem was that if he went up to where the villas and houses were, he had to assume that there would be surveillance cameras all around. He might be viewed as a prowler.

He finished his beer and walked farther along the promenade to a small tapas restaurant with a view straight across the tram tracks toward Repic Beach. He drank a couple of glasses of Rioja with his choices of spicy chicken, croquettes, and Spanish omelet.

Leaving a hundred-euro bill under his empty glass, he picked up his backpack and walked across the tram tracks, over a wooden bridge that led to the pedestrianized zone adjacent to Repic Beach. Opposite the main beach were new whitewashed luxury apartments alongside traditional Mallorcan villas, as well as a few hotels and lively restaurants. A band comprising what looked like local teenagers was playing some old blues standards through a tiny speaker.

Reznick had been taught the importance of reconnaissance in missions. The purpose was to determine the terrain—observing buildings and the topography of the land. What was also important was getting a feel for not only the place but the people.

He was tempted to head up the hill to the cliffside villas later, under the cover of darkness, but decided that he didn't want to arouse suspicion.

Slow is smooth, smooth is fast.

That mantra had been stressed by instructors during his Marines Corps training, over and over again. It was always better—far better—to be accurate and work at a controlled pace in the successful execution of a task. It was no use blustering in, attracting unwanted attention, messing up, and being caught on surveillance cameras. The value of reconnaissance, in his eyes, was integral to any operation.

Reznick made a mental note to head up the cliffs the following morning, when he imagined there would be a lot more people—hikers, people out running, tourists visiting the lighthouse. Then he walked back slowly toward his hotel, across the wooden bridge, past the upscale Hotel Espléndido and the packed Bar Roma.

He decided to continue along the promenade, eager to get a feel for the lesser-known parts of the town. He turned up a steep side street, Carrer de Jaume Torrens. He passed a few more shops, a busy restaurant, Espiritu Libre, then a late-night supermarket and a bustling Chinese restaurant.

Reznick saw up ahead on the corner a group of people sitting around a few plastic tables outside a bar, Es Cantó. It was virtually a hole-in-the-wall. Inside, Reznick could see a couple of young guys playing pool, swigging beer. He pulled up a chair outside.

The barman, a thickset guy, sweating heavily, was collecting glasses. "What do you want, my friend?"

"A cold Spanish beer and a Scotch on the rocks."

The guy winked. "Coming up." He stepped back into the bar. A short while later he emerged carrying the drinks.

Reznick handed him a twenty-euro bill. "Keep the change."

The guy smiled. "Are you sure?"

"Please."

Reznick picked up his bottle of beer and took a swig. He looked through the open window into the bar. A large-screen TV showing a Spanish soccer game, the volume up loud. The excited Spanish commentator talking rapid-fire. The balmy night air was filled with a fug of cigarette smoke and the sound of raucous laughter from the drinkers inside. It looked like a local dive bar. He liked it immediately.

He nursed his drinks for the next half hour, thinking about the audacity of the sniper, the planning. It pointed to the assassin having state-level intel, no question about that. The movement of Muroz, the timing. The killer must have had insider help in some way. He had to have known Muroz was being moved, where, and at what time. This had been a carefully executed and planned assassination, almost certainly involving a highly disciplined team. The shooter was just one part of the equation.

Reznick finished his Scotch and said goodbye to the thickset barman, then jaunted along a tree-lined street, past a beautiful

Catholic church, and turned right. He saw a neon light for a tiny little bar, just yards from the beach.

Reznick headed inside. A small TV was showing the same soccer game. A red-faced guy at the far end of the bar, wearing flip-flops, shorts, and a beer-stained T-shirt was shouting, face beaded with sweat, gesticulating at the TV. The guy was crazy about the hard tackling.

Reznick's cell phone rang. It was Trevelle.

"How's Mallorca?"

"Hot."

"What are you doing?"

"Watching soccer. And drinking."

"Lay of the land and all that?"

"That kind of thing, yeah."

"Listen, Jon, just wanted to let you know that I'm on this. I'm here for you. So if you need anything, just let me know. Any time of day, I'm ready."

"Appreciate that."

"What have you got?"

"Just arrived. Finding my way around."

"What's the plan?"

"The plan?" Reznick picked up his bottle of beer and went outside, cell phone pressed to his ear. "I need to establish where the shooter set up from. And from there, we'll see how it goes. I have an idea where the area might be. But nothing precise yet."

"It's a start. But you've got your work cut out for you, man. I don't know what the hell Black is thinking."

Reznick swigged his beer. "Tell me about it."

"Stay safe, man. I've got a bad feeling about this."

Three

The next morning, Reznick woke at dawn, needing to clear his head. He splashed cold water on his face, put on his running gear, did some stretches outside the hotel, and walked around the corner, past a convenience store, until he reached the promenade. The sun was peeking over the horizon, bathing the water in a burnt orange glow. He did a few more stretches while leaning against a concrete bench, then turned and jogged along the sidewalk toward Repic Beach, following the same route he had taken the previous night, over the bridge and through the pedestrianized area that fringed the beach on the far side of town.

He jogged along beachfront road, Polígon de Sa Platja, until he reached a creosoted hut shaded by a huge towering palm tree. He did a few more stretches for his calves.

Reznick once more took in the winding road that led up to the villas and houses high up on the cliffside. He made a mental note to return later that morning. Then he jogged back the way he'd come and stopped opposite Bar Roma, sweat sticking to his Dri-FIT running shirt.

Workmen were hosing down the dusty side street, emptying the trash from the bins. In the distance was the rattling sound of the first tram of the day arriving in the town.

Reznick ran farther on until he reached the military base, stopping beside a water fountain. He felt his heart begin to race. He splashed cool water on his face and took a few large gulps to quench his thirst. He checked his heart rate on his watch. He wasn't surprised to see that it had risen to one hundred and fifty-two beats per minute. Not bad.

He still felt thirsty and so stopped at a convenience store and bought a bottle of chilled water. He drank it in one long swig, then tossed the plastic bottle into a nearby trash can and walked back to his hotel. He made his way up the narrow side street like he had the night before, past Es Cantó, then turned right and along the shaded street past the beautiful old church.

A stooped priest wearing sunglasses was talking to an elderly woman. She was holding a small dog in her arms. The priest turned and looked in Reznick's direction for a few moments.

Reznick walked on without acknowledging the priest. When he got back to his hotel room, he showered and changed into a pair of Levi's jeans, a navy T-shirt, sneakers, and headed down to the buffet-style breakfast. He picked up a plate and chose some rye toast with butter, a couple of croissants, a glass of freshly squeezed orange juice, and his customary black coffee. He sat alone at a table outside in the sun. The smattering of voices at the adjacent tables were mostly English, a handful of Germans, and a couple of Americans from New York, talking loudly about a planned visit to a local vineyard.

He checked his cell phone, perusing news stories in the New York *Times.* War in the Middle East, the political fallout from Israeli airstrikes amid the rubble of Gaza, Hamas hosting a press conference, a school shooting in Oklahoma, and violent demonstrations outside the United Nations. The stories could have been from any time in America over the last fifty years. The same old.

Reznick finished his breakfast, put on his sunglasses, and picked up his backpack. He had gotten a feel for the town now. He had a strong inkling of the approximate area where the shooter could have fired into the naval base. But what he didn't have was the exact location. That might be tricky if not downright impossible to establish. Still, it was important to narrow down the search. If he could find the where, he could get Trevelle working on why that spot had been chosen, who owned it, and go from there.

He strolled along the promenade as another orange tram rumbled and trundled along the old metal tracks. Just like yesterday, tourists were packed onboard, taking photographs, talking excitedly, looking out across the bay. He immediately felt the sweat running down his back as the temperature edged higher. It was only mid-morning.

He walked past Hotel Espléndido and across the bridge toward Repic Beach. The beach was already getting busy, with people sunbathing, slathering on sunscreen, huge umbrellas shielding others from the blazing rays, and kids dipping into the sea to cool off. He moved past the creosoted hut and then up the steep, winding road.

Reznick had checked a map earlier. The road would lead to the Cap Gros lighthouse, the highest point on the western headland above the harbor. He was eager to establish if it provided an uninterrupted line of sight down to the interior of the naval base.

He passed a few hikers on the challenging route. On and on, twisting higher and higher up the cliffside.

The narrow road led to the villas with the killer views. But first he hiked past them, up the last few hundred yards to the top of the cliffs. The lighthouse, and the whitewashed buildings spread out around it, stood behind a chain-link fence.

Reznick turned around and surveyed the scene. He put down his backpack, got out his binoculars, and searched the naval base across the dark blue waters. He could see the rooftops of the base. He examined the area adjacent to the base, at the eastern side of the harbor entrance. A second lighthouse was visible.

But, despite the elevation, Cap Gros lighthouse was too far back from the edge, and crucially he did not have a clear line of sight to *inside* the barracks.

He walked around the perimeter of the lighthouse and tried various angles to figure it out. But it was the same. There was no clear line of sight into the base.

Reznick took a few moments to absorb this information. It was not what he had expected. He swigged some water and took out his rangefinder. It showed the direct distance between the lighthouse and the naval base was eight hundred and seventy-five yards. But all he could see were the tops of the barracks and the base's office buildings.

He walked for fifty yards, along a path adjacent to the lighthouse, until he got to a tourist hostel, formerly an army telegraph station.

Reznick pulled out his binoculars again and checked the line of sight from there. Nothing. He studied the exterior maintenance balcony on the highest part of the lighthouse. Even if the shooter had managed to breach security, he would have been exposed to passersby and anyone who looked after the lighthouse. And when the shooter tried to escape, it would have been tricky and time-consuming. Besides, if he was a sniper, he would probably not have opted for the exposed upper balcony of a lighthouse if he had the choice.

Reznick turned around and walked back the way he'd come. He had covered maybe one hundred yards when he spotted a winding single-track off the main road. It led to what appeared to be an overlook. Maybe even a passing point for vehicles. The forensic scientist's report had speculated that shots might have been fired from this exposed position.

He took out his binoculars and looked across the water to the base opposite. All Reznick could see from that elevated position was, again, the roofs of the buildings. No direct line of sight to inside the base.

The shooter could not have taken the fatal shot from here. Muroz had been shot after he stepped out of the SUV. The victim had to have been visible to the shooter.

He walked farther down the road, feeling his calves tighten, around a couple of turns, until he arrived back at the row of spacious, modern villas. The clifftop houses had breathtaking views across the water. This place looked a lot more promising.

Reznick had guessed that most of the properties with spectacular views were rental properties. And he was right. He walked past the gray wooden security gates of the first house. Then the next one. And then the next one. Each of the properties had a metal plaque listing the name of the rental company or property company who owned or leased it. He took out his cell phone and saw that at least five of the properties were available on local vacation rental sites.

He wondered if the sniper could have rented a property for a few nights, maybe more. But that would have left a digital trail. Unless he'd had a false passport like Reznick. A false identity.

And another problem from the shooter's point of view was that high-end properties would invariably have internal camera systems and surveillance units. An assassin would think it less than ideal if his actions could be watched remotely by the owner of the property. A hunter would want to be hidden from sight. Leave without a trace.

Reznick felt frustrated and turned around. It was then he spotted—almost hidden by a clump of trees—a narrow dirt track, blue waters in the background.

Reznick was intrigued. It was about as wide as an alley. Huge almond and pine trees mostly shrouded the entrances to a handful of lovely homes. He realized that these properties, perched right at the very edge of the high cliffs, would offer a better line of sight because of the angle. He walked along past the first three houses. But again, all the properties, beautifully painted and presented, were rental properties. Surveilled, twenty-four-seven.

Just as he was about to turn around and head back down the hill, Reznick's gaze was drawn to the far end of the track, maybe another hundred yards along the steep cliffside. He climbed up the path. Overgrown olive trees, Chinese hibiscus and gnarly old oaks, uncut for years, sat behind a rusting fence. He peered through the thick foliage, which nearly concealed the grim-looking property.

A rundown villa was at the farthest end of the unmarked road. In the overgrown front yard, a "For Sale" sign was nearly covered by the chest-high grass spilling over the wall and metal fence. A plaque gave the name of the house. *Paraíso.*

His gaze wandered around the property. It appeared at first glance to be abandoned, a couple of upstairs windows boarded up. He walked a few yards farther along and peered over an overgrown hedge, which was swarming with flies.

Reznick saw a stagnant swimming pool, dark green algae having settled on the water. It looked as if the house was not only empty but had been for a while. Maybe years.

He realized the decrepit property was the perfect location for the shooter.

Just then, the house's front door creaked open. A woman stepped out and carefully locked it before heading down the overgrown path and through the gate.

She seemed surprised to see Reznick standing there. "Hola, Señor."

Reznick smiled. "Do you speak English?"

"Yes, of course. How can I help you?"

"I was just wondering if this property is available to rent or buy? It's a great location."

"It is a great location. But no, sir, at this time, it is not occupied or available. I'm sorry."

"Can you tell me why it's not available?"

The woman shrugged. "It is a bit complicated. It is in poor state, as you can see. The owner died five years ago. There is a court battle later this year to decide who owns it."

"Lawyers involved, right? That could get expensive."

"Very true. I'm just making sure there are no squatters. Properties are expensive for local people, you see. I come once a week from Palma just to check there is no one here."

Reznick turned and looked back at the abandoned house. "It's a beautiful house. It must have great views over the bay."

"It does. Fabulous views. But it is not fit to be lived in. It would have to be renovated extensively."

"I'd love to have a look inside."

The woman checked her watch. "That's not possible. Besides, I'm sorry, I'm late for another viewing over in Sóller." She handed him her card. "Call me in late December. Things might have changed with the court ruling. Excuse me, I must go. I'm late for this appointment."

"Nice meeting you."

Reznick watched as the woman walked along the long dirt road toward the high-end rental properties. There she got into her small red Fiat before she drove off down the hill and out of sight.

Reznick needed to see inside that property.

Just after midnight, Reznick stepped onto the dive boat he had hired a few hours earlier. He had decided to approach the abandoned house from the sea. It would have been easier to hop over the fence and break in. But for now, until he knew more, he was mindful of being caught by surveillance cameras operating in or around the area.

Reznick's instincts told him that the empty house perfectly fit the bill for the assassin, but he needed to see for himself. He had to assume that the realtor may have activated a surveillance system on the property, perhaps hidden from sight. But another reason for caution at this early stage of the investigation was that there was a real chance of Reznick being spotted by alert neighbors with on-street cameras protecting their properties.

With that in mind, he carefully edged the dive boat out from its mooring at the Port de Sóller marina. He had paid two hundred euros in cash to a local fisherman who specialized in scuba trips for tourists.

The full moon in the inky black sky cast a ghostly pale glow on the choppy waters as he ventured out of the harbor. The humidity was like a steam bath. He navigated past the sea wall, weaving between bigger yachts anchored within the bay for the night. He edged beyond the sanctuary of the harbor, the swell getting more pronounced.

He checked his GPS position and the radar as he guided the boat forward.

Reznick looked off to his right, to the lights of the naval base. Then the other way. High up on the cliffs, the lights of the interiors of the villas he had passed earlier in the day. He took out his night-vision binoculars and looked up again toward the villas. Then he methodically scanned farther along until he saw it—the silhouette of the abandoned villa.

Reznick panned down the cliffs and observed a pebble beach directly below the property. He figured it was around one hundred yards from his boat. He pressed a button to drop the boat's anchor.

He took off his shorts and T-shirt before pulling on his wetsuit, flippers, oxygen tank, scuba mouthpiece, and night-vision dive goggles. He also had a waterproof dive bag with fresh clothes, powerful binoculars, and other essentials inside.

He perched on the edge of the boat, his back to the sea, before dropping into the water.

Reznick took a few moments to get his bearings as the night-vision dive goggles kicked in. He checked his GPS coordinates on his diver's watch. The sea around turned a strange aqua-green color, allowing him perfect underwater vision. He dove deeper before propelling himself toward the shore. He kicked hard, his flippers cutting through the water. The night-vision goggles indicated his depth and distance from shore. Seventy-five yards. He breathed hard as he swam in a surreal world, past jellyfish, crabs, lobsters, bream, mackerel, and endless fields of thick seaweed.

Reznick surfaced twenty yards away from shore and swam hard until he reached the rough shingle beach. He scrambled up the pebbles and rough sand toward a rocky incline—ten more yards, well away from the sea. There he took off his goggles, wetsuit, and oxygen tank. He opened his dive bag and took out a towel, quickly drying himself off. Then he put on a pair of black cargo shorts, a black T-shirt, and black sneakers. He pulled on the dive bag and began to slowly ascend the cliff face. He grabbed crevices, fissures, and any cracks in the rocks, as he climbed higher and higher.

A few minutes later, lungs nearly bursting from the exertion, he had already clambered to the top.

Reznick crouched down as he got his bearings. His eyes were adjusting to the darkness after the surreal experience of the night-vision dive goggles. The nearest house with upstairs lights on was nearly one hundred yards away. He hid himself against the treeline at the edge of the overgrown garden behind the abandoned villa and stayed low as he crept down a path. The smell of herbs, citrus fruits, and wildflowers permeated the salty air.

He moved with stealth, slinking up a set of stairs toward the house. No sign of surveillance cameras. But he didn't want to take chances.

Reznick took out a signal jammer and turned it on. It would, theoretically, block out any signals from Wi-Fi, Bluetooth devices, alarms. He headed up another set of exterior concrete stairs and along an elevated narrow path at the side of the property.

He walked up to a glass door and turned the handle. It was locked, not surprisingly. He took out a small penknife, carefully inserting it into the keyhole. He wiggled it around, using the blade as a pick. He heard a click. He put away the knife and slowly turned the door handle.

He slipped into the darkened house. Then he decided to go up as high as he could go, and see what he could see. He found some winding stairs to an attic, French doors leading out to a balcony.

Reznick turned the key in the lock, opening the door. He stepped outside at the highest point of the house. He took off his backpack and reached for the rangefinder, then checked the distance to the naval base. From his position, it showed a distance of six hundred and thirty-three yards. He saw the Spanish flag flying.

He looked through his night-vision binoculars. He could see, with incredible sharpness, plainclothes military personnel moving inside the base. A man spoke to a guard while smoking a cigarette.

Reznick was excited. The position and location of the attic balcony, overlooking the sea and base, gave the most perfect line of sight. He reached into his backpack and quickly assembled the long-range sniper rifle, attached the night-vision scopes, and locked it onto a tripod. He looked through the eyepiece and surveyed the scene. The fine lines of the reticle aligned the pin-sharp crosshairs. The man talking to the guard was in those crosshairs.

This could be it. This might be where it had happened.

Four

Frederick Hicks sat on a packed tram, chewing a stick of nicotine gum, enjoying the morning sun on his face. The tram approached Port de Sóller. He caught a glimpse of the sparkling blue waters as the tram turned along the town's main promenade. The tourists were packed in tight, and the smell of body odor, sweat, perfume, and stale tobacco lingered in the humid air. At his feet sat a black Adidas backpack, as per his instructions.

He wore a Cardinals hat, Ralph Lauren shorts, a white linen shirt, and cheap sunglasses he had picked up at a corner shop in Sóller. He looked like any affluent Western tourist.

A man on the tram with a deep Southern drawl was talking storm systems threatening to become hurricane-force in the Gulf of Mexico over the coming days. His wife just sat looking bored. A Canadian woman was moaning about the cost of living in Quebec, and Germans and Brits could also be heard amid the din of conversations. The Brits seemed in good spirits. Hicks detected a couple of Scottish accents and what sounded like a Scandinavian or Dutch accent among them. It seemed like the whole of the free world was talking at the same time in the open-air wooden tram.

Hicks wiped his sweaty brow with the back of his hand. He ran his hands through his shoulder-length blond hair. A whiff of tobacco smoke and cooking smells drifted through the tram's open windows as they lumbered past restaurants and hotels toward the terminus on the promenade.

He smiled. It felt strangely comforting being back so soon in the small idyllic town by the sea. The scene of the crime. But he doubted the wisdom of him returning. It had only been a matter of days.

Hicks's mind flashed to the crazy aftermath of the shooting that night. It all seemed like a blur. He had driven the white van south across Mallorca to a farm on the outskirts of the neon-lit beach town of Magaluf, before catching a bus to the resort's main drag. It was a paradise for a lot of twenty-something Brits, Scandinavians, Germans, and Dutch. A rite of passage. He had headed to a crummy apartment in the town. The following days had been spent confined in the sweltering room, keeping out of sight, thinking back to the meticulous operation. The planning. The preparation. The inside information he had been passed. Then setting up the Siyavash sniper rifle, the night scope, getting his windage and elevation just right before taking the shot, neutralizing the retired Spanish intelligence operative.

Muroz was the first of a trio of assassinations. A high-value target, he had been told. The decision to kill Muroz had come about when intel chatter in security circles in Madrid, intercepted by the Russian Signals Intelligence Directorate, suggested the Spanish state was worried that Muroz might sell his treasure trove of tapes and recordings to the highest bidder, believed to be Qatar. The Spanish had decided to effectively kidnap Muroz and take him to a naval base in Port de Sóller, before airlifting him back to Madrid to be interrogated and forced to hand over the hidden cache. Hicks had been drafted and trained to take the kill shot, knowing he must also somehow retrieve the tapes and recordings.

But the job of tracking down the precise location of the electronic trove had been left to a specialist surveillance operative.

His handler had been in touch the day after Muroz was killed. A coded message passed by a cutout underneath his door, giving him instructions on where to pick up his next "delivery" ahead of the second assassination. But it was the third assassination that Hicks was looking forward to the most. His handler had hinted that it was the big one. But nothing more than that.

Hicks was still processing his complex thoughts. It was all very surreal. Truth be told, Hicks felt a frisson of excitement to be back in the town. It was slow-paced and upscale. The contrast with Magaluf couldn't have been starker.

Magaluf, in all honesty, had freaked out even him. From the window of his stifling apartment he'd watched the red-faced Brits, being sick after getting roaring drunk on cheap shots and booze, roasting in the unbearable heat until they passed out from heatstroke or went half-crazy.

He couldn't get the sound of incessant bass-heavy dance music pumping from the bars out of his head. The town had been awash with coked-up British tourists challenging locals outside bars on the party strip of Punta Ballena, brawling with each other, squaring up to the Civil Guard, and throwing beer bottles at rival British soccer fans. Albanian and Nigerian gangsters dealt drugs in the streets. Meanwhile trafficked women from West Africa were used as prostitutes for tourists, but also terrorized by organized criminal gangs into preying on drunk tourists.

It was a hellscape he was glad to have gotten out of unscathed.

Port de Sóller was the opposite. Northwest Mallorca, quiet, traditional, locals and tourists sunbathing on the beach as the old trams rumbled by in the scorching sun. It seemed to attract a different clientele. More upmarket. More family-oriented.

Hicks's mind snapped back to the present. He got to his feet, holding on tight to a rail as the tram shuddered to a creaking halt. Throngs of people disembarked in the middle of the town. He waited until most of them had gotten off then stepped from the tram amid the crowds. Tour guides, some with umbrellas to demarcate themselves for their groups, ushered tourists from the tram stop and shepherded them toward the marina.

A woman holding a bottle of water, wearing a tight-fitting Dodgers T-shirt, smiled. "Is this place gorgeous or what?"

Hicks smiled. "Very nice."

"I'm staying in Palma."

Hicks nodded, not wanting to engage in conversation.

"You ever been there?"

"Palma? No, I haven't," he lied.

"Trust me, you'll love it. I'm thinking of moving there. I live in LA. Or rather, I lived in LA. Home wiped out in Pacific Palisades. The only thing I managed to save was my yoga mat, my birth certificate, a bottle of Xanax, and my dad's ashes."

Hicks had to stop himself from bursting out laughing. "Sorry to hear that," he said, barely able to muster any interest in the small talk of a fellow American. "That's tough."

"I consider myself one of the lucky ones. At least we had insurance. Four of my neighbors' houses . . . burned to the ground. But listen to this. Four months before, their insurance companies emailed them to tell them their properties weren't a good risk. And that was that. No cover. Nothing. And they couldn't arrange other insurance to cover them."

"Bummer."

"Where you staying tonight?" she asked.

"I'm not sure," he lied again. "I was thinking of moving around the island a bit."

"I'm free tonight," she said. "You want to hook up for drinks later here in the port? Or maybe in Sóller town itself?"

Hicks couldn't believe this random LA woman was hitting on him. "Got other things planned, sorry. But thank you."

She rolled her eyes and forced a smile. "Story of my life. Take care."

Hicks was glad to be rid of her. He looked toward the boat they were about to board. The chatty woman started pestering a couple who said they were from Little Rock. He ambled down the approach road, past the yachts, toward the largest boat, which was almost as big as a ferry. He pulled out his cell phone. He scanned the bar code of the ticket into a handheld machine and climbed onboard, taking a seat well away from the chatty Dodgers fan.

He bought a bottle of chilled water from the onboard bar. He swigged a few mouthfuls, glad to cool his parched throat after the stifling tram journey from Sóller.

A few minutes later, everyone safely onboard, the boat edged away from its moorings and chugged noisily out of the harbor.

Hicks kept his eyes straight ahead as the boat sailed past the naval base. But he couldn't help but flick a glance up at the cliffside houses. His handler had been specific. *Your work is not finished.* He had accepted the decision, knowing that he always followed orders. *Theirs not to reason why, theirs but to do and die.* The haunting poem by Tennyson he had learned as a child. It was about soldiers and cavalrymen at the Battle of Balaclava, going into battle knowing it would mean almost certain death. Hicks had served as a soldier in the United States Army. A language specialist. He had seen first-hand the terrible sacrifices and costs of war. The deaths, the destruction, the despair. But a soldier always, without question—no matter how crazy the plan from his superior officer—followed orders. Always.

His cell phone vibrated in his pocket. He read the text message telling him to expect a phone call while he was out at sea.

Hicks sipped more of his water, sating his thirst. The boat bobbed in the swell, the sun mercilessly beating down. Farther and farther, it chugged through the choppy open waters away from the port. The waves began to swell and crash on the sides as the boat lolled and rocked. It might have been the height of summer, but the southeast Sirocco winds were whipping up, which would bring red sand in from the North African desert.

Hicks looked at the other faces onboard. A few passengers looked uneasy, eyes darting from side to side as if expecting the boat to capsize at any moment.

He felt comfortable, having gained his sea legs many years back in Galveston, working for the US Coast Guard. He knew tides, currents. He respected the sea. The storms and hurricanes which battered southern Texas in late summer dictated utmost caution while out at sea. This was nothing in comparison.

His cell phone vibrated.

"*How is the weather?*" A man's voice spoke the coded phrase.

"Seen worse." His coded reply.

"Glad to hear it. A woman is on the starboard side of the boat. She's wearing a red silk scarf and a white Yankees hat. Sit down opposite her, take off your backpack, and leave it at your feet."

"What else?"

"You'll see."

Hicks ended the call. Perhaps this was the handover of essential items for the second of the trio of assassinations. He nonchalantly stepped past the other passengers, some taking selfies out at sea. Others sat in their seats, holding hands. He ambled toward the starboard side and studied the tourists. A woman wearing a white Yankees hat and red silk scarf, as he had been told, was speaking into her phone. She was sitting alone at an empty table. He walked over, sat down across from her, and slid his backpack under the table with his right foot. She smiled, talking about sending an email to her lawyer. At least, that's what she was pretending to be conveying.

He felt something touch his leg. He stole a glance under the table. An identical-looking bag sat beside his left foot.

Hicks picked it up.

The woman smiled as she turned away, making small talk about missing home. Her accent was Midwestern, he thought. Her eyes dark brown, features clear, nails impeccably painted.

His phone rang again.

"Yeah?" he said.

"Do you have the new backpack?"

"Correct."

"Move back to your original position on the boat."

The call ended and Hicks complied, the new backpack slung over his shoulder. He went back to his seat, sipping the rest of his water, which was already warm from the heat of the sun.

His vision wandered off to the far horizon.

Hicks held onto the backpack tightly. It felt heavier than he'd expected.

An hour later, the boat returned to the marina. It took a while for everyone to disembark. He caught a taxi from the port back to blazing hot Sóller, the tourists thronged around the church. He walked along a shaded backstreet and into his Airbnb.

He locked the door behind him and closed all the shutters, taking off his sunglasses and Cardinals hat. He went to the kitchen table and placed the backpack on top, unzipping it. He reached inside and pulled out the parts of a new Siyavash rifle, ammo, brand-new night sights, and a new iPhone. He assumed this was for the next kill, not the final kill.

The more he thought about it, the more he felt a warm glow inside. He lay back down on the bed and stared at the ceiling fan whirring the fetid, dead air around the tiny room.

Hicks knew this was his time. His moment. He would make history. He would be infamous. But also immortal.

Five

Reznick asked himself what the hell he was doing as he sat down on a wooden bench beside the marina. He was a trained killer. But here he was, in a sleepy town, mostly cooling his heels, trying to make a breakthrough like a slow-burn private investigator. He'd known from the moment Daniel Black had told him how little intel they had that the operation, if indeed it could be called an operation, was merely clutching at straws. If he had a name of the killer he could eventually find him and neutralize the threat. But he had nothing.

He began to ponder the possibility that him being in the town would attract the attention of the killer. Maybe this was what Daniel Black was planning. Was he using Reznick as bait?

Reznick felt frustrated. That said, he had made one small bit of progress. He took out his cell phone to get any news from Trevelle.

"Hey man, what's going on?" Trevelle said. "Any progress?"

"I wish."

"You must have something."

"Maybe. I might have found the shooter's location last night."

"That's something. A step forward, right?"

"I don't know."

"You don't sound your usual self."

"This whole thing stinks. We have nothing to go on. We're just scratching around looking for a lead."

"Hang in there, Jon, you'll figure it out."

"Hope so. Let me ask you something, Trevelle."

"Sure thing."

"The guy that carried out this hit. We don't know who he was, right?"

"Correct."

"I'm curious, has there not been any chatter in the Civil Guard or Spanish intelligence circles? Electronic communications, that kind of thing?"

"From everything I've seen, they're as clueless as we are."

"That's bullshit. How is that possible? Muroz was in their care, on a secure naval base."

"Jon, I swear, they've drawn a blank."

"Let me get this straight. This shooter managed to get into position and take out this highly guarded intelligence asset, on a secure naval base, without any surveillance cameras in or around the base or town picking up any clues? Is that what you're telling me?"

"Correct. He's like a ghost. What are you thinking, Jon?"

"I'm thinking this guy is a pro," Reznick said. "He's in, he's out, not a trace. But it's hard to believe there's nothing."

"You established where you believe the shot was fired from?"

"High degree of probability. It's an abandoned villa. I'm going to check it out for a second time in daylight. One thing's for sure—this guy's not acting alone. He'd need hard intel. A comms team on the ground. There has to be a digital trace somewhere."

"I've worked with NSA tools, my own software, but not a trace. Spanish intelligence appears to have nothing."

Reznick thought about that for a few moments. "What if that's the point?"

Trevelle paused, then said, "What do you mean?"

"There's been a media blackout on this shooting. What if they have more but they don't want anyone to know about it?"

"I hadn't thought of that."

"Listen, I'm playing devil's advocate here. But it's interesting and notable that they appear to have locked down any media chatter about this. Someone should be reporting on it, but no one is touching it. Why?"

"It would be acutely embarrassing for the Spanish. Deeply unnerving."

"Damn right it would be. The assassination of a retired intelligence operative on a Spanish military base? It would scare people. Was this terrorism?"

Trevelle said nothing.

"Okay, I need you to do me a favor. The abandoned villa is called Paraíso. Spanish for Paradise."

"How did you find it?"

"I walked around the port. I looked for the best positioning. It looks promising."

"I'm listening."

"I'd like you to access surveillance systems of nearby villas. Cami del Far. It's a long, winding, elevated street above the port on the west side of the harbor entrance. The abandoned villa, I believe, has perfect line of sight."

"But it could be one of the other villas?"

"It could be. But my money, at least for now, is on Paraíso. No one there. Isolated, and maybe a hundred yards or so from the nearest villa."

"That would be your choice?"

"It makes sense. But I'm guessing this shooter also has a handler. Maybe a team who helped put this together. He has to have backup."

"This is sounding more and more sophisticated. This is no lone wolf. State-level?"

"Quite possibly. Check surveillance systems around midnight Mallorca time, when the assassination was carried out. Triangulate any cell phone towers with the coordinates of the abandoned house. Any messages or phone calls from in and around that area. That's what I'm interested in."

"I'll take care of it."

"I also want you to find out more about this dead guy, Muroz. A lot more. I've read the CIA file on him. But the intel's all routine background, no personal details. All about his politics and his work. There must be more about this guy. Personal stuff. I want you to dive into his family. Connections. I don't think he had kids. Did he have a spouse? Girlfriend? Mistress? I'm thinking this guy who lived in the shadows for decades still had acquaintances. Friends. A drinking partner. Colleagues in Spanish intelligence. Someone in the town who knew him well. Someone has to know more about him. He lived in this goddamn town after all."

"I'm on it, Jon."

"Get me what you can. And get back to me ASAP."

Reznick ended the call. He got up from the bench and walked along the promenade, stopping for a coffee at a sidewalk café. As he sat down at a table the tram rumbled by. Scores of tourists swarmed over the port like bees to honey.

The waitress smiled. "What can I get you, Señor?"

Reznick looked over a menu and ordered a Mallorcan pastry specialty, an *ensaïmada*, with a large black coffee.

"Good choice, Señor."

A few minutes later, she returned with a delicious, sweet pastry, drizzled with frosting. He wolfed down the pastry in a matter of seconds and washed it down with the coffee, wiping his mouth with a napkin.

Reznick ordered another black coffee and a water, and sat watching the world go by. At the restaurant across from the tram stop, he spotted cameras mounted high up, surveying the area. He marveled over how it was possible for the hitman to have assassinated the intelligence operative without any digital trace in the twenty-first century. He wasn't buying it. There had to be something. But so far, no encrypted messages or video surveillance clips had been unearthed. Then again, this was a small town on an island in the Balearics. This wasn't Manhattan, London, or Berlin with best-in-class surveillance, everywhere, twenty-four-seven. Maybe the local cops or Civil Guard were slow, relying on their colleagues in Palma for forensic support.

He hung around for half an hour, drinking coffee, knowing he was a little bit closer to finding the shooter. At least he had pinpointed a probable location. But nothing more. That was his only lead, if you could even call it that.

Reznick watched a group of Spanish girls wearing pretty dresses, laughing and giggling. Other teenagers, locals, carried soccer balls under their arms, a couple wearing Barcelona soccer jerseys.

A Civil Guard cruiser edged into view, one of the officers checking out Reznick and the other café customers. The car crawled farther down the promenade as another tram departed the port, trundling away toward Sóller in the broiling sun.

Reznick paid the bill and turned up Carrer de Jaume Torrens. He headed inside Es Cantó, the bar he had visited on his first night. A couple of old guys were playing pool, smoking. The TV was again showing a soccer game.

He sat down on a stool at the bar and ordered a bottle of Estrella Damm, a classic Spanish lager. He had taken a liking to it. He took a large gulp, sating his thirst, and smiled at the thickset barman.

"Hey, how are you, Mr. American? You like our beer?"

"Excellent." Reznick finished the rest of the beer in one go. "Man, that was good."

"You thirsty?"

Reznick ordered a couple more bottles, giving one to the barman. "Cheers."

"You were in here the other night, right?"

"Guilty as charged."

The barman laughed as he sipped his beer, perspiring heavily in the heat. He was in his forties, a tough-looking guy, arms like lamb shanks. "Where are you from?"

Reznick shook the barman's vise-like grip. "I'm from a small town like this."

"Here on vacation?"

"That obvious, huh?"

The barman smiled. "Most Americans go to the restaurants on the main street by the promenade, then head off on the tourist boats. Which is fine. But they seem in so much of a hurry."

"I know." Reznick surveyed the smoky, hot bar. "I like it here in the town. This area. What about you?"

"What about me?"

"Where you from?"

"I'm from a small town, near Santiago in Chile."

"You're a long way from home, my friend."

"Trust me, I love it here. It's paradise. My brother lives here too. He moved over about fifteen years ago. I moved twenty years ago."

"You move for work?"

"I move for better prospects for not only me but my family."

"Good for you."

"Everyone speaks Spanish. The sun shines three hundred days a year. Nice place. People are nice."

"Apart from us tourists, right?"

The barman smiled. "It's all fine with me. No one bothers me here. It's a friendly town. Good people. I love Mallorca."

"I don't blame you."

Out of the corner of Reznick's eye, an emaciated bespectacled man with a scraggy beard came into view. Reznick turned to face the character. The man glared at him. He wore an open shirt, stained in beer and sweat. He staggered forward, unsteadier on his feet as he got closer.

"*Mierda!*" the guy shouted, staring at Reznick.

The barman pointed at the man as if to warn him about his behavior.

"What did he say?" Reznick asked.

"It means 'bullshit.' He's drunk. He's always drunk."

The barman remonstrated with the customer in Spanish, flushing crimson in the face.

The drunk man squared up to Reznick and poked him in the chest.

Reznick grabbed the guy's arm, twisting it sharply. "Tell him that I'll break his fucking arm if he lays a finger on me again."

The scraggly man yelped, muttering under his breath.

The barman shouted some aggressive-sounding words in Spanish. "He apologizes."

Reznick slowly loosened his grip as the guy managed to carefully extricate his arm.

The drunk man rattled some cobwebs from his skull and approached the barman, who turned and looked to Reznick. "He's harmless. But he's been annoying everyone. He's talking crazy stuff."

"What sort of crazy stuff?"

The barman hemmed and hawed. "He's raving . . . he's crazy. Talking about a guy being killed in the town. Inside the naval base. It's what crazy people say, right?"

Reznick's senses were on high alert. "What?" he said, feigning ignorance. "He said something happened on the base?"

"His sister is a cleaner. She comes in here too and started talking about this guy being killed. It's just a rumor he's spreading around. I think he's just wanting attention."

Reznick swigged some beer. "But is it true? Was someone killed at the base?"

"No." The barman shook his head. "That's just what he says. I think it's bullshit. He's the resident alcoholic."

"What's the guy been saying exactly? Kind of a wild story."

"You're telling me. So, he says his sister is talking about a coverup. But that's his words, not hers."

Reznick looked closely at the skinny guy—bloodshot eyes, jaundiced scaly skin.

The barman learned forward, dismissively. "No one believes him. I don't believe her either. She's a bit crazy too, if you ask me. Spreading bullshit. Her brother said she was told to stay quiet about it or she would lose her job. That's what he said his sister told him. So, it's secondhand. Don't listen to him. I wouldn't worry about it."

The drunk man sipped his beer and turned to stare at Reznick. The man began to speak in broken English, eyes rheumy, sad. "My sister . . . she saw his body . . ."

"Whose body?"

The barman interrupted. "He's told me the same thing. That his sister watched from a window at the base as the man's body was taken away by the Civil Guard."

"Humor him," Reznick said. "Ask him where it was taken."

"It's bullshit."

Reznick shrugged. "Did he say where the body was taken?"

The barman relayed the question in Spanish and the guy gave a gruff reply. "His sister told him that the body was taken to Palma to be cremated the following day. He said it was a coverup."

Reznick ordered a couple of shots of Scotch, handing one to the drunk.

The man hugged Reznick tightly before he crossed himself. "Forgive me, Señor. I'm tired." His warm breath was loaded with liquor and cigarette smoke. "But my sister saw it all. She no lie. She is a good, honest woman."

Reznick turned and looked at the barman. "Interesting story."

"He doesn't know what day it is. His sister has been taken away to a psychiatric hospital. Last night. That's what he said. The whole thing is a pack of nonsense."

Reznick looked at the sad, tragic, drunk guy. "I'm sorry."

The man began to cry, babbling in Spanish.

"What did he say?" Reznick asked the barman again.

"He said the Civil Guard said she was having a breakdown. They said she was hallucinating. She saw the man being shot. Then they took her away; he said he doesn't know which hospital. No one will tell him if his sister is dead or alive."

Six

It was just past midnight as Juan Pinto walked down the main corridor within the labyrinthine headquarters of Spain's Civil Guard, in central Madrid. He swiped his ID card then stepped into the control room. Huge screens showed four intelligence operations underway in locations across Spanish territory: Madrid, Tenerife, Malaga, and Mallorca. A few other screens showed real-time footage of ports, including Barcelona, and border crossings into France and Portugal. Sitting at a conference table was his second in command, Pedro Mendes.

Pinto sat down beside his colleague. Mendes was smart. An American-Spanish lawyer who had spent his formative years in New York before relocating to Spain to join the Civil Guard, following in his father's footsteps, Mendes had enjoyed a meteoric rise since he had arrived in Madrid five years ago. A highly intelligent, strategic thinker, and cold as ice. Pinto liked him, and could see that Mendes was going to go far. His father had been the Spanish Consulate General in New York.

While Pinto's Spanish was obviously fluent and Mendes's Spanish was competent and functional, Mendes still preferred to speak in English.

Pinto didn't mind. The added bonus was that hardly any of his subordinates knew what the pair of them were talking about. In intelligence circles, that had its advantages.

"Okay, so tell me what this is all about," he said to his colleague. "You said you wanted to talk."

Mendes picked up a remote control and pressed a couple of buttons. The face of a steely-eyed white guy at Palma airport. "We've got something of importance developing in Mallorca."

Pinto pointed at the guy on the screen. "This guy?"

"Yeah." Mendes checked a file he had flipped open. "I've done some analysis on this man. And I think we have a serious problem on our hands. Another one which might very well complicate our investigation into the assassination of Luis Muroz."

"Don't tell me. CIA?"

"Not officially, but we believe this guy is working off the books. Passport says this is William Nader."

Pinto looked at the features of the man on the screen. "How did we get alerted to this?"

"A security officer asked a few basic questions when he walked through the gates. Our latest voice analysis software picked up the conversation from the officer's camera on his lapel, and it indicated there is a high probability this is a man called Reznick. Jon Reznick. He has worked on highly classified operations for America. Black-ops specialist. This is not William Nader."

The huge screen showed the man identifying as William Nader with a backpack and suitcase, wearing sunglasses, arriving at Palma airport.

"Why am I only hearing about this now?"

"The voice analysis software was being updated over the last forty-eight hours. It only just went live in the last three hours."

Pinto leaned back in his seat. "That's bullshit."

"I know."

"Let's focus on this guy. And also the timeline of events. First, an assassination in Port de Sóller eight days ago. Maybe a foreign government. We still don't know. And now we have this CIA operator, if he is working for Langley, arriving on the island, presumably under a false name. This isn't a coincidence, is it?"

"Not a chance. The killing of Muroz was carefully planned. That's why we've had to keep it under wraps—a media blackout. But the Americans are onto this."

"Shit. And we still have no leads on who carried this out?"

"The intel indicates Basque separatists may have reformed with a new, younger, more radical leadership. We've also heard that there might be a Russian link."

Pinto brushed it off. "I can't see it. They have enough on their plate right now."

"It wouldn't be the first time. Consider this: Muroz had a pathological hatred for all things Russian. A lot of guys of his generation did. Muroz detested communism. Socialism. He loathed Moscow and everything it stood for. And the FSB are very active across Europe. We know this. We also know that paramilitary units are working in support of Catalan groups. Not to mention hundreds of foreign nationals working for Russian disinformation initiatives, especially in relation to Ukraine. Make no mistake, Russia's Main Intelligence Directorate influences operations, and is active in Madrid and Barcelona. That's GRU. So, they're here, in our midst."

Pinto studied the face of the American. "Point taken. We have also arrested several cyberwarfare specialists from Russia in Mallorca in the last two years, right?"

"Correct. Six men."

"Here's the problem. I really don't see this as a Russian operation. This would be heavy-handed even for them."

Mendes's face was impassive.

"Which still leaves us in the dark. The reality is we're nowhere near finding out who killed Muroz, much less who was behind it. Why is that?"

Mendes stared coldly at Pinto. "The assassin, sniper, whatever you call him, is not acting alone. That much is clear."

"What're your thoughts? Not about this Jon Reznick guy, but about who would carry out such an audacious assassination? I've been giving this some thought. Inside a naval base? I would bet my house that this was not the work of Moscow. So, if that's the case, what are we left with?"

"Consider the man who was neutralized. Muroz was a man who attracted attention. He had strong opinions. He wasn't afraid of sharing those opinions. He wrote columns in right-wing newspapers. He was not averse to rattling the cages of left-wing politicians. In fact, he reveled in it."

"It's not illegal, and it's hardly worth killing an old man over."

"Maybe, maybe not. But it made him many enemies in leftist circles. He was part of the old guard. Didn't seem to bother him that the world has changed. Spain has changed. He also had a Substack where he wrote about global challenges in the modern world. Everything from secularism to Marxism to Spain's growing levels of mass illegal immigration. He was ultra-strident on North African immigration."

"What's our best bet on what happened?"

"Our best analysis talks about a Red Brigades cell slowly emerging in Barcelona, aligned with the Catalonian independence movement. Backed by Cuba, Venezuela. No trace of Russia in the analysis. You want to see the report?"

Pinto waved the offer away. "Not buying it. Doesn't feel right. Zero strategic point for goddamn Cuba."

"So what do you think, Juan?"

"What do I think? I think this person, whoever killed Muroz, this ghost, might be working on behalf of a state actor, on behalf of a country."

"I agree."

"A country that has issues with our country. Maybe a country that has a problem with NATO."

"There is that. Which leaves Russia, China and Iran. The problem is that we have nothing to go on. Local police looked over the location they believe the shooter may have had access to. Civil Guard too. A cliff on the other side of the bay. But they've got nothing forensics-wise. He might have been able to fire from a parked van. We just don't know."

Pinto looked again at the man on the screen. "And now into the fray comes this man. Reznick, right?"

Mendes pinched the bridge of his nose, dark shadows under his eyes. "I've spoken to a few contacts of mine in the FBI. He's known to them."

"Shit, that's all we need. American intelligence services plugged into this."

"He used to work in the background for the FBI, apparently on sensitive, classified cases for a former assistant director named Martha Meyerstein. Reznick is as cold as it gets. He's a former Delta Forces operator. He lives in the shadows. After Delta he came under the auspices of the CIA. Disappeared after that."

"What's the American military attaché at the embassy in Madrid's involvement with this Reznick?"

"We don't know. The attaché we tailed, Chuck Glaser, landed in Palma the day after the hit."

Pinto nodded. "Do we know Glaser's purpose?"

"We don't know. But we can make an educated guess. We put a tail on him, and he quickly traveled back to Madrid. But when

I called Glaser a few hours ago, he doubled down that Nader is an American. Businessman. Likes to travel."

"That's bullshit. He's lying."

Mendes shrugged. "Absolutely."

"We need to confirm who sent him here. Where is he staying?"

"He checked into an Airbnb in the town of Port de Sóller, where the assassination was carried out."

"Seriously?"

"Yeah. But he's already moved to a boutique hotel, a block from the promenade. Quiet; more privacy. We also have footage of him inside a bar in the port. Hanging around. Asking questions apparently."

Pinto studied the face on the screen. Inscrutable. "There's more to this than a guy on vacation. Is he gathering intel? He's a killer, right? None of this adds up."

Mendes shut the file. "Correct. Reznick is an assassin. That's what he does."

"And the reason for his sudden arrival in Port de Sóller?"

"If I had to hazard an educated guess, Reznick has been hired to track down and kill the man who killed Muroz."

"But why?"

Mendez shrugged.

"Like I said, there's more to this than meets the eye," Pinto said. "What if the CIA has intel on this dead Spanish spook? What if Muroz was supplying intel to Langley? Was Muroz working for the CIA at one time?"

"We've searched Muroz's home in Port de Sóller top to bottom. Inside and out. Ripped up the floor, the walls, garden, concrete. There's nothing."

"Who wanted Muroz dead? And why the hell would the Americans want his killer dead? We need to find out. I don't like being blindsided."

"Where do we go from here?"

"First and foremost, we need to head to Mallorca. We can't allow this to get out of hand."

"Agreed."

"Besides, with Reznick's arrival, I fear anything could happen."

Seven

Reznick was already up and about, thinking about a daylight visit to the abandoned property. It posed risks. No question about that. But he needed to have a good look inside and outside, in natural light, to see if he was missing anything.

Something was gnawing at him. His focus on the abandoned property made sense. But he still had no concrete proof that it had been the shooter's location. Maybe he'd missed some evidence in the darkness that could confirm it, one hundred percent.

He began a series of stretches opposites Bar Roma before running along the wide promenade.

The early-morning sun was at his back, his T-shirt sticking to his sweaty skin. He jogged past a cop car, the policeman in the passenger seat staring long and hard at Reznick. A young woman on an electric scooter, backpack on, sped by, headphones on.

He ran on, beyond Hotel Espléndido, well-heeled tourists sitting at tables and sofas outside enjoying breakfast, and continued on over the bridge to the pedestrianized zone by Repic Beach.

He stopped for a few minutes and watched as the sun bathed the water and houses and hotels all around in a beautiful, dreamy, tangerine hue.

Reznick swigged some water and looked over to the naval base. He contemplated, once again, the sheer audacity and inside knowledge that would have been required to carry out the cold-blooded assassination of a retired Spanish intelligence chief on official soil. A man who would by the nature of his work have had secrets. A man who had known the value of intelligence.

The operative who had gunned down Muroz was clearly military-trained. And the shooter had to have had technical backup. Whether it was intercepted communications within the Spanish military or sources with the intelligence community. Maybe an insider who'd passed on the information.

He wondered if the Spanish intelligence services had intercepted some sort of electronic communication that had indicated an imminent threat to the life of Muroz. Was that what had prompted them to get him to a place of safety?

The irony was that Muroz hadn't been safer behind the walls of a military base. It was a major and humiliating intelligence failure, which was probably why it was being covered up.

Reznick finished the bottle of water and tossed it into a nearby trash can. He needed to look at the killing from a different angle. He could come up with a plausible theory as to why Muroz had been the target. But why the location? The Spanish government wasn't surrounding a retired intelligence officer with a large security detail. So why kill him when he was, in theory, in a more secure location?

Reznick considered whether the operative or his handler had some inside knowledge, or if the shooter had been initially instructed to neutralize Muroz at his villa up above Port de Sóller, and the base had been plan B. Had Muroz been closely guarded at his house? If so, then why move so suddenly to the base?

The more he thought about it, the more the questions kept piling up.

Reznick pushed those thoughts to the back of his mind as he turned around and jogged back across the wooden bridge. The rumble of the first tram of the day arriving in the port shattered the sultry calm, tourists leaning out of the open windows. He easily outran the old Franco-era tram as it trundled along.

When he got back to his hotel room, he showered and changed into a white polo shirt, navy shorts, and sneakers, and made his way down for breakfast. He loaded up at the buffet with a mug of fresh black coffee, a bowl of granola, a banana, and a couple of croissants. He took a seat outside on the outdoor patio adjacent to the pool area.

Reznick ate faster than he should have. He got a second coffee, and finished it in no time. He sat for a few minutes enjoying the hot Mallorcan sun. The warmth felt great on his skin.

When he was finished, Reznick left the hotel and walked to a nearby coffee shop. He sat down and ordered another coffee, his third of the morning.

He pulled out his cell phone as he watched the promenade slowly come to life.

"Afternoon, my friend, how are you?" he said to Trevelle.

"Good morning. Working away."

"Do you ever get a good night's sleep?"

"Not for a long time."

"Listen, Trevelle, I asked you to investigate a cleaner at the naval base. Any more on that?"

"Nothing on the cleaner. But I'm working on it. However, Muroz, I have an update."

"That I want to hear."

"You're going to love this. His body was indeed taken to the crematorium in Palma by the Civil Guard."

Reznick sipped his coffee, thinking back to his animated conversation with the drunk Spanish guy.

"That side of the story you heard stacks up," Trevelle continued. "So the cleaner might very well be telling the truth."

"You mind me asking how you know for sure?"

"I've done a deep dive into this base. Surveillance videos inside and outside, along with cameras inside the crematorium confirm this. I managed to retrieve the footage from a cloud server in Alicante."

"Great work. But we seem to be missing a step here. What about the autopsy?"

"If you like what I just told you, you're going to love this."

"Try me."

"They seem to have cut out the middleman in this case."

"What do you mean?" asked Reznick.

"Muroz's body was driven to Palma in the middle of the night, under the cover of darkness. Three hours after the shooting. Straight to the crematorium."

"So no autopsy? No medical examination of the body for forensics? Toxicology? What the hell is going on?"

"Nothing. A drive to the back door of the crematorium. Cameras inside the rear entrance show the makeshift coffin, which we can only assume contained Muroz's body, loaded into the incinerator. No body, no bullet. No forensics. Nothing. It's like it never happened."

"Sounds like a classic coverup. Very Franco-esque."

"You got it. No other explanation."

"So, when I arrived in Palma a few days after the killing, there was no funeral, it had already been incinerated. Without due process. No protocol followed."

"Correct," confirmed Trevelle.

"What about any family? No military funeral?"

"Zilch."

"I read that an aide to Muroz, one of his senior officers in the secret police, was blown up in a terrorist attack in the late 1960s by ETA."

"Maybe this is the link. They fucked up by blowing up the lower-level officer by mistake. Maybe they finally got their target. But the Spanish state is covering it up."

"I'm not buying it. Not for one minute. Have you established anything on potential friends, contacts, colleagues from Muroz's work in the intelligence service or the secret police?"

"He was born and brought up in Sóller. Other than that, I'm working on it. However, there is better news with regards to surveillance footage and cell phone triangulation around the time of the assassination."

Reznick sipped his coffee. "I thought there would be. What've you got?"

"A text message was received at a cell tower three minutes before the assassination. Triangulation pinpoints the recipient within a proximity of ten yards of the abandoned house."

"You've got to be kidding me."

"Nope. And the house has been in probate for years. Dispute held up in court."

"Good to know. The realtor said as much."

"At least someone is honest."

"So the text came from what device?"

"A burner phone I believe. Nokia."

"Location the message was sent from?"

"The sender was using a Swiss VPN. But I managed to strip all that away. The text came from a café in Paris."

"Paris? Are ETA in Paris? What about surveillance from the café at that time?"

"Wasn't working. Dead. Besides, we can't know for sure if it actually originated in Paris."

"If you had to put money on whether the text originated in Paris, what would you guess?"

"I'd guess the message originated in Paris."

"International dimension. Interesting." Reznick looked over the promenade, across the sparkling blue water, to the houses high up on the cliffs.

"Where do you go from here?"

"I think a second visit to the house is overdue."

"Be careful. None of this is good."

Eight

The mid-morning sun was streaming through the open windows of the top floor of Maria Garcia's townhouse. Maria assessed her reflection in the full-length mirror. She wore black, as she invariably did. Tired, rheumy eyes; lined face and cracked lips. She felt the solitude more and more. Her heart was aching. It would always be aching. The years of emptiness. She was in her eighty-ninth year, having lived alone for decades, with very little reason to go on. But she would endure. She always had. A quiet determination forged in childhood. Her father had endured, despite his trials and tribulations. She would too.

She would endure not only the loneliness, but the typical ailments of the old. Aching joints, aching limbs, and the pancreatic cancer eating her alive. The slow-release morphine kept it at bay for now. But she sensed the end was nigh. She was scared. Scared of dying. Scared of living.

She felt a sharp twinge in her arthritic knees. It wouldn't stop her kneeling down in church. Her beloved respite. A sanctuary from the secular world which had infected every corner of Spain. The Mallorca she had known as a child was gone. The country was gone. She longed for the certainties of the old Spain. The traditions. The faith. The religion. Now, in the twenty-first century, rampant, unashamed secularism was the new religion. No one believed in God. Not like they used to. No one believed in anything.

Sóller still had the most beautiful, exquisite church, centuries-old, located in the medieval town square, soaring majestically to the heavens. She had worshipped and prayed there throughout her life. The church loomed over the historic town like a sentinel. She remembered a quieter time. A more peaceful time. But it was all so different now. The month of August was peak tourist season. Locals had begun to rent out their properties to tourists throughout the year. The whole character of the Sóller had changed. It was younger, more belligerent, more in-your-face. A sense of entitlement from young Germans, Scandinavians, and, of course, the British. A movement had begun in Spanish society, objecting to being overrun and outpriced in their own towns and villages. She had read about large anti-tourist protests in Barcelona. She understood the sentiment. Locals unable to afford to stay in the towns their families had lived in for generations.

Maria just needed to look out of her window to see how things had changed. Not for the better, in her eyes. Thousands of visitors from wealthy Northern European countries, sitting around in cafés and bars in the plaza, drinking, sprawling over a place she had played in as a child.

The more she thought about her beloved Sóller, the sadder she got. What had become of the deeply Catholic town she had known? The respectful men. The farm workers. She felt vulnerable. Men and women drinking excessively, swearing in public. Sóller was not Magaluf, it was true. Nowhere near it. Its saving grace was that it had attracted a far better class of tourist. A more respectful tourist. But the God-fearing people she had grown up with were either dead or had moved away. The secularism was even creeping into the children growing up here now. Fewer went to church. More went to bars. It saddened her.

Maria adjusted the silver crucifix under her dress, clutching her rosary in her left hand. She shuffled downstairs, locking the door behind her, then turned and walked down the narrow street, keeping to the shadows. She brushed past a group of German tourists wearing football shirts. The smell of sunscreen, cheap perfume, and sweat lingered in the boiling air as she headed around the corner and out onto the plaza.

Maria did not make eye contact with anyone. She passed the water fountain. A young woman wearing a tight, see-through top, breasts partially exposed, sipping a beer from the bottle, sat with her bare feet in the water. It had been unheard of in Maria's time. She hurried up the steps of the church and through the huge, ornate wooden doors. She was glad to feel the still, cool air inside. She was in the sacred heart of the town.

She bowed her head and walked somberly toward the front of the church. She sat down, alone, in her usual spot. She glanced back for a moment. Three rows behind her was an old man she didn't recognize.

She closed her eyes, rosary clutched tight, the smell of incense and candle wax in the chilled, stony air of the ancient church. She imagined she was back here as a child. A little girl, holding her mother's hand. The Latin Mass. The liturgy. The solemn communion with God.

Maria slowly opened her eyes. She noticed a few regulars who turned and nodded, smiling, in her direction. She did likewise. She was a regular at Mass. Later, she would attend the Vigil Service. She was comforted by and devoted to the rituals. They gave her peace in her heart—a sacred connection with earlier generations, and with God almighty. She would give thanks and prayers to St. Bartholomew. She would say the catechisms. She would read her Bible when she got home.

She got up from her seat and kneeled inside the Gothic edifice, thinking of what she had lost, tears cooling her wrinkled skin. She thought of her beautiful daughter who had disappeared from her life. A daughter who wanted nothing to do with her. A daughter who had seemed to enjoy tormenting Maria when she was around. Now her daughter—Maria didn't even know if she was alive or dead—had made no contact since leaving home and never coming back.

Maria grieved for her. She also grieved for her late husband whose death had overshadowed the last fifty years of her life. She feared God was punishing her.

She sat in her seat for a few moments after the service. Maria spoke briefly to the priest in passing, then went straight back to her home, her memories all she had left. Photographs, images burned into her mind of family, long gone. The daughter she had cradled in her arms, soothing her with gentle prayers. The husband she had held. She had nothing but regrets now. But there were still memories. Memories, and secrets she had been entrusted with.

Secrets she would take to the grave.

Nine

Reznick decided he needed to try to visit Muroz's house on the outskirts of Port de Sóller before he made his second trip up to the abandoned house. It was late morning as he turned right along the promenade, backpack slung over his shoulder. A couple of sweeper trucks and garbage collectors emptied trash cans and cleaned the street. Reznick turned up a steep winding road, along Carrer de Santa Caterina. Past Bar Albatros on the corner. He walked on, higher and higher, the road getting narrower.

He pulled his baseball cap half an inch lower, shielding his eyes from the brutal sun. Heart rate rising, endorphins kicking in. He checked his watch. It showed a temperature of thirty-two degrees. Eighty-nine degrees Fahrenheit. Another hot one.

Reznick climbed up more steps, past renovated old fishermen's cottages, most converted into fancy apartments and townhouses. Pastel painted shutters. He was on the same side of the water as the naval base. But at a far higher elevation.

As he continued up the winding path, he passed breathless, overweight tourists who had already hiked up to the top.

Reznick stopped outside a low-rise apartment complex and took stock. Two police cars and a Civil Guard car blocked off the entrance to the large, detached villa. Blue and white tape cordoned off the area. It was still locked down. Maybe they were still searching the property or the grounds.

A police officer walked down the hill toward Reznick and ducked under the tape. "Señor? Can I help you?"

"I wanted to visit the maritime museum at the end of the road," he lied.

The officer gave a sharp shake. "No, Señor. Not possible. It's closed until further notice."

"Why, what happened?" he asked.

"I'm not able to tell you that, sir. I'm sorry. It's a Civil Guard matter."

Reznick could see he wasn't going to make any headway. "Appreciate your time."

"No problem, Señor."

Reznick turned and walked back down the hill. Halfway down he stopped beside a metal fence and looked out over the dazzling blue waters of Sóller Bay. His experience had told him that trying to push an investigation would be fruitless. Far better to quietly, slowly, and deliberately build a picture of what had happened. Small steps. *Slow is smooth, smooth is fast.*

Off to his right, inside the naval base, the yellow and red Spanish flag fluttered at half-mast. He found it interesting that the base was marking the death of Muroz—assuming it was the passing of the former secret police chief they were commemorating.

Daniel Black had set Reznick a virtually impossible task. He had questioned the wisdom of one man being sent in. But despite the formidable challenge he faced, his mindset always, invariably, defaulted to *there is always a way*. He had been taught to figure stuff out. There was always a solution. Sometimes you just needed to hang around long enough.

He thought back to the hardcore Delta Force selection process. The punishing runs, brutal hand-to-hand combat, elite marksmanship, the need for gut-wrenching stamina. You had to go above and beyond, even when you felt like you were going to die. And you needed a deep resilience, a mental strength, so you were ready to go again. To fight again. Never give up.

Delta was full of tough, smart, and highly self-motivated type-A personalities like him. But they were also problem-solvers. It was a prerequisite. They had to figure shit out. Many were perfectionists. They trained like crazy until it was second-nature. Trained to kill. But also trained to think. It could save their lives. What to do in the middle of a firefight in Ramadi in Iraq, surrounded by a baying mob—how did you extricate yourself? How did you reach a target? How to fight back without killing everyone in the town? There was always another way. You just had to figure it out.

Reznick had been taught to work a problem. Failure was not an option. It had been drummed into him. Be flexible. Take charge. Figure it out. If you can't figure it out, find someone who can.

Reznick charged along the promenade to the other side of the bay, then up the steep, winding road, the blazing midday sun burning the back of his neck. He eventually reached the row of clifftop villas. He walked along the narrowing dirt road to the abandoned villa, then took a few moments to check that he hadn't been followed.

The first thing he noticed was that there was no realtor's car nearby or outside the property this time. That boded well, he thought.

Reznick opened the creaking metal gate and crept down the overgrown path and around the side of the house to a weed-strewn terrace. He needed to be in and out in less than five minutes. That's the time he had allotted himself.

Reznick took out his knife and inserted it into the lock of the French doors, twisting it hard. He leveraged it back and forward before the doors clicked open.

He pushed open the doors and stepped inside.

Reznick took a long look at the interior of the villa in the daylight. Hardwood floors, no furniture, floor-to-ceiling windows, all left to rot. He bounded upstairs in the dusty, airless house. No art on the white walls. Blank, as if all the possessions had been taken out until the court case was resolved.

He climbed up another flight of stairs. The attic—ceiling low, angled.

Reznick stood on the terracotta tiles of the attic floor. He turned the key, opened the doors and stepped out onto the terrace. He looked down at the weed-strewn terrace below, grass and algae growing in between the cracks of the tiles. He was looking for any clues, signs of life, evidence of the sniper that he had missed. But there was nothing.

Reznick felt frustrated. He slipped back inside, keeping the doors open. His gaze searched the empty attic room. Light flooded the space. He walked to the rear of the room and turned around. He took out his binoculars, turning to face the base.

Goddamn it. This is the spot.

He had perfect line of sight set back in the room. Crucially, the sniper would have been well concealed from view, hidden in the rear of the attic. It was perfect for a sniper. The terrace, on reflection, wasn't the obvious choice after all.

Reznick sensed that this was indeed the room, the exact spot, from which the assassin had taken the fatal shot. One shot. It would have required a highly proficient marksman. It wasn't ultra-long-range. But the difficulty the shot presented couldn't be underrated.

He went back out onto the terrace and looked down onto a concrete patio area adjacent to the filthy pool, flies and insects buzzing around the green-brown water. He turned around and carefully examined the lock. A few scratches, but not from Reznick gaining entry. Maybe the scratches had been caused by the sniper opening the doors.

Reznick went back inside, carefully shutting and locking the French doors. He checked his watch. Two minutes left. He went back downstairs to the first floor, through the kitchen, and out a door directly under the attic's balcony.

He crept through the overgrown grass covering the ceramic tiles that fringed the stagnant pool. He kneeled down, looking for anything that had been missed by the local police. Closer and closer. It was then that he saw it—a gray, waxy substance. A thick wad of old, heavily chewed gum.

Reznick pulled back the tufts of grass as he leaned in so he was just inches away, staring at the piece of gum. Then he noticed something even more interesting. Indentations.

Teethmarks.

He took out his cell phone and zoomed in with the camera, snapping a photo. Then he took a pen out of his backpack and gingerly turned over the gum. Teeth imprints—three upper teeth, maybe a molar missing, and an incisor. He took more photos. Different angles of the gum.

It was a long shot. Then again, it was worth exploring, even if there was a remote chance of finding a match. Trevelle had told him that the villa hadn't been occupied for years. Maybe he was grasping at straws. But he didn't have anything else to work with.

Reznick sent the photos over to Trevelle.

"You taking up dentistry, man?" Trevelle laughed when he answered the phone.

"Good one. No, I found this lying below the upstairs balcony, in thick grass and weeds, below where the shooter might have been standing before he took the shot. I'm guessing whoever owned this place or lived here last didn't spit gum out into their garden."

"Jon, that's a super-long shot."

"Maybe. But I still want you to check it out."

"How?"

"Get hold of a forensic odontologist."

"Jon, you've gone crazy."

Reznick was beginning to wonder if he had. "Get the very best there is. Make sure they're a government scientist, maybe working for the Feds, or someone who's worked for the government. Security clearance is important."

"Copy that."

"Once you've found the best forensic dentist you can, who has the required security clearance, send them the photos."

"Of teeth imprints in a piece of gum?"

"I know . . . it's crazy. But you never know. If it's nothing, we can rule it out. But if we get lucky and we get a match, it could be the opening we're looking for."

"I don't want to rain on your parade, Jon, but has it occurred to you that it might have belonged to the owner of the property and been there for years? Maybe it was their kids. Maybe friends of the kids."

"Can't rule it out. But I want you to get going with that. Do what you can. And do it fast. Let's see where it takes us."

Ten

The window was wide open but the blackout curtains were drawn tight, and there was hardly a breath of air.

Frederick Hicks lay on his bed and tried to follow the spin of the noisy ceiling fan, waiting for a call. The stifling third-floor apartment was situated above an alley in the heart of Palma's Old Town. Sweat beading on his back, his mind in feverish anticipation. In the distance, he heard church bells. The sound took him back to his childhood in the Midwest. A world he had left behind.

His family had been regular churchgoers. For all he knew, his parents still were. He hadn't reached out to them since his disappearance in Mosul. He had been told that his parents would have been advised by the Army that Frederick, in all likelihood, was probably dead.

He sensed he was about to be activated again. The thought of that made his heart beat that little bit faster. He was ready. But he suspected they were testing him. Making sure he was mentally strong enough. Making sure he wouldn't slip up. Making sure he would stay the course.

Hicks had completed the first of the trio of assignments. He had been given one shot to kill Muroz. And he had done it. But he knew that he would have to complete the second assignment here in Palma before he would be allowed the opportunity to carry out the third crucial assassination. He had no specific idea what the targets would be. But he knew the third was going to be big.

His handlers were toying with him. It was a game they were playing. It was almost as if they knew what he was thinking. How he was feeling. For all he knew, they might have preinstalled cameras in this sweltering apartment ahead of his arrival. Nothing would surprise him.

The smell of spicy cooking wafted in to his room from the Indian restaurant below.

Hicks had been rather glad to get out of Port de Sóller and the Sóller area in general. He had traveled to the city of Palma by motorbike in the early hours of the morning. Through the warren of narrow streets and alleys of the capital's Old Town, past the smart boutiques, bars, tapas restaurants, upscale hotels, art galleries, late-night drinkers, cafés still buzzing in the night, then he'd slipped up the dusty stairs and into the rundown apartment.

He yawned, having managed only a few hours' sleep since his arrival, thanks in part to the broken air-conditioning.

Hicks was restless. He got to his feet and did some stretches, getting rid of the knots of tension in his back and neck. He did a hundred push-ups. Then a hundred crunches.

The endorphins kicked in, elevating his mood. He felt sharper. He raced to the tiny bathroom, splashed lukewarm water on his face, and dried it on a towel. He was wired. He had been cooped up long enough. He needed to be outside, on the move.

He put on a pair of shades, a navy baseball cap, and his old Adidas sneakers, and tucked his phone into his back pocket.

Hicks charged downstairs and into the narrow street. The smell of cigarette smoke and fish from a nearby paella restaurant wafted his way. He walked around the block, soaking up the ambience. Well-heeled locals and tourists flocked to the glass-fronted shops. The modernity was juxtaposed with beautiful Renaissance architecture, as well as Baroque, Gothic, and, in a sign of the influence of the Moors, arched ochre stonework. Cartier, Louis Vuitton, Carolina Herrera, Hugo Boss—the brand names were everywhere. He took a shortcut through a courtyard and then down an alley to a delightful square. He found an empty sidewalk table outside a café.

The waiter approached. "Señor?"

Hicks perused the menu slowly. He ordered avocado toast and a cappuccino.

A while later, the waiter returned with his food and drink.

Hicks devoured his brunch, then sat watching the world go by. Cyclists pedaled down the impossibly narrow, ancient street, followed by cops on mopeds. A pair of police officers walked by, eyeing everyone with suspicion.

A Moroccan street vendor approached a lady outside a café farther down the street. He was selling African beads, silk scarves, smoking his unfiltered cigarette, shouting from time to time in Arabic. It was a matter of seconds before the poor guy was set upon by cops.

Hicks watched as the man was grabbed by the two cops who had passed by only moments earlier. He felt sorry for the unfortunate bastard, having to hawk his wares to tourists. He sipped his coffee, grateful to be in the shade of the narrow Old Town street and out of the blinding, fierce sun. His cell phone rang. Maybe this was the call he had been waiting for.

"How are you today, Freddy?" The voice of his handler. "Everything okay?"

"You mind booking some decent accommodation in future? Air-conditioning is broken. Again."

"Can't get the staff these days."

Hicks wasn't in the mood for jokes.

"I'm sorry. It won't happen again," his handler promised. "So, you decided to get out of your apartment."

He assumed that they'd been tracking him. "I was roasting alive."

"I understand."

"What've you got for me? Any updates?"

"I have a time."

"When?"

"Not long."

"Can you be more precise?"

"It will be in eight hours and six minutes."

Hicks checked his watch. He wondered why the second hit was in the late hours of the night. "Location?"

"Bar Artemis on Plaça de Cort. Popular square, other bars and restaurants around. It will be very busy, according to our research."

Hicks knew where the bar was. It was only yards from a six-hundred-year-old olive tree, close to the town hall. It made sense. At that late hour, the bar would be thronged with tourists and locals, soaking up the intoxicating atmosphere. When it was dark, the temperature dipped enough to be far more comfortable. He had passed the bar last night as he made his way to his crummy apartment. It had been standing-room-only, inside and out. "Copy that. Very interesting."

"Do you know it?"

"Passed it. Perfect. Have we got any background on the target?"

"The man is a politician. He frequents that bar."

"One less politician. What's not to like."

"Indeed."

"What else?"

"We have been watching him for months. This bar is a regular haunt. I mean, this is where he goes to get loaded."

"Why?" said Hicks.

"He's lonely. And that's why he's there four nights of the week."

"Is he married?"

"Yes."

"So he's in town during the week, attending the Parliament of the Balearics, right?"

"Correct."

Hicks felt as if he knew the politician already, although he didn't yet have the name.

"He never misses a session of parliament. But he is a big drinker. Two years ago, he was diagnosed with liver damage. But it hasn't stopped him."

"And when he's not getting drunk or in parliament?"

"He returns to his home in Cala Bona for the weekends with his family."

Hicks shot his eyes over to the Moroccan street vendor, who was now being hustled, noisily, into the back of a police car. "What does this politician look like?"

His cell phone pinged. A photo of a portly, ruddy-faced seventy-something man.

"You get it?"

Hicks memorized the face. "Copy that. The guy looks like he needs to go to the gym."

"Anything else?"

"His name?"

"Javier Perez. He's a far-right politician on the rise. Married for twenty years to his third wife, who lives in Cala Bona. A former member of the European Parliament. Neoconservative. His grandfather was a confidant of Franco, no less. Virulently anti-immigration. Anti-Islam, same as Muroz. Has also called for the bombing of Tehran. Hence why they were both chosen as the warm-up to the main event. He has called for a Crusade against non-Christians. And we believe he has views that might get traction at the next election. There's speculation he might even become the next prime minister of Spain."

Before his eyes, the photo of Perez dissolved on his phone.

"Are you ready?"

Hicks looked at his watch. "A lot of time to kill until then."

"Stretch your legs for an hour. When you return to your apartment, you will see that a parcel has been left for you. It will be lying at the bottom of the wardrobe in the bedroom."

"You want me to go for a walk?"

"Yes, a long walk. Head down to the marina, look around, stop for a coffee. Then go back to your apartment."

Hicks's mind began to race to the hit in the early hours. "How are we doing this?"

"We have thought about this. You will wait for an opening. Maybe a bathroom break. He drinks a lot, and his medical reports show he has had prostate problems. So he'll be needing to piss regularly."

"That's a fair assumption. Question is, how do we neutralize this guy?"

"It's going to be made to look natural. You will have the necessary equipment delivered to you within the hour."

Hicks ended the call and felt his stomach tighten as he thought ahead to the second hit.

He paid his bill and sauntered off, through the narrow medieval streets of the Old Town. He stopped to glance in the window of a boutique displaying women's fashion, practicing countersurveillance techniques. He did this on three further occasions. A few hundred yards away, he walked into a bar and exited through the kitchen. No one said a word.

Hicks took a circuitous route to the marina, walking along the Paseo Maritimo, Palma's seafront promenade. He then headed counterclockwise, staying in the shadows of the narrow streets of the Old Town for as long as possible, past a beautiful church on a corner, then he walked parallel to the gardens of Can Fontiroig, site of the remains of the Arab Baths, before he returned to his suffocating apartment. He made his way up the stairs, swiped the card for the door, and shut himself inside. He triple-locked the door, closed the external shutters, and drew the curtains. He opened the wardrobe. Inside, below his jeans and shirts hanging on the clothes rail, lay a bulky North Face backpack. His handler was as good as his word.

He took out the backpack and carefully unzipped it. Inside was a Ziploc bag with two ballpoint pens. He knew what they would contain. A special ingredient—sux. A paralyzing drug. The victim would be unable to move, and it would induce a heart attack. Also inside was a new iPhone, a tiny earpiece, a Glock, a carton of ammo, and a cardboard box containing a white shirt, a tailored navy linen suit, expensive-looking dark brown Italian loafers, a spectacle case with tortoiseshell glasses, and a set of electric hair clippers. Business casual. Nice.

He loaded the magazine and racked the Glock's slide. Then he placed the gun on the bedside table and lay back down on the bed, his mind ablaze.

It was dark when Hicks's cell phone alarm vibrated by his bed. He had been waiting for this moment. He checked his watch. It was just past eleven-thirty. But just as importantly, the watch also showed his blood pressure was perfect. 110/68. No nerves. Ice cold.

Hicks took a tepid shower and felt invigorated, alive. He shaved off his beard and trimmed his tousled shoulder-length hair. He put on the white shirt, suit pants, and loafers. He checked himself out in the freestanding full-length mirror and smiled. Very clean-cut.

Hicks put on the stylish navy linen jacket, carefully placing the ballpoint pens in an inside pocket. He powered up his new iPhone and placed it in his pants pocket. He put on the tortoiseshell glasses then checked his reflection in the mirror for the final time. He looked like a suave German or English tourist popping in for a drink or two before bed.

He had a mental picture in his head of how it was going to go. The environment, a packed bar, was going to be a challenge. There were multiple variables. Drunk people were unpredictable. They approached strangers. They bumped into people. Besides, the bar was tiny. He would also need to find the right moment. There couldn't be anyone in the bathroom apart from himself and the target.

Hicks knew this was going to be tricky. It wasn't as simple as a long-range sniper shot. And this was all assuming that the target would turn up. He was relying on the intel on the target's movements and habits to be correct.

He needed the atmosphere in the bar to be busy—noisy, but not chaotic. He would have to wait for the right moment—a window of opportunity in a vibrant, packed, unpredictable environment.

Hicks lingered in the room for a few more moments. He couldn't believe he was at the center of it all at this moment. He would make history. But he felt relaxed in himself. He was where he was always meant to be. Guided by a higher power. The blue-eyed assassin, they called him. He liked that.

He picked up the miniscule earpiece and inserted it into his left ear, then departed his sweltering apartment just before midnight. The air was sticky, high humidity, but still more pleasant than that suffocating apartment. He locked the door behind him, skipped down the stairs and out onto the buzzing, cosmopolitan backstreets of the Old Town. Brushed past tipsy tourists and locals at the teeming sidewalk cafés and bars. Street hustlers selling beads, hash, coke, grass, cigarettes, whatever.

He threaded through the crowds and down an alley, then into the ancient square. Up ahead he saw the neon sign for the bar. A few tables outside, people drinking, some eating small plates of tapas. He hadn't eaten for hours. He felt famished. But he knew he would have plenty of time to eat when the job was done.

Hicks headed inside. He brushed past a group of affluent young Spanish guys, laughing, joking. He padded across the flagstone floor in his leather-soled loafers, through the bar into an alcove area, past the chatter of noisy Spaniards talking politics, tourists, and, of course, soccer. He spotted the last empty table and was grateful to sit down.

A waitress approached, flashing a huge smile. He ordered a half-bottle of rosé, tipping the waitress twenty euros when she brought it over. "Gracias, Señor."

Hicks sipped his glass of chilled wine. He had never felt crazier. Never felt happier. He soaked up the convivial atmosphere, the bonhomie. He hadn't been into a bar like this in a long, long time. In a way, it seemed a shame for such a pleasant evening to be cut short. He sat quietly, mind churning, as he imagined what was going to unfold.

The adrenaline rushed through his body, his nerve ends twitching in anticipation.

Hicks checked his watch. It was ten minutes after midnight. The place was packed but he wasn't sweating, thanks to the welcome blast of air from a cooling unit behind his head.

His earpiece buzzed. "Good evening. I'll be guiding you over the next few moments. Do not speak. Just listen. Clear your throat if you understand."

Hicks cleared his throat as instructed. It was good to hear the voice of his handler again. A man he trusted with his life.

"The target is sitting at the far end of the bar with a young lady friend. Take a look in a few moments."

Hicks's gaze wandered around the bar until it fixed on the rumpled, sweaty old guy, arm draped around the petite young woman in a low-cut red dress. The man was partially slumped over, as if he were already wasted. Hicks watched surreptitiously as the man pawed clumsily at the woman's thighs.

"The woman he is with is not his wife," the handler said.

A married man touching a woman who was not his wife in an intimate way repulsed him. In many ways, Hicks held ultra-traditional values. One man, one woman. He couldn't abide infidelity of any sort. It reminded him of his father. A father who had attended church but beaten his wife until Hicks intervened as a strapping teenager and stopped it. He was only fourteen. A short while later, his abusive father had broken down and apologized, humiliated.

He pushed those thoughts to one side. He watched the man kiss the girl on the cheek, stroking, caressing her silky hair, laughing.

Hicks observed this exchange while nursing his glass of rosé. The man's eyes were glazed, face flushed.

"Choose your moment. We have all the time. Good luck, my friend."

The earpiece clicked off. The group at the next table were talking excitedly as they watched the highlights of a Barcelona and Valencia soccer game, gesticulating at every perceived foul.

Javier Perez ordered another bottle of white wine. He toasted the pretty woman at his side, then proceeded to knock back his glass in one large gulp. The barman filled up his glass as the girl giggled excitedly. All around, the bar's patrons were raising their voices, shouting. The noise was like a cacophony. But it wasn't out of control. The portents were favorable.

Hicks glanced up at the TV. The commentator seemed to explode into life. The commentator screaming, jabbering away. A player had been badly fouled, leading to uproar on the pitch and a commotion in the bar.

Hicks watched and waited. Quietly. Patiently. He observed Perez lean forward again and kiss the girl on the neck, then her cheek, before whispering in her ear. She laughed at whatever he said.

Perez slid off the stool and blew her a kiss before he stumbled away toward the restroom, pulling his tight-fitting pants above his waist. A red neon sign—*Bano*—was situated above a mirror at the rear of the bar.

Hicks sensed this was his opportunity. He waited a few moments to make sure no one else was following Perez, then glanced around. Everyone seemed to be enthralled by the soccer highlights on the TV. He slowly got up from his chair and made his way to the restroom, along a long passageway at the back of the bar.

Perez was standing, swaying slightly, his back to him, peeing loudly into the ceramic urinal. He looked around and grinned, face red, sweating. The guy was blazing drunk, eyes bloodshot, heavy and glazed, as he attempted to zip up his pants.

Hicks reached into his jacket pocket, took out the pen and pressed the cap, activating the needle inside. He sharply jabbed the man with the needle through his dark jeans, into his backside.

The man turned briefly, taken aback, mouth open.

Hicks watched as the man's bloodshot eyes fixed on his—terrified, unable to comprehend what had just happened—before he collapsed on the tiled mosaic floor. Eyes wide open, staring. Paralyzed. Unable to speak, move. Not even to blink.

The pinprick on the man's backside would look like a spot. The suxamethonium chloride had worked its magic. Assassination didn't have to be a gunshot. Sometimes a victim could look as if they had died of natural causes.

Hicks gazed down into the politician's unblinking eyes. The target didn't know it, but he would soon be dead. The autopsy would simply show a heart attack. Classic. Hicks knew Perez would be dead before he had left the bar. He put the pen back in his pocket, turned, and walked nonchalantly out onto the street, not catching anyone's gaze.

A girl wearing a full-face crash helmet on a powerful Kawasaki motorbike was waiting for him. He climbed on the back and she accelerated away, through the winding backstreets of Palma. The night-owl revelers continued drinking wine, laughing and joking, as Hicks disappeared into the sultry night.

Eleven

The backstreet in Port de Sóller, Carrer de Canonge Oliver, was deathly quiet as Reznick returned to his hotel. It was just past three in the morning. Not a soul around. But he sensed he was being followed.

The low hum of an electric car was almost imperceptible at first. He walked on past the church across the street. But then he stopped and turned around.

The headlights of a Civil Guard car bathed the street.

Reznick pretended to lurch a little as the car pulled up sharply beside him. Let them think he was tipsy, on his way home from the bar. He was tempted to pull out his Beretta that Trevelle had sent to his hotel. But he knew that would have him arrested, deported, or simply shot.

Three cops wearing jeans and T-shirts and sneakers stepped out.

The smallest of the three, sporting a neat goatee beard, flashed a Guardia Civil ID. "Señor, a moment please. You need to come with us."

"Why? What's the problem?"

"No problem. We just have some questions, Mr. Nader. Nothing to worry about."

Reznick's instincts told him he should worry. If they were calling him by his fake name, he sensed they knew who he really was. "So, what do you want to know?"

"Señor, not here on the street, we will explain it all soon. But you need to come with us, otherwise you will be arrested. *Comprende?*"

Reznick could see from the expressions of the three armed Civil Guards that they were in no mood for any bullshit, especially from a belligerent American. He decided to play along. "I don't know what this is all about. I was just out enjoying a couple drinks."

Despite his protestations, he was directed into the back seat of the Civil Guard cruiser, sandwiched between two of the officers.

The car sped away from the port toward central Sóller, just over three miles away. There, the vehicle pulled up outside a nondescript Civil Guard office down a quiet side street, not far from the main plaza.

Reznick was brought in through a side door and escorted to a windowless room.

The Civil Guard officer with the goatee pointed to a chair. "Sit down, Señor Nader."

Reznick sat down. A young woman walked in and handed him a bottle of water. He took a sip. "Thanks. Well, this is nice. This where you guys hang out at night?"

Impassive faces all around as the young woman left the room. His stab at humor had gone down like a lead balloon, not surprisingly.

The door opened and a wiry, tough-looking man, wearing a white button-down shirt and navy chinos and boat shoes, walked in. The man's face was like stone, dark shadows under his eyes. He carried a manila folder.

He sat down across from Reznick and sighed, putting the folder down on the desk. He fixed his gaze on Reznick for a few moments. "Well, here we are. Are you enjoying your vacation, Mr. Nader?"

"I was until I got brought here. What's going on?"

"We were hoping you could tell us, Mr. Nader. That is your name, right?"

Reznick dead-eyed the man. "Who are you?"

"My name is Juan Pinto, Civil Guard intelligence unit in Madrid. We report directly to the Ministry of Defense."

"Good to know."

"But right now I'm working on a taskforce set up by our National Intelligence Center. The *Centro Nacional de Inteligencia.*"

Reznick shrugged. "That's all very impressive."

"You see, I concern myself with national security and intelligence, transnational threats. Terrorism. Organized crime. And I've got some questions for you. We believe there are irregularities in your passport. We were hoping you might be able to help us out."

"What's the problem?"

Pinto opened the file and pulled out some black-and-white photos. He pushed them across the table to Reznick. The images showed Reznick outside the abandoned house talking to the realtor. "Your passport says you are a business consultant from New York. Your name is William Nader? Is that right?"

"Correct."

"Where in New York do you live?"

"I live here and there. I work remotely a lot of the time."

"Help me out here, William. Why is a business consultant from America showing such an interest in a broken-down, abandoned house in beautiful Port de Sóller. A house that is not even for sale."

"Well, to be honest, I was thinking about buying a retirement home in Europe."

Pinto smiled, shaking his head. "Don't take me for a stupid man. I know who you are. You are not William Nader, are you?"

Reznick took his passport out of his back pocket and handed it to Pinto. "Look for yourself. It's all fine. Most folks call me Bill."

Pinto opened the passport and studied the photo and details. "It's an interesting story. But we believe it is a cover story. And that's a problem for not only us, but also you."

Reznick shifted in his seat. "I don't follow."

"There is no person called William Nader. Certainly not in this room."

"You need to take this up with the State Department. They deal with passports for American citizens."

Pinto leaned back in his seat.

"Listen, I haven't a clue what you're getting at," said Reznick. "I'm assuming this is all just a big misunderstanding. You've seen my passport and it's all in order."

"The passport most certainly is not all in order. Maybe I need to make myself clearer. We know your true identity. Your real name."

Reznick said nothing as Pinto put his cards on the table.

"Your name is Jon Reznick. You work for the American government. Am I right?"

Reznick folded his arms.

"Don't be shy, Mr. Reznick." Pinto flicked through the folder. "I managed to procure all your details through a friend of mine. Your file makes for fascinating reading."

"This is all very interesting. I'm guessing mistaken identities happen all the time. But is there a point to all this? I looked at a house that's not for sale?"

"My patience is not infinite. You need to tell us precisely why you are here. If not, you will be deported with immediate effect."

"I don't understand what you're getting at. I'm on vacation. I was looking at a property. True, it needs a lot of work from what I saw of the outside. So what's the problem? A retirement home in the sun."

"You look too young to retire."

"I like to plan ahead. That's my motto."

Pinto gave a rueful smile. "Why that property? It's not for sale. It isn't advertised as for sale. But I'm guessing you already knew that."

Reznick shrugged.

"I believe you have other reasons to be looking at that property, Mr. Reznick. And I'm wondering why that would be."

"I'm not following."

"I would appreciate it if you were a little more forthcoming about your interest in that property."

"Listen, I don't want to be disrespectful. I love Mallorca, I love Spain. I don't know if some wires have gotten crossed or something. But the fact of the matter is I'm an American citizen. Check with the American Embassy in Madrid or the consulate in Palma."

"We will."

"I'm visiting this beautiful island like millions of others. I literally have no idea why you pulled me in. This all seems so unnecessary."

"I'll tell you another reason we pulled you in. I can sense trouble a mile off, as you Americans like to say."

"You can sense trouble? What trouble?"

"I like order, Mr. Reznick. Or . . . Mr. Nader. We don't welcome outside interference in our country. So, I'm going to ask you again . . . why are you here?"

"Outside interference? What are you talking about?"

Pinto slammed the palm of his hand hard onto the table. "You know what I'm talking about," he said, raising his voice. "You know your story is a lie."

"I've already answered your questions, Captain Pinto. You've seen my passport. I have no idea what you're talking about, and this is eating into my vacation."

"Eating into your vacation." Pinto leafed through the folder in front of him again. "Do not fuck with us."

"I am a law-abiding American."

"So you keep telling us. We have also learned that you checked into an Airbnb on the promenade down in Port de Sóller."

"That's not unusual, is it?"

"What is unusual is that, for some unknown reason, within a few hours you left and checked into one of the town's nicest boutique hotels. Why is that?"

Reznick considered this, steepling his hands. "I'm very picky about my accommodations."

"So, what was wrong with the apartment?"

"I wasn't happy with the size of the television. Besides, a lot of the channels are preset with German TV shows."

Pinto smiled. "Very droll, Mr. Reznick. I like a man who can find humor in adversity."

"Listen, let's cut to the chase. Charge me with changing accommodation if you must. But just so you know, I don't welcome being hassled while on vacation. If I'm not released, my next call will be to the American Embassy in Madrid. And trust me, they don't fuck around with niceties. So, what do you say?"

Pinto stared long and hard at him. "Your mask seems to have slipped, Jon. We know what you're all about, Mr. Reznick. Don't think you can come to our beautiful country and undermine our democratic institutions, our way of life. We have a balanced society.

We believe in freedom but also structure. We have laws. And we have our own ways of doing things."

Reznick leaned back in his seat. "No disrespect, but I have literally no idea what you're talking about."

Pinto pressed his hands on the table. "Let me be clear, just so there is no further misunderstanding. We know what brought you here."

"What was that?"

"We don't take kindly to foreign governments meddling in our domestic affairs."

"What domestic affairs are you talking about?"

Pinto's face flushed crimson. "Play games all you want, Mr. Reznick, but I want you to know that we will be watching you very closely. We have been watching you. We know who you are. We know what you do."

"Am I free to go?"

"You need to think long and hard before you decide if you want to continue this vacation. We don't want you here. I'll leave it at that—for now."

Within a few minutes of the surreal interview-cum-interrogation, Reznick was released into the deserted Sóller streets. It was just after four in the morning. He walked back to the main plaza and caught a cab back down to the port. He asked to be dropped off outside Es Cantó, which was still open, a few locals sitting outside on stools.

Reznick ordered a cold beer as a Spanish news channel showed police taping off a bar. He sipped his drink, staring at the screen. A photo of a plump guy in a suit flashed up.

The barman wiped the top of the bar with a dirty cloth. He pointed at a clean-cut guy in the corner. "He was asking for you earlier."

Reznick looked over at the man sitting by himself, sipping a glass of white wine. "Me? Who is he?"

"He's the brother of the crazy guy who was hassling you last night. You know, the loudmouth. He's harmless but he can get argumentative when he's drunk. The brother is a nice man. A policeman."

Reznick expected this was related to his interrogation. His mind flashed back to the conversation with the drunk man about what his sister claimed had happened inside the naval base. He knew that what the man had told him was true.

"Why does he want to speak to me?"

"He's worried something might happen to you. He's a cop. But he's a good guy."

Reznick ordered two more bottles of beer, and walked over to sit down beside the middle-aged, clean-shaven man with piercing gray eyes. He was wearing a black T-shirt and jeans.

Reznick handed him one of the beers. "I hear you want to speak to me."

The man leaned in. "Gracias, Señor. I didn't know if or when you would turn up."

"Here I am."

The man's gaze wandered around the bar. "I am a policeman."

"So I heard."

"Twenty-four years. I live here in Port de Sóller. But I wanted to warn you."

"Warn me?"

"You need to be careful. People are watching."

Reznick knew that already from the conversation with Pinto. "What people?"

"The Civil Guard. I know that for a fact."

"They're watching me? What seems to be the problem?"

The man gulped some beer from the bottle, glancing up at the TV. "The police, people like me, we're not like the Civil Guard. We are local. They take their orders from Madrid. They close ranks. You have to be very careful."

"I understand what you're saying. Can you talk about your brother? He spoke to me last night."

The man's eyes became guarded.

"Quite a character," Reznick prodded.

"He's an alcoholic, Señor. A smart man, but a hopeless drinker. But he is not a bad man. Sadly, my sister also has her problems."

"Your sister cleans at the base, he said?"

"Correct."

"What do you know?"

"I know something is very wrong. My sister tells the truth without fail. I hear things too. I believe they have tried to hush up what happened. It is scary what has happened in the town."

Reznick feigned ignorance. "Hush what up?"

"The killing. The shooting."

"Inside the base?"

"They don't want anyone to know."

"Why not?"

"It's a sensitive subject. The man who was killed was a controversial figure. He worked in intelligence in Madrid for decades. But he was killed on a military base. You see the problem."

Reznick sipped his beer and waited for him to continue.

"I heard that the murder was carried out by a foreign government."

"Which government?"

The man grew more antsy. "I've said too much. What do you know?"

"I heard the man was shot. Long-range. Right?"

"Absolutely correct. All hell has broken loose. No one is supposed to know. But stuff like this gets out eventually."

"What else do you know?"

"I came to warn you. I think your life might be at risk if you stay here. You need to think long and hard before you get involved. I know for a fact that there are intelligence operatives from Madrid who have arrived in the town within the last few hours."

"Civil Guard?"

"*Centro Nacional de Inteligencia*. And others."

Reznick knew that to be true.

"I was told a team of four are here, in the Sóller area. They answer to the Ministry of Defense. These guys. They can make people disappear. My sister has been taken away."

"Your sister? Where did they take her?"

"A hospital. A psychiatric hospital in Palma. They said she's mad. But she's not. She's my sister."

"I'm sorry."

"I cannot visit. They will not allow me to visit. I'm scared for her. And I'm scared for me too."

Reznick patted the man on the shoulder. "I appreciate you reaching out."

"Be careful, my friend. None of this will end well."

Twelve

The early-morning rays peeked out over the dusty, sunbaked rooftops of Sóller. Maria Garcia was up bright and early, as always, sitting at her favorite café, drinking her black coffee, sunglasses concealing her rheumy eyes. She watched the first tourists disembark from a German tour bus which had pulled up outside the police station, adjacent to the town's church—a place sacred to her.

She watched a little girl skip beside her mother, who was pushing a stroller, singing a sweet nursery rhyme. The girl ran toward the fountain and dipped her small hands in the water, splashing her face to cool herself down.

Maria smiled as she watched the innocent child—a local girl by the look of her. The mother beckoned the girl back and she ran to her mother's side. She held her mother's hand and continued to skip and sing her little song. Maria thought back to her time as a young woman in Sóller. She'd had a child then. A child she had been told she could never have. A daughter she had loved unconditionally despite all the challenges. Despite the doubts from her closest friends in town. There was a time when it had all seemed so perfect. But then her world had collapsed. She was married, then she was widowed in her thirties.

She saw the hope and innocence of the child playing in the fountain, and recognized that feeling of joy and freedom. She had felt that for a brief moment in time. Now an emptiness and anger lingered and gnawed at her soul. She often sat alone in her home, late into the night, thinking of what could have been. But any dreams Maria had once had were crushed by the death of her husband. She hoped and prayed the little girl would not experience such pain.

Her solace back then was that her own daughter would one day marry, have children, and her daughter would have a family around her. A warm, loving family she could fuss over. But that was not to be. Her daughter grew up resentful of Maria. She began to drink and take drugs. Maria had felt as if she had done something wrong. Then her daughter had said she didn't want to marry. She dabbled in Eastern mysticism. She wanted to travel to India, she said. Then she wanted to move to the Far East.

Maria had tried to hang onto her for as long as she could. But the daughter she'd once known was gone. Now she didn't even know if she was dead or alive.

Maria had retreated into the only world she knew. Her town. Her church. She'd shut herself off from the world. Her friends no longer wanted to see her. They thought she had become cold-hearted. That nothing made her happy anymore. It was true.

The priest emerged from the Church of Saint Bartholomew, the magnificent church that towered over the Plaza de la Constitución.

He was a kindly man who Maria very much respected. A local man. She had known his parents. Good people. He looked across the square and waved at her. She waved back. But as she did so, she saw the priest turn to talk to a couple of Civil Guard officers who had pulled up in a car outside the church.

She grew curious as to what the priest and the officers were talking about. She knew the soft-spoken priest was very loved in

Sóller, highly thought of not only among the congregation, but in the town. The priest knew the tradesmen, the café owners, the director of the main citrus fruit-producing company which harvested the valley's oranges, and also the police and the Civil Guard. He knew what was going on. He made it his business to know what was going on. She was intrigued. She worried the priest was sharing titbits of information with the officers. She knew there had been a spate of thefts and mindless graffiti scrawled on a wall behind the church. Was it related to that? Or maybe it was related to the murder of another son of Sóller, Luis Muroz. The news was not public knowledge. But in a town like Sóller, she suspected it would be only a matter of time before the story trickled out. Maybe it already had.

Maria sipped her coffee. She had learned of his terrible death only two days earlier. She had overheard a hushed conversation a housekeeper from Port de Sóller was having in a local café, only yards from her home. Maria had not responded. She had just listened to the woman relay the news.

Maria felt a terrible sadness at Luis Muroz's death. She had grown up with him in Sóller, attended the same school. She had no idea who would have wanted such a clever man, who'd had such a glittering career working for the government in Madrid, to be killed under such circumstances.

Her gaze was drawn to a blond-haired German couple, or maybe they were Scandinavian, who were posing in front of the fountain. She enjoyed watching what was going on despite her reservations about the impact of mass tourism on her beloved Sóller. She was interested in people-watching, but she far preferred seeing the occasional familiar face. Autumn and winter were best—most of the tourists long gone. The town seemed slower, quiet. That's what Maria craved.

She felt the sun on her weathered face as it edged higher over the roofs. Her breathing was shallow. Her joints ached. Her heart was empty. But still she held on. More and more she counted how long she had on this earth. Her doctor thought she was clinically depressed, yearning for family. For her late husband. For her daughter who had disappeared from her life. She would not tell the doctor that she would also miss Luis Muroz. They'd had a special bond.

Maria had written out a new will the day before, after learning Luis had been killed. She was leaving all she had to her brother. A man who shared her values. She was taking the passing of Luis as a sign. A portent of things to come. She sensed she herself was close to death. She didn't know for sure. But what she did know was that she was in God's hands. Only God knew how long she had on this earth.

She also knew that God, and only God, would look after her. She prayed on what He had in store for her. She felt as if her life was closing. Maybe she was yearning for another time, another place. She yearned for her old life. But still she endured, day after day, mostly alone. Her younger brother was a balm to her soul in a scary world of uncertainties.

The tram trundled by and chugged farther up the hill to the terminus. She drank her coffee and watched as the early-morning tourists from Port de Sóller alighted from the rickety old tram. The fancy sunglasses, indecently short skirts, crop tops, boys with earrings. It was all so different.

Maria saw a familiar face step off the tram. A stooped old man. Her brother. The beloved priest down in Port de Sóller, face flushed, perspiring in the brutal heat of an August day. She had been expecting him. She watched as he walked, hunched, down the hill and across the plaza, past the fountain, toward her. He smiled as he caught her eye, sitting down opposite her.

He bowed his head as she clutched her rosary under the table.

Maria knew what he wanted to speak to her about. He touched her cheek and smiled.

"God bless you," he said.

She smiled. "You look tired."

"I have a lot on my mind."

"Luis Muroz?"

Her brother nodded. "I just wanted you to know," he said, "that Luis stored his diary and such that he had kept in the town."

"His diary? Where is it?"

"I have it."

"Where?"

"I have it in a safe place. He instructed me last week, just before his death, where it was kept. I have it. And I will bring it up to you very soon."

"Why not now?"

"Luis stressed caution. He lived his life for his country. You must guard his legacy. And his work. It will be soon, I promise. And he stressed the diary is for your eyes only."

Thirteen

Reznick sat on his balcony until mid-morning, facing the imposing mountains in the distance, deciding the investigation had run into serious headwinds. He had come to the attention of the Civil Guard. He knew that wasn't good. In effect, his cover had been blown. And he figured it was just a matter of time before the CIA called him back home.

He walked downstairs to the hotel's outdoor pool. He swam fifty lengths. He felt energized and more alive. Afterward, he returned to his room, showered, and changed into a fresh linen shirt, jeans, and sneakers. He returned downstairs where he feasted on a brunch of granola, scrambled eggs on rye toast, a glass of fresh orange juice, and black coffee.

He could only imagine how this would be viewed by Daniel Black and the CIA team who were running the operation. But until Reznick heard otherwise, he knew the drill. He would stay in place until he was instructed to return. Only Black could pull the plug on the operation. No one else.

Reznick might have felt like throwing in the towel. He had considered it. But only for a fleeting moment. Besides, it wasn't his way. He stuck things out through thick and thin. The rough with the smooth.

He put on his sunglasses and a Red Sox baseball hat before leaving the hotel, the sun burning the back of his neck. He had only walked a few yards when his cell phone rang.

"What did the Civil Guard want with you?" Trevelle Williams asked.

"This and that."

"Yeah . . . but what exactly?"

Reznick explained the terse conversation and exchange with Juan Pinto.

"That ain't good."

"You got that right. They know exactly who I am. Which poses a whole new set of problems and questions."

"Fuck. I'll pass this news to Langley."

"I'm guessing they already know."

"Maybe. Listen, Jon, I've got a couple developments of my own. First, I thought you might want to know about something that happened in Palma. I think it's interesting."

"What've you got?"

"It may or may not be related to what happened to Muroz in Port de Sóller."

Reznick stepped onto the promenade as a tram left the port, packed with tourists. "Yeah, I'm listening."

"So down in Palma, late last night, a controversial far-right Spanish politician died of a sudden heart attack in the bathroom of a bar. It's splashed all over this morning's papers across Spain."

Reznick's mind flashed back to seeing the news footage. "Yeah . . . I saw a clip of that. The news was on the TV in a bar. But what's the connection? Old guys die all the time. It happens."

"Sure. This guy was a mess. He was out of shape and seventy-eight years old. But he had no history of a heart condition."

"None at all?"

"Nothing."

"It's not too convincing. He was old, arteries furring up, drinking too much . . . heart gave up, right?"

"Maybe. But this is where it gets interesting. He was a Spanish politician, but he was also ex-military intelligence in Madrid. He appeals to nationalists, former Francoists."

Reznick contemplated the news. "Ex-military intelligence? Similar backstory to Muroz."

"That's what I'm saying. There's chatter online, supposedly encrypted message boards . . . political staffers and cops talking like it was made to look like an accident. Which is dynamite."

"Now you've got my attention. And this happened in the bathroom of a bar? Someone must have seen something."

"This is where it gets downright weird. Apparently not. No witnesses."

"What about surveillance footage? There has to be something in or around the bar."

"Not working, inside or outside."

"Gimme a break." Reznick stopped and looked out over the sparkling blue waters of the bay. He sensed that Trevelle's analysis was right. The death in Palma was no coincidence. "It does feel too convenient. Two retired former Spanish intelligence operatives dying within nine days of each other. One a definite assassination."

"You want to know the latest?"

"Sure."

"Spanish intelligence has reached out to Interpol for help. And this is where it gets doubly interesting. A message from the coroner in Palma revealed a suspicious pinprick mark on the dead man's backside, found during autopsy three hours ago. As if he had been jabbed. You know what I'm talking about."

Reznick knew immediately what Trevelle was talking about. A method of inducing a heart attack. A sux attack. He himself had used the same assassination technique—an auto-injecting syringe disguised as a fountain pen or ballpoint pen—against jihadists in Europe and the Middle East. It also reminded him of a similar attack in 2010 of a senior Hamas operative in Dubai who'd been neutralized by an Israeli hit squad. Tasered first to subdue. Then injected with sux. Then, to top it off, the guy had been manually suffocated. "Any other links to the dead intelligence guy in Port de Sóller?"

"This only just came through in the last few minutes. The pair were not only at one time senior intelligence operatives in Madrid. They were, by all accounts, close personal friends."

"Bullshit."

"It's true, Jon. This politician was a high-ranking operative within the *Centro Nacional de Inteligencia.* They worked together for decades. Both served in the sixties and seventies under Franco."

"Now that is interesting."

"There's chatter in military circles about ETA. I can't keep up with all the rumors and speculation. It's blowing up big-time. But the mainstream media is reporting this as a simple collapse and heart attack of a popular Spanish politician."

"ETA? . . . I'm not buying it. Not their MO, is it? With them it's usually bombings, close-range shootings. This is an altogether different league. This is way more sophisticated. Way more knowledge. It would take a state-level actor to get in and out again without anyone seeing a thing, or there being any footage."

"I think so."

Reznick could see the potential link between the two deaths was compelling. "So who the hell is doing this? Is this house-cleaning? Maybe taking care of business, government-style?"

"That's what it looks like."

"What's your second bit of news? You've already got my juices flowing."

"You're going to like this. I've been doing a deep dive into the world of forensic dentistry. Who knew?"

"The photo of the teeth marks on the gum . . . That was a long shot. Has it actually yielded anything? I was just grasping at straws."

"The results are in. Forensically analyzed by a lab in Arlington used only by the Agency. We got a perfect match for one individual. It's believed to be nicotine gum."

"Go on."

"He's American. And we have his records."

Reznick was dumbstruck for a few moments. He wondered if he had heard right. "Can you repeat that?"

"He's American. Former US Army. We know who it is."

"You're fucking with me."

"Nope."

"Are you sure?"

"Positive. The dental records are held by Department of Veterans Affairs. A perfect match because of the distinctive missing teeth."

"Have you got a name?"

"Frederick Hicks."

Reznick made a mental note of the name. "What else?"

"Former United States Army language specialist. Fifty-two years old."

Reznick had needed a breakthrough. And now he'd gotten one. "I need a photo."

"We've got that too. The only problem is that it was taken two decades ago, in Iraq."

"There's nothing more recent?"

"Nothing."

Reznick felt his heart rate hike up a notch. He'd thought realistically it would be a million-to-one chance to get a match for the dental records. "He's one of us? An American? I did not expect that. Not in a million years."

"I guess if I was playing devil's advocate, I might say that him being there doesn't prove that Hicks killed Luis Muroz."

"True. It's circumstantial. But unless he was squatting in the place, doing some much needed gardening, this indicates or at least points to Frederick Hicks being the probable shooter."

Trevelle was quiet for a few moments. "The military background certainly makes him the prime suspect."

"I'm satisfied this is our guy. But this leads us to the next question—what was the motivation? Where the hell has Frederick Hicks been for the last few years? Was he stationed abroad?"

"That's a whole other can of worms, Jon. His backstory is going to freak you out."

"What've you got?"

"Frederick Hicks speaks seven languages. English, North Mesopotamian Arabic, Modern Standard Arabic, Farsi, Gelet Arabic—which is a nomad language used in southern Iraq—Azerbaijani, and Kurdish. Very high IQ."

"Who do we think he's working for?"

"Hicks's last known whereabouts were in Iraq."

"Where was he after that?"

"We don't know."

"Why not?"

"Iraq was the last anyone saw or heard from him. It's the last *anyone* heard from him."

"What the hell does that mean? Did he just disappear?"

"Pretty much. He went missing some time in the middle of the night from his base near Mosul. There was speculation that he'd had a breakdown. But it was classified, officially, that he went AWOL."

"So, now he's resurfaced all these years later?"

"That's what it looks like. Dropped off the grid for a couple of decades. No sign of him. But now we've got that dental match."

Reznick was struggling to get his head around the chain of events. He tried to understand how and why an American soldier had disappeared in Iraq and then resurfaced as a potential killer in Europe. "I have so many questions. Who's he really working for? That's the main question. Is he a gun-for-hire? Is he a political assassin, killing right-wing politicians in Spain? There's so much we don't know."

"The military records make for interesting reading. Hicks had been acting weird for weeks before he disappeared, according to his commanding officer. He had been studying the Quran every waking hour."

"Maybe it helped with language skills."

"Maybe."

"You don't sound so sure, Trevelle."

"I'm not."

Reznick walked on for a hundred yards and sat down on the wall overlooking the beach, trying to figure out the rationale for Hicks's actions. "What if there's another explanation."

"What are you thinking?"

"Radicalization. I saw that plenty there. Killing Iraqis left, right, and center. It takes its toll mentally. People flip. Tough guys flip. Happens all the time. I don't think the ordinary man in the street fully understands the traumas of war. Seeing friends getting blown to pieces. The enemy getting their heads blown clean off. It takes a heavy toll."

"Are you saying Frederick Hicks might have converted and been radicalized? Switched to the other side?"

"We can't rule it out. It's important to keep an open mind." Reznick contemplated the incredible intel which had come from a piece of discarded gum. "Run the last photo you have of him through facial recognition, against everyone who's entered Mallorca, by air or sea, over the last couple years. Let's see if we can get a match with a different ID."

"That could be tricky. We'd be looking at age-induced changes on face recognition technology. The technology isn't perfect. No guarantees."

"Death and taxes—the only guarantees. Listen, this is great info. But we need to find this guy. And quick. I sense this whole operation is going south. We need to get a fix on him fast."

"On it, Jon. I'll get back to you ASAP."

Reznick ended the call. He had worked with Trevelle for years, and his advanced cybersecurity and IT hacking skills could access information that was beyond the realms of most. And Jon had come to rely on him. Time after time, year after year. He remembered meeting Trevelle, at an old, abandoned warehouse in Miami's Overtown neighborhood, Trevelle's original nerve center. His pal, an ex-NSA math and computer genius, had since located to Captiva Island in Florida. The guy was nuts about cybersecurity. End-to-end, military-grade encryption. Future-proofing encryption to guard against threats from quantum computing. Reznick was lucky to have him on his side. Never once had Reznick heard that Trevelle could not solve a problem. He came through each and every time.

Reznick's cell phone pinged. It was Trevelle already. He tapped the message. A photograph of a bearded blond man with shoulder-length hair; a Canadian passport. He studied the rugged features, the ice-blue eyes. His cell phone rang.

"You get it?" Trevelle's voice was excited.

"Oh yeah."

"The photo we have from his military days 99.98 percent matches this guy's face. This is Frederick Hicks. I would bet the house that it's him."

"What name did he use on the passport?"

"Warren Litt. He didn't fly into Palma. He caught a ferry from Barcelona six months ago."

"This is our guy. This is the shooter. Great work, Trevelle."

"What else can I do for you?"

"Keep this intel locked down. Run the photo of Warren Litt through every surveillance system you can access in Spain, especially across the Balearics."

"You think he's fled the island?"

"I don't know. Maybe. He might be abroad already. High probability, I would say. But he might be in Palma if he was responsible for the politician being neutralized. We're making progress. Pass on what we've found to Daniel Black. Keep him in the loop at all times. That's crucial."

"I'm on it."

Reznick ended the call. He looked again at the photo on his phone. He was sure that this was the shooter. He would bet his life on it. But something was still bothering him. If it was him, why had he been so careless as to leave a forensic trail. It was sloppy. Perhaps the guy had been stationed in the abandoned house for not just hours, but days, waiting for the chance. Maybe he had simply spat out the gum at night and forgotten to clean it up. Then again, the shooter might not have thought that something as innocuous as a piece of gum could be traced back to an individual.

It was a misstep.

Reznick, by contrast, had had it hammered into him during his Delta years, time after time, not to leave any trace behind during surveillance operations. It could be physical waste, shit, litter, cigarette butts—anything that indicated a human had been there. This mistake by Hicks, or Litt, might indicate that he hadn't had foreign special forces training. Maybe he was just a long-range sniper as well as a language specialist. Then again, maybe Hicks had been trained but was just sloppy.

The more Jon thought about it, the more he understood why the local police had missed it. A piece of gum in thick, overgrown grass. It was part chance and part good luck that Reznick had stumbled on it. But it had opened up the investigation.

A person of interest, Frederick Hicks, was now on his radar. He was onto something. It would give the CIA, crucially, a name and a face.

But Reznick's brief was not just to track him down. He had to kill this guy, if indeed Hicks was responsible, and find Muroz's cache of tapes. Wherever the hell they were.

Reznick still felt behind the curve. Despite the breakthrough, he had been compromised. His identity was now known to the Civil Guard, and he sensed he hadn't heard the last from them. He would have to be prepared for them to arrest him and deport him in the middle of the night.

For now, Reznick was absorbing all that he'd learned. Hicks being ex-Army was a troublesome development. He pulled out his phone and looked again at the photo of a grizzled Hicks in Palma after disembarking from the Barcelona ferry. With the scraggly beard, he looked as if he had been behind enemy lines for months. Who was this guy? Who was he working for?

This level of sophistication, planning and intel pointed to this operation being a rogue state action. Was Hicks a sleeper agent that had been activated for a mission? Why Spain? Why were the targets retired Spanish intelligence agents? What were the strategic geopolitical aims of these two assassinations in Mallorca? Was the assassin's work done? Was it over? Was he working for Russia?

Despite this morning's breakthrough, Reznick felt frustrated at his progress. He still needed to track down Hicks. And he sensed that the highly targeted killings would not stop until Hicks himself was neutralized, upping the pressure on Reznick to find a solution.

He picked up his cell phone and texted Trevelle. *Get me something. Anything. Before it's too late.*

Fourteen

Reznick awoke in darkness, sitting on the stifling balcony, cell phone vibrating on the table. He picked up his phone and went inside, shutting the doors behind him. The cool air-conditioned room was a welcome relief.

Reznick was groggy as he checked the caller ID. He didn't recognize the number. "Yeah, who's this?"

"Trevelle, who do you think it is?"

"New number?"

"No. Doing some frequency hopping."

"You need to get out more."

Trevelle laughed.

"What's happening? Anything else on Frederick Hicks or Warren Litt?"

"Not so far. I'm working on it. But I thought you might want to know something. Just an update. I'm your eyes and ears after all."

"I'm listening."

"Police just took down the tape around Muroz's villa in Port de Sóller."

"When?"

"An hour ago."

"I was just up there earlier. Cops were still there. Anything else?"

"This might be of interest. Surveillance footage from a townhouse down the hill showed a solitary figure heading up there shortly after the tape came down. I can't identify who it is, since it was dark, and poorly illuminated. Anyway, this person—looks like a man, slightly stooped—was walking up the hill thirty-two minutes ago, not long after the barrier was lifted and the cops drove away."

"Might be a tourist?"

"Maybe. But the only house up there is Muroz's empty villa. And the museum. And the museum isn't open."

"Could be someone out for an evening walk?"

"I don't know. The timing is interesting. I just thought you'd want to know."

"Appreciate that." Reznick ended the call and went to the bathroom. He turned on the light and splashed cold water on his weather-beaten face. His eyes looked more hooded than usual.

He left the hotel, heading down the narrow street and along the promenade. He turned after Bar Albatros and started walking up the steep incline toward the museum and Muroz's villa.

He felt a trickle of sweat on his neck, his heart beating fast after hiking through the glue-like humidity. On the brow of the hill, the villa was silhouetted against the inky black sky.

Reznick stopped and leaned back against a stone wall, standing in the shadows, watching and waiting. It was possible the person Trevelle had spotted on the video footage might be gone—just a passing tourist or a local enjoying an evening walk. But something made Reznick hang around a little bit longer. He was as patient as he had to be.

Twenty minutes later, a spectral figure emerged through the external security door, carefully locking it behind them.

Reznick quickly headed back down the hill, not wanting to spook the person. He saw a couple of wooden benches overlooking the marina, about halfway down. He sat on one, facing the sea and the yachts, his back to the narrow road. He took out his cell phone as if he were scrolling through messages.

He sat in silence for a couple of minutes, and listened. The sound of soft footsteps. He sensed the figure close by, walking faster, only a few yards behind him, then continuing down the road. He waited a few moments before he turned around.

Reznick saw the stooped priest from the church in Port de Sóller, briefcase in hand. He waited until the priest had gone down the hill before he began to tail him along the promenade, keeping his distance as the priest shuffled up the side street past the supermarket and Chinese restaurant. He saw the priest turn right at the top of the road where Es Cantó was located.

Reznick wondered for a moment if the priest might be going inside for a late-night tipple. But he didn't. Instead, he scurried along the quiet side road that led to his church. There he crossed the street and trudged up a path next to the church, before disappearing through a side door.

Reznick walked on for half a block until he was at a pedestrian plaza, a couple of late-night shops and eateries open. He sat down at a café, ordered a beer and a burger. He had line of sight to the side door of the church. He watched and waited to see if the priest would be staying inside for the rest of the stifling evening. Perhaps the priest had just been running an errand or two. But why had he been inside Muroz's house at that particular time, so soon after the police barrier was lifted?

Reznick wondered if the priest had been picking up personal papers from the house. If not that, then what? But the police and Civil Guard had searched the house. They must have searched carefully for any stash of papers, films or electronic devices. Was it something personal to Muroz that only he and the priest knew about?

The priest might very well be a cutout, Reznick thought. A go-between. It made sense to him. A cutout was old-school tradecraft. Or perhaps the priest was a relative of Muroz.

Reznick expected the dark shadow cast by the Franco years still lingered for some more traditional Spaniards. The last remnants of the regime that had ended with Franco's death had been overtaken by a new Spain. But Muroz and other former employees of the regime, or its sympathizers—men and women now in their seventies and eighties—still held its secrets, all these years later. But that didn't answer the central question of why anyone would get someone like Hicks to kill Muroz in Port de Sóller or the politician in the bar in Palma.

He remembered a Delta mission to try and find two soldiers who had been ambushed and captured in Yusufiya, near Baghdad. Reznick and his Delta team had found them dead a week later. They had been horribly brutalized, their innards eaten by dogs. The sickening scene had imprinted on his brain.

It was highly unusual for soldiers to become separated from their units. But when they did, in places like Iraq, the consequences were invariably a terrible death. Which made Hicks surviving all the more remarkable and difficult to believe. The story didn't add up. It couldn't add up.

Reznick knew from his raw, brutal, first-hand experience of Iraq that American soldiers who went missing, or got separated from their units, would be killed by jihadists. No ifs, ands, or buts. Almost certainly tortured before they were killed. Maybe even filmed and sent out to the world's media as a warning.

Reznick's thoughts turned again to the suspicious death in the bar in Palma. He knew the tell-tale signs of a sux assassination. A pinprick on the backside was all that an autopsy would be able to find. Only by analyzing the brain would a medical examiner find any traces of the paralyzing agent.

Hicks, in Reznick's eyes, was a double assassin. The link between the two dead men, killed so recently on the same island, seemed undeniable. But that meant Hicks was getting intel at the highest level. Someone was allowing him to operate, telling him where the target would be, guiding him into position at the right time. This was advanced inside knowledge.

Just then, the side door of the church opened. The priest emerged, still stooped, clutching the briefcase, looking around furtively. He turned the corner, toward the promenade, no more than fifteen yards in front of Reznick.

Reznick slid a twenty-euro bill under his empty bottle of beer to cover the check, and watched as the priest got into the back of a white cab outside Ca'n Tati bar, the tiny bar he'd been to on his first night. The cab drove off. Opposite the bar, a group of guys milled around beside their mopeds and motorbikes, a popular method of transport around the town.

He spotted Peter, the barman, smoking and laughing, leaning on a Kawasaki trail bike. He walked over to the burly Chilean. "Hey Peter, how are you?"

Peter grinned. "My American friend. I'm good. You not at the bar tonight?"

"Sightseeing." Reznick pointed at the bike. "Hoping you can help. I wanted to rent one of those. Is yours available for an hour or so?"

"Right now?"

"I'll pay you."

"Take it man. I'm about to do a few hours at the bar. The walk will do me good, right? Drop it off there."

Reznick laughed. He handed Peter fifty euros. "I appreciate that, thank you."

"Man, it's free."

"I'll have a beer when I bring it back."

Peter handed him the keys and the helmet. "Be careful. It's fast."

Reznick sat on the bike, then did up the helmet. He inserted the key and turned the ignition. The bike roared to life. He sped off, turning left, and rode along the near-deserted promenade, the white cab carrying the priest disappearing into the distance. He opened the throttle and sped past the bars and restaurants adjacent to the beach.

Up ahead he caught sight of the cab and the silhouetted figure in the back.

Reznick followed the cab out of Port de Sóller. The taxi sped up, overtaking a lorry, heading through the Sa Mola Tunnel. Reznick leaned low and kept the cab in his sights.

The taxi exited the tunnel and snaked through the grand streets of Sóller town, before it came to a stop in the main plaza.

Reznick slowed and pulled up on the edge of the square. He watched as the stooped priest got carefully out of the cab and headed straight across the square, down a side street. He edged the bike quietly down the narrow street as the priest stopped outside an opulent townhouse. The priest knocked three times on the huge ornate wooden door. A few moments later, the door opened.

Reznick craned his neck but was unable to see who was inside. The priest briefly turned around to check he wasn't being followed, before entering the house and shutting the door. Reznick turned off the bike's engine, took off his helmet, and called Trevelle.

"Man, you get around. You're in the town? Sóller? What've you been doing?"

"Following a priest, if you believe that."

Trevelle laughed. "You can get arrested for that kind of behavior, Jon!"

Reznick grinned. "Yeah, yeah, all right."

"So what do you need?"

"The church in Port de Sóller."

"Saint Ramon de Penyafort?"

"Correct. Who's the priest? I need a name." Reznick waited as Trevelle tapped away on his keyboard thousands of miles away in Florida.

"Let me see what we've got. Okay . . . so the guy is Father Anthony Garcia."

Reznick looked around and saw a sign on the narrow street in front of him. "Carrer de la Rectoria in Sóller. Who lives at number seven?"

"It'll take me a few minutes to do a proper check."

"And get what you can on this Father Garcia. He left Muroz's villa with a briefcase. Then he went into Sóller to this rather grand old house. Who's he visiting at this address, just off the main plaza?"

"I'll also have to translate my findings."

"Get on it." Reznick ended the call, put his helmet on, started up the bike, and rode it around the block. He returned to the street, but with a different vantage point. This time facing south. He maneuvered the bike so it faced away from the townhouse's imposing front door. He adjusted the mirror on the bike so he had a reverse line of sight.

He watched and waited. But not for long.

A few minutes later, a hunched Father Garcia left the house. But Reznick could see that the briefcase the priest had been carrying was no longer there.

Reznick watched in his mirror as the priest hiked back down the narrow street and disappeared into an alley.

As Reznick rode back to the port, his mind raced as he struggled to put all the pieces together. The priest had passed on the briefcase to the person inside the townhouse. The briefcase presumably held something from Muroz's villa that the priest had picked up after the police had finally left.

Reznick rode the bike along the promenade, then up the street to Peter's bar. He pulled up outside and switched off the engine, hanging the helmet on the handlebar.

Peter grinned as Reznick entered the bar. "You want that beer?"

"As long as it's cold."

Peter reached into a fridge and pulled out a bottle of Estrella Damm, prying off the metal top. He handed it to Reznick and got a set of keys in return. "You have a nice ride on the bike?"

"Very good, thank you."

Peter smiled before he turned to serve a customer.

Reznick sat down near a couple of young guys watching sports highlights on the bar's TV. His cell phone rang. "Yeah, Trevelle."

"Okay to talk, Jon?"

"You got something? Already?"

"The person that owns and lives in the Sóller property?"

"Go on."

"You're going to love this."

"Try me."

"It's the priest's sister."

"I did not see that coming. What's her name?"

"Maria Garcia."

"What else do we know about her?"

"Quite a lot. There's a political connection. Her grandfather was the head of the Falangists during the Civil War."

Reznick looked across at Peter, who raised a glass of beer in a toast. "Now that is interesting. Is that a thread emerging?"

"I'm not done. The dead intelligence chief?"

Reznick sipped his cold beer, quenching his parched throat. "Yeah."

"Maria was rumored to be his lover. Back in the 1980s."

"You're kidding me."

"Her political sympathies were the same as her grandfather's. Devout churchgoer. Very religious. Her husband was murdered in the seventies by a section of the Red Brigades. Had one child, a daughter, who seems to have left Spain."

"How do we know all this?"

"I've accessed classified intelligence files related to Muroz. A source, a one-time friend of Muroz within the intelligence services, was concerned that Muroz might be compromised in some way. He was openly fraternizing with Maria Garcia in the eighties and nineties in Palma. But never in Sóller."

Reznick was stunned by the news.

"Maria Garcia and the assassinated man, Luis Muroz, were lovers. The question is, what was in the briefcase?" Trevelle said.

"What indeed."

Fifteen

Frederick Hicks scrutinized his reflection in the full-length mirror as he went through his slow, deliberate tai chi moves. His body glistened in the stifling heat trapped in the apartment in the Old Town of Sóller. He felt the endorphins kicking in. He was in an elevated state of consciousness. It felt transcendent. He had learned the ancient Chinese martial art when he was in his late twenties, after he went AWOL in Mosul. It helped him relax as he struggled with flashbacks of the scenes of carnage across Iraq. Along with devotional prayer, it brought a sparkling clarity to his inner world, enriching his life. But mastering the art of tai chi was also useful for combat and defense, if and when it might be required. It kept him supremely fit and focused.

Hicks felt the rivulets of sweat run down his back. He grimly wondered why his handlers insisted on using apartments without air-conditioning. Maybe they were pushing him to his limits. Maybe they were fucking with him. Maybe it was part of a plan. But really it was a minor inconvenience. After enduring summers in Baghdad and Mosul, nothing could compare with those brutal temperatures. He had seen people go mad with the heat. It had hit one hundred and twenty-three degrees Fahrenheit on multiple days. When power outages happened, air-conditioning units went quiet.

Westerly winds whipped up dust in the atmosphere, making it impossible to breathe. Children, babies, the vulnerable elderly were rushed to overwhelmed hospitals. No power. No lights. Insanity. The screaming in the dark, dusty streets.

He remembered once during a heatwave, being sick as a dog in the back of a Humvee, hurtling through a trash-strewn backstreet in a dirt-poor Shia district. The temperature outside had been one hundred and twenty-two degrees. In the metal box, it felt as if he was on fire. He didn't think he'd make it out alive. By comparison, a stifling apartment in a beautiful, medieval town in northwest Mallorca was nothing.

He finished the rest of his moves, methodically, carefully, as he felt himself becoming free of his conscious being. He felt lighter. He was on a higher plane. It was as though he were floating above the clouds. Above consciousness. Drifting.

Hicks sensed a presence watching him. An overseer. An overlord. Not in a physical sense. In a metaphysical sense. He was inhabiting a space outside day-to-day reality. Outside of the confines of his mind, body, and soul. Outside of the confines of science. Outside of the confines of knowledge. Maybe even outside the confines of what humans could understand.

Hicks stretched his calves as he stood, staring at his reflection. His eyes sparkled in the mirror. He sat down cross-legged on the mat and closed his eyes. He began his morning meditation routine. Twenty minutes, it usually took. Deeper and deeper he felt himself falling into a cocoon of calm.

When he was sufficiently relaxed and clear-headed, Hicks opened his eyes, allowing a few moments to gather his thoughts. It would take a while for the outside world to encroach on his state of bliss.

Hicks felt reborn again. He got up and showered. He put on a fresh gray T-shirt, jeans, sneakers, and a Sóller baseball cap like any tourist. He checked his reflection in the mirror and put on the Tom Ford sunglasses he'd bought in Barcelona.

His cell phone vibrated on the dresser. He picked it up and checked the message.

Sóller train station, locker 5. Code 9975

Hicks put his phone in his pocket and stepped out into the broiling heat, careful to lock the door. He trekked down a narrow, cobbled side street, grateful for the shade of the townhouses on either side. He took a circuitous route, mindful to avoid the main town square which would be full of tourists. Finally, he emerged from a backstreet and walked into the entrance of the train station, then over to a bank of lockers, his eyes on locker five. He entered the four-digit code and pulled open the door. Inside was a backpack. It felt heavy, bulky. He shut the locker door, turned around, and left the station with the backpack on his shoulder.

Down the hill, a sharp right, and around a series of shaded, cobblestone alleys, flanked by more grand townhouses and upscale boutiques, away from the main square. Then across a pedestrianized street before he turned back down an alley toward his apartment.

Hicks ascended the stairs to the second floor and, in the apartment, placed the backpack on the bed. He carefully unzipped it. Inside, once more, were brand-new parts for a Siyavash rifle, ammo, night sights, rangefinder, a Canadian passport with the name Charles Edgar on it, and a brand-new iPhone. The first thing he did was turn on the cell phone.

A few moments later, it rang.

"Good morning," a man's voice said. "The package safely received?"

"Yes indeed, thank you."

"Three days."

Hicks closed his eyes, knowing that this was referring to the third of the trio of assignments. Three days was a long time to wait.

He assumed they would only give him details when it was time. But who exactly?

"Will I return from this mission?"

"It's doubtful you will return, my son. But your duties will have been completed. Your work will be done."

"What else can you tell me about the third assignment? There must be something."

"I can tell you the importance of patience. Trust in us. We are preparing a plan. All in good time. Have faith."

"I have faith."

"Very well. Sit tight. Await instructions. But know this—you are exceeding our expectations of you. What I can tell you is that you won't be disappointed when you are given the target. You will have an opportunity to live forever. Eternity awaits."

Sixteen

Reznick sat on his hotel balcony, drinking a cup of coffee, staring out over the Tramuntana mountain range towering in the hazy distance. The bedside phone inside his room began to ring. He went in and picked up.

"Good morning, Mr. Nader, this is Gabriella in reception. Sorry to bother you. I have a visitor for you."

"A visitor?"

"He says he's a friend of yours. His name is Juan Pinto."

Reznick recognized the name of the Civil Guard intelligence officer. His heart sank. He had hoped that he would have made greater progress in tracking down Hicks. Pinto turning up at his hotel was an unwelcome distraction. Maybe he was going to be arrested and charged. Maybe Pinto would have him whisked off to the airport and forcibly deported.

"Mr. Nader, are you still there?"

Reznick snapped back to the present. "Yes, sorry. Is Mr. Pinto alone?"

"Yes, sir, just him. He's sitting opposite me at reception."

"Tell him I'll be down in a couple minutes."

"Very good, sir."

Reznick ended the call. He had to keep up the pretense that he was William Nader until the operation ended. The problem was that Pinto knew exactly who he was. It was a problem he could do without. He wondered what Pinto was really here for. Was Reznick going to be given an ultimatum? Was Pinto fishing for information that he wouldn't be able to provide?

He took the elevator down to the airy, light-filled lobby.

Pinto stood smiling. He wore jeans, a short-sleeve white shirt, and sneakers. Urbane, relaxed, and chilled out. "William," Pinto said, extending his hand somewhat theatrically, as if greeting an old friend, "I heard you were in town on business. I hope you don't mind that I dropped by."

Reznick shook Pinto's hand. "I thought we were done."

"A few minutes of your time. I just want to talk. It won't take long."

"I'm on vacation. Can't it wait?"

"It won't take long. Just walk and talk. It's no big deal. Besides, it's a beautiful day. Thirty-one degrees already."

Reznick was wary. His instincts told him to keep his guard up. He had to keep up the pretense. Of course Pinto didn't buy it. But here he was having to take time out from finding and neutralizing Frederick Hicks to assuage Pinto's suspicions. He put on his sunglasses as they stepped outside.

The pair walked out into the blinding sun and headed to the promenade.

Reznick felt the rays already burning his neck. The sparkling waters beside the beach looked inviting in this heat. But he assumed Pinto wasn't going to be inviting him in for a dip.

"I hope you don't mind me taking up some of your vacation time."

"Why would I mind?" Reznick drawled.

Pinto smiled as they rambled along the wide pathway next to the promenade. "This is the first time I've been here," he said. "I'm from the city you see."

"Madrid?"

"I work in Madrid. But I'm originally from Seville. They say it will hit forty-one degrees in Seville this afternoon. My mother was telling me all about it this morning."

"I'm guessing you didn't come here to exchange pleasantries about the weather?"

"That's a specialty of the English I believe," Pinto said.

Reznick smiled. "What exactly do you want from me? I'm just trying to get some peace and quiet on my vacation."

"I want to let you in on a little secret of mine. I believe in giving people a second chance."

"Is that what this is? A second chance?"

"Yes. No matter who I'm dealing with, I can give a person the opportunity to change their mind. Time to reflect. Time to put the record straight."

"It's all very admirable. But is there a point to this discussion? I thought we covered everything in Sóller."

"I want you to know a little about me. I'm not too dissimilar to you."

"How do you figure?"

Pinto's hands were clasped behind his back in a semiformal manner. "My father was in the Army. And he was a tough man. Like your father."

"You don't know the first thing about me."

"That's where you're wrong. My father taught me the importance of fairness. Give a man a chance, he used to say. Don't rush to judgment."

Reznick said nothing as he walked alongside Pinto.

"I believe your father was in the Army too. Vietnam. Now that would have been a baptism of fire, fighting there. No doubt about it."

"Don't play games with me, Pinto."

"I'm not playing games. I'm just using this little walk to let you know a little about me. And hopefully I get to know you a little bit better in the process, Jon. I know you're not Mr. Nader. But I think it's important we iron out any differences, man to man."

"You asked me the other night why I was here. I explained all that."

"Yes, you did. And for that I thank you. The problem is I don't believe you. You are not a business consultant. And to insist that you are . . . well, it insults my intelligence. Please do not insult my intelligence."

Reznick's patience was ready to snap. He wasn't used to being called out in such a manner. His cover was blown. But he could only abandon the operation if he was told to by the CIA, directly from Daniel Black himself. He had to follow protocol, and see the mission through unless he was taken off the job. "I thought I explained why I'm here in Mallorca. There's only so many times I can tell you."

"That's fine. I can look into your eyes and see the type of man you are."

"And what kind of man am I?"

"You are a man of strong character. Strong moral fiber. But you need to be honest with me."

Reznick glanced at his watch. "This is all very nice, shooting the breeze like this, Juan, but I'm due for some breakfast. I'm starving."

"Perfect. Me too. Do you mind if I join you? I've been told about a great spot a bit farther along."

The Beach House was located over the wooden bridge at the far side of town, adjacent to Repic Beach.

Reznick and Pinto sat down at a table under a huge umbrella, shielded from the full force of the sun. They ordered black coffee, crepes with maple syrup, and Greek yogurt with sliced bananas.

Pinto took off his shades. "I don't get out of Madrid as much as I should. My wife is always telling me I need to take a vacation. I find it difficult to unwind. I find it difficult to sleep."

"You're an insomniac?"

"A lot of the time I am. I work a lot. Just like you."

Reznick could discern that Pinto was trying to either create a rapport or, more likely, bait him into saying or doing something he would regret.

The server returned with their order. She set down the plates and the mugs.

Reznick thanked her and sipped his coffee, taking a mouthful of his crepe. "This is very good."

"I told you."

"I thought you'd never been here before."

"I haven't. A local officer recommended it." Pinto took a forkful of his own crepe, then a small sip of his coffee, finally dabbing his mouth with a napkin. "Can I be candid?"

"Whatever you want."

"I want you to understand, first and foremost, that this is not personal, Jon. This is purely business. We cannot tolerate your presence here. You seem a very personable man. But this is the second occasion when I've had to try and explain my position. Maybe you didn't get the message when we talked in Sóller. You see, Jon, I've got to say, for the second and last time, that you must leave not only the town, but the island of Mallorca, today."

"Is that an ultimatum?"

"More like strong advice you should heed. Look around you."

Reznick's gaze took in the tourists walking by, joggers, families on the beach.

"We are a peaceful town. Your mere presence greatly concerns not only me, but my bosses in Madrid. They spoke to me first thing this morning. You know what they said? *He must leave with immediate effect.* They did not want to discuss the matter. They did not want to reach out to our American partners, either in Madrid or in Washington. So, I am following orders."

Reznick dragged his crepe through the syrup, contemplated his next move.

"I just checked," Pinto went on. "The last direct flight to New York from Palma leaves at 1320 hours today. That's just before one-thirty this afternoon. Just over three hours away. You have time."

Reznick checked his watch. "And why would I want to leave this beautiful island?"

"Because I know what you are. I know what you do. And your presence is not something we welcome. I just explained all that. As I said, it's nothing personal, Jon. I hope I'm making myself crystal-clear."

Reznick sipped his coffee.

"My patience isn't infinite, Mr. Reznick. Neither is that of my superiors. You must heed this advice. Actually, I'll be more candid. Get on that plane, and we're good. Hell, I'll even pay for your ticket back home."

"What if I don't make it on time? What if I don't want to?"

"Don't disappoint me, Mr. Reznick. I'm trying to help you."

"I'm curious. What if I ignore your advice? What then?"

"I would not recommend that course of action."

"Why is that? What will you do if I'm still here tonight?"

"I'm an optimist, Jon. I believe in the good of people. And I also believe in people being rational. I'm sure you'll make the right decision."

Reznick looked at his watch. "I don't think that gives me enough time to pack. Say my goodbyes."

"Don't test my patience more than you already have. If you haven't left the island on that flight, the consequences will be swift and I won't be able to help you."

Seventeen

Maria Garcia was clutching her rosary beads as she opened the shutters in the upstairs bedroom. The last remnants of the evening sun dipped behind the old rooftops of Sóller. Particles of dust were visible in the fading light. The sound of laughter drifted up to her room from the plaza below. She often stopped and took in the view from this window. The room where she had grieved for months and months after her late husband's murder. She remembered the time well. She had felt as if she were going mad. A slow descent into darkness. Her soul blackened.

While her husband's life had been extinguished, the love lived on. Long days, longer nights. The years rolled by and the anniversary of his death came and went. Time did not stand still. The love she had was replaced by a harder edge to her heart. She became colder. More distant. When her daughter said one day that she hated her life and never wanted to see her again, Maria had been inconsolable. She had blamed herself. She had tried to reason with her daughter. But she didn't want to hear it.

Maria sometimes took out a dress belonging to her daughter, smelling the lingering perfume on the fabric. It had last been worn thirty years earlier. Her daughter might have a family somewhere.

But it was the lack of not knowing, the lack of connection, that was like a knife in Maria's heart.

The sound of bells snapped Maria out of her dark thoughts. She breathed in the sultry evening air. She gazed out at the church as the sky darkened, her cotton dress sticking to her sweaty skin. She fanned herself in a vain attempt to cool down. The church was soon silhouetted against the inky black sky, the stars bright around it. The sun may have gone for the day. But there was no let-up in the oppressive heat.

Maria Garcia fanned herself one more time before she left the sanctity of her home. She carefully locked the front door behind her as she always did. She was on her way to evening Mass. She muddled across the packed square and up the stone stairs of the church. She brushed past a group of British tourists at the rear of the church as she made her way to her seat.

She sat down, eyes closed, as the sacred words from the Bible flowed out of the priest's mouth. She felt the comfort and safety they gave her. The feeling that she could go on. Being here reinforced her. It was a balm to her soul. When the service was over, she said a silent prayer to her dead husband. And another for her daughter, wherever she was.

The priest approached her afterward and she made small talk. The weather, the wine harvest that would begin soon, the upcoming fundraiser for the church's upkeep. She pledged to do her utmost and had promised one thousand euros to the fund. She complimented the priest for his steadfastness and thirty years of service to the town. The priest asked about her arthritic knees. She brushed away his concerns and thanked him for the passages from the Bible. Passages she had been taught in the same church all those years ago.

She left the church and walked back across the plaza, past the men in their tight-fitting shorts and sleeveless shirts lounging outside the bars and cafés, drinking bottles of beer, the young women with large glasses of wine. It was all so jarring.

Maria kept her eyes straight ahead. She strode down her street and was relieved to get back to her townhouse, again carefully locking the door with the huge rusting key once she was inside. Relieved to get back to the memories. The sanctity of her home. A world that had not changed.

She climbed the steps into her living room, her old bones creaking. The sticky evening air filtered through the gap in the shutters. She switched on the large fan, stirring the warm air. Then she pulled down the large screen on one wall. She felt strangely nostalgic.

She sat down in her favorite armchair. Then she reached over and flicked the switch of an eight-millimeter film projector.

Up on the screen appeared grainy black-and-white footage from the early 1970s. Her husband holding her hand, looking handsome in his Army uniform. He was rarely home then. But when he was, Maria had cherished the time. Her mind flashed back to that golden era. Tourism was in its infancy, at least in the northwest part of Mallorca. Sóller hadn't been affected. Life was slow. Not until the 1990s did things change in the Sóller valley. The creation of the tunnel that had opened up the link to the port.

She pushed those thoughts to the side as she admired her husband's imposing, handsome features. The kind eyes. She studied her own expression. Joy. Pure happiness. Her eyes alive. She watched as her husband took off his tunic, sitting on a chair, drinking a small glass of wine. Maria attended dutifully to him. On the screen she handed him a plate of Gori de Muro, traditional Mallorcan cookies made with rosemary. He laughed and bit into the biscuit. The memories flooded back like it was yesterday. And then it was gone. Flickering film and cherished faded photographs were all she had left.

It was hard to believe that only three short years later, her husband was gone for good. Assassinated like a dog in the street. Her husband had been laid to rest in the church in Sóller. Full military honors. She remembered senior members of Spain's military had been in attendance. She had received their condolences.

The film strip ran out, flapping wildly until she turned the projector off. She reached over and switched reels to another film. A favorite of hers. Color footage of her daughter's First Communion, aged seven. Wearing white, the little girl turned and stared at the camera as if resenting the intrusion. Maria wondered if, even then, that was a hint of her daughter's dissatisfaction with her life. She had never seemed happy or settled despite Maria and her husband's best efforts.

The film went on, then ran out, another tail flapping until Maria leaned over, switched off the home movie, and bowed her head. Her precious world that had once existed, a world of tradition and faith, had ceased to exist. But her love for her husband and daughter still endured. It would never be extinguished.

She still kept their clothes in the wardrobe. His uniforms, pressed and clean, in the attic. She would occasionally touch his military tunic. It was her way of remembering him. Having him with her after all these years. His presence lingered.

He had valued discretion. A quiet-spoken family man. She had admired that. They had lived a quiet life. She had not shared her innermost fears with her family. She kept her life and her feelings close to her chest. Her husband had always instilled in her listening more than talking. And she had observed.

Maria opened the fridge and poured herself her favorite tipple, a glass of white Rioja. She preferred the dryness of the white wine as opposed to the darker red Riojas. Her late husband, if offered, had preferred red. She remembered serving up his favorite pie with a glass of red wine made from Tempranillo grapes. It had smelled of black cherry and plum. She had loved the way he smelled his wine before he savored it.

So long ago. So far back in time only the photographs and short, grainy films, only the clothing and other objects, remained.

Maria picked up her glass of Rioja and made her way carefully down to the basement through a locked door. Then down a set of winding, stone steps to a sub-basement, buried underneath the townhouse. She tapped the code into the keypad and stepped into the converted seventeenth-century wine cellar. She shut the door from inside. Her secret world.

Maria sat down in the easy chair. She often headed down to the old cellar when she wanted time to luxuriate in that bygone era. A place of absolutely privacy. A place of secrets. Her innermost sanctum.

She picked up the remote and pressed a button.

A huge white screen opened up on the wall. She pressed another button and started up the projector behind her.

The red and yellow flags of Spain fluttered in the breeze alongside American flags. It was 1970 again. The fashions had been so different. Wide collars, simple fabrics, long dresses. The colors seemed so vivid. The men and women of the country looked so, so familiar, but yet so different.

Maria marveled at the footage as it played. Into focus came Richard Nixon, the American president, alongside the much-lamented General Francisco Franco. The leftists and socialists said Franco had been a dictator. They talked of disappearances and torture. But she still believed in the conservative vision for her country. A country at peace. A country not in thrall to the Soviet Union. A country free of Bolshevism. A country aligned with the West. With the United States.

The covert footage was date-stamped. Shot on the second and third of October 1970 in Madrid. Franco and Nixon laughed, looking away from the cameras for a few moments. She paused the footage. She remembered being there that day. Her husband had been honored with an invitation to attend the state visit. A banquet in Nixon's honor. A trusted friend of Spain was paying homage.

She sipped her chilled wine, feeling the alcohol warm her belly, soothe her soul. The footage had been shot by her childhood friend. A man who had entrusted her with a veritable treasure trove of hundreds of reels of film footage and countless photographs and sound recordings. She had been sworn to secrecy.

The man, with whom she had grown up in Sóller, had moved to Madrid. But when she saw him again, after her husband's death, a bond was re-established. A sacred bond. He was a man she had grown to love after her husband was murdered. Their platonic relationship had turned more intimate and loving. The relationship had stayed in the shadows, and now he was dead. She was mourning two men.

The man behind the camera had visited Mallorca once a month since 1977. She had never allowed him into her house. It would not do. She was a widow. Instead, Maria had traveled on the train from Sóller to Palma, where she would visit him at his hotel, far from the prying eyes of the town square. They would talk. And laugh. And share stories of their childhood. They had played together as children.

He had trusted her. He could see she was a very private woman. A woman who, like him, cherished a world that was fast disappearing. She was a nationalist. She was a monarchist. A conservative. A traditionalist. A Catholic. She saw communists, socialists, and anarchists as insurrectionists who would bring chaos to the sacred soil of Spain.

Maria continued to watch the footage as the memories flooded back.

Eighteen

Reznick felt as if he was in limbo. He hadn't been called to end the mission despite his identity being known to the Spanish intelligence service. He had to assume Trevelle had told his handlers by now and that everyone was in the know that his cover had been blown and he was in jeopardy. He assumed he might be under surveillance in and around the port. But to compound matters, he still hadn't made any further progress in tracking down Frederick Hicks.

It had been another frustrating day and night, and he was still hanging around Port de Sóller as midnight approached. He was mindful that he had ignored the warning from Pinto earlier in the day. But since Reznick had not heard anything to the contrary from the CIA or from Trevelle, the mission was still on. He started to think about contingency plans, about disappearing to stay in the country.

Reznick was trekking along a deserted side street, the questions about Hicks and his whereabouts still ricocheting around his head, when a white van slowed down as it passed. He saw two men inside, both staring back at him. He sensed trouble. The van turned around quickly and pulled up beside him. Four masked men armed with nightsticks jumped out of the van's side door.

The first pressed a gun to Reznick's head. "Señor Reznick?"

Reznick realized the time for the Civil Guard to play nice was over. "I think you've got the wrong guy."

A second man jabbed his nightstick hard into Reznick's guts.

Reznick felt a sharp pain in his stomach as he crumpled to the ground. A boot smashed him hard in the face. Once. Twice. Pain exploding behind his eyes. He tasted warm blood. "Motherfucker."

Blows from the nightsticks rained down on his head and neck. He tried to cover his face, his hands smashed, trying to protect his head from being caved in.

Reznick felt electric shocks of pain as the blows rained down. Then two of the masked men hauled him to his feet, pulling his arms tight behind his back. He was handcuffed and bundled into the van.

The men strapped him into a seat. The smell of cologne and cigarettes was heavy in the air.

Reznick sat bleeding in the middle seat, one man on either side of him, a third man opposite.

The driver accelerated away and they drove off at high speed.

The men talked rapidly in Spanish. Reznick hardly knew a word of the language. His mind flashed back to the chat he'd had on the promenade with Juan Pinto. He assumed these guys were following Pinto's orders. It would make sense. These guys were clearly not in the mood for bullshit stories.

The masked man sitting opposite him said, "Señor Reznick, you need to answer our questions, yeah?"

"I'm not Reznick. You must have the wrong guy."

The masked man leaned forward and grabbed Reznick's throat, squeezing tight.

"Listen to me, Mr. American. We will get answers to our questions. And we will find out who you really are." The guy slowly released his grip. "We don't take kindly to outsiders interfering in our country."

Reznick cleared his throat. "Who are you?"

"Who do you think we are?"

"Civil Guard?"

"Maybe. Maybe not. I don't know. What I do know is that we will get answers. So, I would advise you to get your story straight before we get down to business."

Reznick knew he was in for some rough treatment. The van accelerated around a few corners and then drove hard on a highway as if to the interior of the island, away from the coast, away from the tourists.

"Where are you taking me?" he asked.

"We ask the questions, Señor. Learn to shut the fuck up unless you are spoken to."

Reznick shifted in his seat. The minutes dragged. He felt himself drifting off as if passing out. But he didn't. He sat, head bowed, an open wound above his left eye, metal handcuffs pressing tight against the bones in his wrists.

He wondered where the hell they were taking him. Maybe they were taking him to Palma. Maybe to the Civil Guard barracks there. Maybe directly to the airport to have him deported. But he sensed this was going to get real ugly. His instincts told him that he would soon find out what was in store for him.

The van pulled abruptly to a stop. The driver jumped out and walked around the side of the van, sliding open the doors.

Reznick saw that the vehicle was inside an old, abandoned warehouse, the lights of the van illuminating the vast concrete space. The huge doors were shut and locked. He was dragged out of the van and over to a chair which was bolted to the floor. He was tied to the chair with nylon rope.

A glint of metal. A knuckleduster. One of the masked men stepped forward and threw a shuddering punch to Reznick's jaw. The blow nearly caused him to black him out immediately. But he straightened up as searing pain erupted on the side of his head. A second punch smashed into his mouth. He groaned. He rode out the waves of pain, tasting blood again. He spat out some bloody teeth.

The same guy slapped Reznick with the back of his hand. Excruciating shocks behind his right eye grew in waves like an electric current.

The sound of deafening music began to play at ear-splitting volume. Maybe Metallica. He felt himself screwing up his eyes to try and block it all out. The waves of sonic overload were making him sick. The seconds became minutes, which became a void of time. But then he began to feel himself drift away.

He felt disoriented, masked men staring down at him, strobes flashing in his face. It reminded him for a fleeting moment of Delta's brutal SERE training. Survival, Evasion, Resistance, and Escape. The sleepless assault on the senses. Flashbacks ran through his skittish brain. But this was real. They had caught him cold. These were pros.

Reznick squinted as a flashlight was shone in his face. Then a stun gun was pressed against his neck. He felt the electricity making him convulse, his movements out of control as he went into violent shock, the world turning upside down. Then a black curtain came down.

When Reznick came to, he was unable to see out of his right eye, tied up and handcuffed to the chair, which was still bolted to the floor. He squinted across at one of the masked men.

The man opposite shifted in his chair as he leaned forward. "Señor, it doesn't have to be like this. We give you chance, but you don't take it. What are we supposed to do? We need some straight answers. Why are you here?"

"I don't know what you're even talking about. I was just hanging out at a couple bars."

The masked man sighed, like Reznick was disappointing him. "I think you're not telling the truth."

Reznick grinned, tried for charm. "I had a few drinks. This is crazy. You must have the wrong guy."

"I think we know who you are, Jon. But we need to hear it from you. We want to hear from you. You are no stranger to us. You have been spoken to twice already. But still you play these stupid fucking games, Jon."

Reznick's befuddled brain knew they had to be Civil Guard. Were these guys from Madrid?

"We have a problem. And we need to establish why you are using a false identity. Who sent you here? Was it the American government? Which agency? Pentagon? State Department? CIA?"

Reznick spat out some warm blood from his throat onto the concrete floor.

"You were sent here at the behest of the CIA, were you not? Talk to me!"

Reznick let himself vanish mentally, knowing what lay ahead. He would ride it out. The fear of pain was sometimes worse than the pain itself. He began to compartmentalize. It was as if this was happening to someone else.

A man behind him punched him in the side of the head.

Reznick's vision blurred as pain erupted behind his eyes.

"Passport violations are very serious. We believe you are concealing your true identity, Jon. Just admit it. Then tell us who you're working for. Then we can move forward, and everyone gets to go home."

A slap across his cheek. Screams in Spanish, spittle on his face.

Reznick sat and took it. He was zoning out. He had been trained to withstand just about anything. Pain. Discomfort. A lot of pain. Terror. Violence. Torture. It was all about the ways to deal with it. Fighting the fear. Overcoming primitive instincts to give in, to survive. His mind flashed with images of his house in Rockland, Maine. The breakwater on Penobscot Bay. The peace and tranquility of the sandy cove. The sea crashing onto the rocks below. He was visualizing the place where he was free. The place where he was at peace.

The man in front of him picked up a nightstick and prodded it hard into Reznick's stomach.

Reznick gasped, struggling to catch his breath. Then there was a violent slap to the face. A second slap. Again and again. Fifteen hard slaps. More screaming. Incessant screaming.

"What's the matter with you, Señor?"

The masked man took out a serrated knife, steel glinting under the hard lights. He stood up and cut the rope that tied Reznick to the chair. He lifted the knife to Reznick's throat.

Reznick felt the pointed end pressed hard against the soft flesh of his neck.

"How does it feel? You like that? Or do you want to talk instead?"

Reznick knew the guy wasn't fucking around. He braced himself.

The man moved the knife away from Reznick's neck and down to his chest. He then moved it expertly across to the left triceps. The knife cut into his skin, carving. Blood spilled onto the floor.

Reznick felt himself scream as he felt a sickening, excruciating, shooting pain. He was being cut expertly as if by a butcher carving a particular cut of meat. He closed his eyes, trying to ride out the waves of pain erupting in that localized area. He clenched his teeth. "Motherfucker!"

Two men stepped forward and grabbed Reznick by the hair, dragging him toward a trough of water.

Reznick knew what was coming. The guys grabbed his face and thrust it deep into the freezing trough. He swallowed some fetid water. It filled his lungs. He struggled as he feared he had taken his last breath. His primitive instincts kicked in, the deep fear of drowning instilled in human DNA. Again and again, down and down, the men forced his head into the metal base of the trough. He gasped for breath, lungs filling with water, feeling as if they were going to burst.

He held on. And on, willing himself to think of his daughter. Her beautiful face. He saw her smiling at him. *Hold on, Dad. Hold on tight.*

He was pulled from the water. Reznick gasped for air, swallowing more and more water.

"You are making this very difficult for yourself, Jon. You need to tell us who sent you and what you are planning to do. Are you going to Palma for any reason? Have you got instructions? Are you on a time-critical mission? You need to tell us everything. And quick."

Reznick shook his soaking, bloody head. He managed to get some vital air into his lungs before he was dunked hard under the water again. Held down, gasping for breath, face pressed into the steel bottom of the trough. He felt himself drifting away. He knew they were getting closer to drowning him. He sensed they were not nervous about killing him. But he knew that these were just tactics to instill fear, scare the average Joe into submission.

He endured. Ten seconds. Twenty seconds. Thirty seconds. Forty seconds. Lungs nearly bursting. He expected his rib cage to burst open. On and on, longer and longer.

The men held him down. He counted seventy seconds in his head. He got to seventy-one seconds. His head was once more yanked from the water by his hair.

"Señor, you enjoying this?"

Reznick's face was dunked into the freezing water. Over and over again.

He counted twelve submersions before he was finally dragged from the trough and placed on his knees.

The man kneeled down as Reznick retched water and bile onto the concrete floor.

"You're showing rather amazing resilience for a business consultant, Jon. Can you explain why that is? Why are you snooping around the port? Why were you following a priest in Sóller? What are you planning, Jon? Are you the shooter? Do you know what I'm referring to?"

Reznick denied, denied, denied, falling back on his training. "I'm not planning anything."

The men dragged him across the concrete and into the middle of the warehouse. "One last time, you crazy son of a bitch! Who sent you?"

Reznick looked up at the masked men, squinting out of one eye against the harsh light. He was breathing hard, shaking, going into shock.

"We asked you a question! Who sent you?"

Reznick felt himself grinning like a crazed jackal at the absurdity and futility of the situation. "Who sent me? My travel agent. He recommended the trip. You want his number?"

The blows and kicks rained down once again.

Reznick could not fight back, hands still cuffed behind his back. He looked up at one of the men. Then a huge fist smashed into his face.

And his world turned black.

Nineteen

Frederick Hicks was in his apartment in Sóller's Old Town, chewing a wad of nicotine gum, staring through an open window. Moonlight bathed the houses in a ghostly hue. He swigged from a bottle of water, ignoring the incessant dripping of the toilet's faulty tank.

Hicks checked his watch's luminous dial. It was nearly four o'clock in the morning. He caught a glint from the steel slide of the Glock on the table. He picked up the handgun, enjoying the warm, solid feel of the polymer grip on his skin. He closed his eyes. He could hear his heart beating. Fast. Faster.

Hicks held the gun in his hand and pressed it tight to his temple. He knew his time on earth was coming to a close. He had resigned himself to his fate. He would shortly take his last breath. Not at a time of his making. But it was part of the deal.

He put the gun back down on the table. He hoped and prayed that, before his time came, he could complete the mysterious third and final part of his mission.

Hicks felt it was like a calling. He was special. He had been chosen to carry out the operations in Mallorca. No one else. He was the guy. The one who had been told that if the first two assignments were accomplished, he would carry out the third. It was difficult not to get too excited, thinking ahead.

Hicks had been trained for years to be used as and when required. He had subsumed himself to each mission. The mission was everything. He was diligent to a fault. He never questioned his orders. He did as he was told. Without question. Without fail.

He had been told time and time again, by his handlers and his trainers before them, that patience was required. Infinite patience. He was a sleeper agent. Inserted into a country to wait until he was activated. Eighteen months earlier he had slipped onto Spanish soil near Cádiz in the dead of night after being dropped off by fishing boat from Tangier, Morocco. And from there, carrying his new identity, he had backpacked across to Málaga, where he had hunkered down for six months. No one there knew him. No one had bothered him. He'd lived alone in the *Centro Histórico* neighborhood. Málaga had once been a Roman city. Then occupied by the Moors. He had passed his time studying its history, waiting for the call.

He'd stayed indoors during the blistering heat of the day. Like most people in southern Spain, he ventured out after dark; eating at tapas bars in back alleys, reading, watching, listening, waiting. He'd observed and moved around the dusty streets, returning to his apartment before dawn.

Then Hicks had moved to Mallorca after getting the ferry across from Barcelona. He'd lived for months at an old townhouse in the town of Sant Joan, in the center of Mallorca. There he had been surrounded by wheat fields and fruit trees. He had received messages at dead-drop locations, usually a deserted farmhouse just outside the town. Coded messages, provisions, instructions, orders, weapons. His handlers were very careful. Almost to a fault.

Hicks had no regrets. He had been warned by his handlers that the mission, especially the third part, if he lived that long, would inevitably result in his death. He had resigned himself to that fate.

He knew his remaining time on earth was precious. Sacred. He was a long way from home.

Occasionally, very occasionally, his thoughts turned to his elderly parents in the small Iowa town of Williams, population three hundred and seven. They'd be in their mid-eighties by now, tending to their five-acre farm. He often thought of them, rising before dawn, milking the handful of cows, eking out a modest living, occasionally asking themselves or their God what had happened to their son more than two decades ago.

Hicks was a different person to the brilliant language student who had excelled in school and then college, having won an Army scholarship. His parents could never have afforded the tuition otherwise.

He thought of his friends at high school. He remembered the Lutheran church on Beech Street where he had sat with his stern-faced parents. He'd loved them so much. But it had all begun to change after he was deployed overseas. He was never, ever the same again. His mother noticed first. She tried to coax him out of his shell. But it was no use.

She saw how withdrawn he was after his first tour of duty in Iraq. He didn't drown himself in booze. He just sat in his room, staring at the wall, having flashbacks of torture victims strung up from bridges, trying to figure out if he wanted to live or die. He could never sleep. He lay on his bed most of the time, gun in hand. His third tour of duty was the one he never returned from.

His mind flashed back to the year he was kept in a safe house in Mosul. American special forces had hunted for him, going house to house. But the whole time, he had immersed himself in the culture of his Shia hosts. The traditions. He had brushed up on his Iraqi Arabic, which some called Mesopotamian Arabic. It was the most widely spoken language across Iraq, including among the large population in Baghdad. He studied how the language was influenced by Sumerian, Mandaic, Turkish, and other ancient languages. The year he spent in Iraq, amid the violent war being inflicted on the people by his country, shook him to the core. Shook his belief system. He had always been taught to believe in American exceptionalism. Liberty, freedom, individualism, meritocracy, and good old capitalism. But when he saw the blood on foreign soil flowing like a hellish river and life becoming a living nightmare, he could see it was just a myth. His inner world began to crumble. He began to re-evaluate his life. He listened to those around him in Iraq, praying five times a day. The world he knew dissolved. In time, it became a distant memory.

The vibration of his cell phone snapped him out of his reverie.

Hicks moved into the cramped living room, picked up his phone.

"Are you watching the television?" said his handler.

"No. Should I?"

"Turn it on. CNN."

Hicks did as he was told. He picked up the remote control and turned on the small television in the corner. He skimmed through the channels until he landed on CNN. A few minutes later, the President strode down the steps, where he was greeted by a Spanish military guard of honor. Hicks watched the Secret Service detail fanning out all around, as the President was escorted to The Beast, the bulletproof and bombproof car he would travel in.

"What do you think?"

"I'm intrigued."

"You should be. How do you feel?"

"I don't know what to feel. My head feels scrambled. I need details. Times. Places. I'm assuming they will be forthcoming."

"All in good time."

"What can you tell me?"

"I can tell you that this is the big one. And the time is nearly upon us."

Hicks felt a blizzard of emotions rush through his head.

"Stay alert. We'll be in touch."

Twenty

Reznick floated in darkness, a brilliant white moon above, a galaxy of stars like pinpricks in the ink-black sky. He sensed he wasn't alone. A woman's voice swam to the forefront of his mind. He struggled to open his eyes. Blurred vision. Pounding head like a jackhammer. He looked around. Then, finally, everything came into focus.

A woman kneeled down next to him, holding his hand. "Señor? Please blink twice if you can hear me."

Reznick blinked twice. In the distance was the sound of sirens. Closer and closer. Blue lights approached. The ambulance pulled up sharply in front of him. Paramedics jumped out and rushed to his side.

"Señor, stay still!"

Reznick tried to get up but failed. Sharp, shooting pain in his side and his face. His gaze wandered around. He appeared to be in the middle of nowhere.

"Señor, you need to go to hospital. We will take you."

Reznick felt himself floating and drifting as the paramedic spoke. In and out of focus. The man touched Reznick's face with his blue latex gloves. His blood was on the paramedic's hands. He tried to stand up again.

"Señor, you need the doctor. Hospital."

Reznick amazed the paramedics by struggling to his feet. He felt light-headed. But he brushed away their concerns. "Just a bad fall, that's all." He walked a few steps, his legs wobbly and weak. Then a few more yards, away from the ambulance.

The paramedics tried to coax him to come with them. But he wanted no part of it, brushing them aside.

"I'm fine," he lied, putting on a brave face. "I'll get a taxi home. Just a little fall."

Reznick took out his cell phone and ordered an Uber. It arrived five minutes later as the paramedics looked on, incredulous. He got into the back of the car.

The Uber driver's face in the rearview mirror told the story. "Señor," he said, "what happened? You need medical help. Why are you not in the ambulance?"

"Little fall. I'm fine."

"You don't look fine to me, Señor."

Reznick smirked at the man. "Trust me, I'm fine. Probably need a drink."

The driver smiled. "I will take you to hospital, my friend. You should not drink. My sister is a nurse."

"I'm fine."

Reznick sat in the back of the Uber for what seemed like an eternity. Every pothole and uneven surface jolted and jarred. It was a painful twenty-five-minute journey back to the port from the wasteland on the outskirts of Palma. He was dropped off outside his hotel. He tipped the driver fifty euros.

"Gracias, Señor," he said. "Are you sure I cannot take you to hospital?"

"It's nothing. Thank you."

The driver, bemused, gave a little wave and drove off.

Reznick walked through the automatic doors of the hotel. The night desk clerk was alarmed.

"Señor, please, you need a doctor. What happened?"

"Nothing happened. Just a bit clumsy. I'll shower. I'll be fine."

"What happened? Were you attacked?"

"You don't want to know, trust me."

"Please, let me call the doctor."

Reznick took the elevator to his floor and was grateful to get back to his room. He locked the door and limped into the bathroom. He cringed at his messed-up reflection in the mirror. Blood streamed from multiple head wounds, his right eye was puffed up, swollen, and blood seeped through his T-shirt where he had been cut on the triceps. He took a warm, painful shower, dried himself off, and put on a hotel robe. He took out three miniature bottles of Scotch from the minibar. He struggled to grip the bottle top on the first one before unscrewing. He gulped down the contents, warming his belly, burning his throat. He winced as the pain erupted in his back again. He drank the other two Scotches straight and collapsed on his bed as the walls began to close in.

Light streamed through the blinds of his hotel room like shards of glass piercing his eyes. The sound of his cell phone vibrating on the bedside table roused him from his sleep.

Reznick winced in pain and coughed. Blood was splattered across the bedsheets. He reached over and picked up his cell.

"Jon, what the fuck happened?" Trevelle.

"I had a disagreement with a few masked guys."

"Jon, this is nothing to joke about. I just saw the footage of you entering the hotel lobby. What the actual fuck? Someone messed you up bad."

"I need to sleep it off. I'll be fine."

"I want to FaceTime you."

Reznick ended the call and it rang again. He pressed the FaceTime icon. Trevelle's eyes widened as if shocked at what he was seeing. "It's not as bad as it looks."

"Jon, what the hell? I'm going to get a doctor over there."

"We can't jeopardize the mission."

Trevelle tapped a few keys. "This is not about jeopardizing the mission. The mission can't be completed if you're incapacitated."

"Forget it."

"No, you forget it. I just booked an American medic, a person we can trust. He lives, lucky for you, on the other side of the port."

"That was my call, Trevelle."

"Too bad. He won't be long."

Reznick seethed and ended the video call as he tried to sit up straight. The last thing he needed was some busybody medic who would inform a nearby hospital, maybe the police, maybe the Civil Guard. He couldn't become the story. He had a job to do.

He got gingerly to his feet. He hobbled into the bathroom and studied his bloodied reflection in the mirror. He dragged himself back to the bedroom, slumped down in an easy chair, blood seeping through the white dressing gown.

They'd given him a systematic beating, not to mention the simulated drowning. He felt waves of nausea wash over him. He rushed to the bathroom again and dry-heaved into the toilet bowl. And again. He flushed away what little bile and Scotch had come out of him, still feeling woozy and nauseous.

Reznick stayed on his knees. Time dragged. Maybe twenty minutes, half an hour. He couldn't say. The phone beside his bed began to ring, snapping him out of his stupor. He walked back over and picked up.

"Mr. Nader, I have a doctor here at reception. He said he has an urgent appointment with you."

Reznick groaned as the pain kicked in around his ribs. "Send them up."

A few moments later, a knock at his door.

Reznick got up tentatively and winced as he walked across his room, quietly opening the door. He squinted out into the hallway, seeing a tall, casually dressed man.

"William Nader?"

"Come in, Doc."

"Dr. Simon Schwarzman. You're an American, I believe?"

"That obvious, huh?" Reznick said.

The doctor smiled. "I'm from New York City, currently residing in Port de Sóller."

Reznick felt himself gritting his teeth. "How did my friend Trevelle hear about you?"

"I'm the closest English-speaking doctor to you. I live here in the port. I have a penthouse apartment overlooking Repic Beach. Wake up to the sunshine, blue skies, and the sea every morning. Sure beats Staten Island."

Reznick went out to his terrace and slumped down in a seat.

"So, what happened?" the doctor said.

"Rather not say, Doc."

"You get worked over bad?"

"And then some."

"They did a helluva job."

"I'll be sure to give them a good review."

The doctor laughed as he opened his bag and took out antiseptic wipes. He carefully pressed one against the deep cut on Reznick's temple.

Reznick winced at the nipping pain. "Fuck's sake, Doc."

Over the next hour, Schwarzman carefully cleaned and treated Reznick's wounds, abrasions, cuts, and bruises. Then he used an applicator to apply silver nitrate to chemically cauterize the bleeding of the wound above his left eye. "Motherfucker!"

"Language, Mr. Nader."

Reznick winced at the searing pain as the chemical burned into his skin. "Stings like hell!"

The doctor ignored Reznick's protestations and stitched a three-inch gash on his head as well as the deep cut above his eye. He handed him antibiotics, checked his blood pressure and blood oxygen levels.

"That wasn't so bad, was it?" Schwarzman said.

Reznick grimaced. "Are you kidding me?"

"You really should go to the emergency room. There are several great private clinics I would recommend."

"I'll get over it."

"You need an MRI, maybe a CT scan. You said you were knocked out? You've been sick? That's not a good sign."

Reznick nodded. "I know all that."

"Please, get yourself checked out. You might have a brain bleed."

"I'll think about it."

"What's with the aversion to hospitals?"

"I've got work to do."

"Work? Mr. Nader, work is secondary to your health."

"I'll get myself checked at the end of my visit, I promise."

Schwarzman tutted at him, but finished by cleaning and stitching up the wound on his triceps. "What the hell were these guys up to anyway? Did they torture you?"

"I don't know," Reznick lied. "Bad losers or something. Tell me, you got any strong painkillers? This is hurting like crazy."

"I've got some codeine for moderate pain. That should at least take the edge off."

"You got any on you now?"

Schwarzman got out a packet of codeine. He took out two and placed them in Reznick's hand along with a bottle of water.

Reznick knocked back the pills and gulped down some water. He felt himself wincing. "Son of a bitch!"

"They'll kick in soon. Don't overdo it."

Reznick slumped back down on the bed. "What about Dexedrine?"

"You use that?"

"Now and again," Reznick lied.

"Everything in moderation. Rest and more rest. And an appointment at the clinic."

When Reznick finally managed to stand up, the pain slowly subsiding, he patted the doctor on the back.

"How much do I owe you, Doc?"

"It's all taken care of by your friend in Florida, Mr. Williams."

"Mr. Williams, huh?" Reznick smiled. "Thanks for helping me out, Doc."

"Look after yourself. And try not to get into any more fights."

Twenty-One

The footage from various locations had been pieced together for him. Juan Pinto studied the surveillance footage taken for the third time that morning. He lit up a cigarette as he sat behind his temporary desk within the Civil Guard's small office in the town. He watched Reznick navigate the narrow streets on a motorcycle registered to a Chilean who worked at a bar in Port de Sóller. On the screen, Reznick pulled up, having followed the slightly stooped priest from the port all the way into Sóller town.

Why?

Pinto lived in Madrid, a big metropolitan European city. He didn't know the nuances and ways of small-town life in northwest Mallorca. He believed in hard facts. Intelligence-led operations. He needed to know why Reznick had followed the priest. A trained American assassin tracking a priest, a well-thought-of man, born and bred in Port de Sóller. A hard-working and much-loved priest, he had been told. More than one parishioner had said something to the effect that the priest was a quiet man who always gave everyone he encountered the time of day. A man who raised funds for numerous charities in the Sóller valley.

Did Reznick, because of his access to US intelligence networks, know something Pinto didn't? Did the priest have connections in the town that interested Reznick? The more he thought about what such a feared man as Reznick, masquerading as an American businessman, was doing tailing a Mallorcan priest, the less he understood.

He assumed Reznick had fresh intel to track the old priest up to Sóller. But what?

Pinto rewound to the beginning of the footage. It began down in the port, as the priest caught a cab late at night. Reznick watched the priest leave his church as if he had the old man under surveillance. The footage then cut to the priest arriving at the home of an elderly Sóller lady, Maria Garcia. Pinto had learned that she was the priest's sister, a widow—a regular, churchgoing, long-time resident. A perfectly innocent visit. A kindly brother visiting his elderly sister. But he also saw the priest enter with a briefcase but leave without one.

That itself was intriguing.

Pinto pulled up the priest's file, which had just been sent through. He had been described by a cardinal who knew him as a quiet, reflective man, whose political sympathies were shared by his whole family—staunch nationalists. The priest's brother-in-law had been blown up by ETA way back in the 1970s. Maria Garcia's late husband. This had only further hardened the family's views.

Pinto had already gotten a court order to bug the priest's church in the port, as well as his cell phone, looking for further clues.

Then he saw a handwritten note in the file, dated sixteen years ago, that said the priest had been a close personal friend of Luis Muroz. That was a connection. A thread. No one had connected the dots because the information was contained in a tiny note within the priest's file. The priest had evidently also been a regular at Muroz's house in Port de Sóller. Both had shared a penchant for nationalistic views, a shared love of all things Franco, as well as a liking for Johnnie Walker Blue Label.

Pinto's thoughts returned to Reznick. He assumed, if Reznick was indeed working for the CIA or some special program, that Reznick had access to stellar intel. But he couldn't figure out why the Americans weren't sharing it with their NATO partners in Spain's intelligence community. Did they not trust the Spanish? Was there a reason they weren't sharing? He knew the capabilities of the NSA as well as the CIA, and he was aware of their vast resources and worldwide reach, unrivaled around the globe. They operated on a higher plane. Their way, their rules. Maybe Reznick had a defined operation, and that didn't include collaboration.

He clicked around on his computer, bringing up the file on Maria Garcia. A model citizen, patriotic, a proud Franco supporter back in the day, almost a relic of the ancient regime which had ended when Franco died in 1975. She had led a good life. She had been a faithful wife, according to those that knew her. Her husband had been assassinated a few months before Franco's death.

Pinto read on. The widow was described as a reliable Civil Guard informer on her neighbors in Sóller who showed republican, leftist, socialist, or communist sympathies. He hadn't expected that. The file also noted, much to his amazement, that Maria Garcia was rumored to have been the lover of Muroz in the 1980s, when she worked part-time in Palma as a translator. But there had been no mention of Maria Garcia in Muroz's file. A strange omission.

The more he read, the more intrigued he became by this old woman. He pulled up her most recent photo. It showed her collecting money for the church at a luncheon. Her financial records showed her imposing townhouse was valued in the region of one and a half million euros. A sizable asset by anyone's standards. No mortgage. Her assets in her bank amounted to eighteen thousand euros, and she lived off her small government pension and her husband's pension.

Maria seemed to live a frugal life. On the surface, it was the typical life of an elderly, well-off Spanish widow. She attended church. She had a brother, the priest, who visited. Her political affiliations were clear. Pinto asked himself if there was something that he was missing. It intrigued him that she and her brother had been informers for the Civil Guard. Not the local police.

The connection between Muroz and the priest seemed like a meeting of minds, the quasi-fascist Muroz and the quietly spoken priest.

Pinto clicked a few more times and pulled up footage of Reznick's brutal interrogation. It didn't sit well with him. The amount of blood turned his stomach. Torture was not allowed in Spain or across the EU. At least officially. But the old habits died hard. The directive from on high in Madrid was quite clear: whatever it takes, find out what Reznick knows and who is giving him his orders. *Whatever it takes.*

Pinto had passed that on to a shadowy group attached to the Ministry of Defense, who had taken him at his word, doing whatever it took to get the information out of him. And yet, despite the drowning, stabbing, and systematic beating, Reznick had not yielded. Not one bit. He had given them nothing.

What the torture had proven beyond a doubt was that this person who had been interrogated was no business consultant. This was not William Nader. To withstand that kind of torture took training at the highest level. The man subjected to the harsh, shocking interrogation was Jon Reznick, ex-Delta operator. A government assassin. But then, he had already known that. So really they were no better off than before.

Pinto admired the bloodied, battered, but unbowed expression on Reznick's face. He felt a sense of awe at his stoicism. His toughness. Reznick must have felt he had made a breakthrough pinpointing the priest as a person of interest. The son of a bitch hadn't given them anything. Not a morsel. This was a man who had been trained to take punishment. Severe punishment. Pinto watched as Reznick was submerged into the trough filled with water. Held down, struggling, drowning. It would have killed most men. Forced them to confess. Not Reznick.

Pinto slowed down the footage. He watched as Reznick was pulled by the hair out of the water. He paused the video. Reznick's face, teeth clenched, blood pouring from his nose, temple. Eyes ablaze. This was one tough fucker. He wasn't going to crumble for anything. Maybe he would if Pinto had weeks or months to work on him. But he didn't have that luxury. Time was not on his side.

He leaned back in his seat and dragged hard on his cigarette. Plumes of blue smoke filled the tiny office.

Pinto could see a new picture emerging. He knew full well that Reznick was also trying to find Luis Muroz's killer. First and foremost, Reznick was a hunter. That's who he was. A ruthless hunter. And more than anything, Pinto thought, a hunter needed patience.

Reznick was showing a great deal of patience. He was still around. His cover was blown. But he hadn't disappeared like Pinto had advised him to.

Pinto's biggest problem was that the sniper was still at large. The triggerman was like a ghost. Not a trace of him. Maybe he was still around Mallorca. Maybe even closer than Pinto suspected.

The apparatus of the Spanish state—the intelligence services, police, Civil Guard, and the Ministry of Defense—was also looking for the sniper. But the hunt for the man, assuming the shooter was a man, had stumped everyone.

Pinto still didn't know the identity of the person who had killed Muroz. And now the sniper was still on the loose just before an important geopolitical meeting in Spain. A meeting being held on the island of Mallorca. Some of the most powerful people in the world would be in attendance. He had read the latest intelligence report. All police, Civil Guard, military, and intelligence leave had been canceled across the country.

Pinto was feeling the pressure in both his work and his home life. His superiors were pressuring him on why he hadn't caught the killer. He wasn't sleeping. He was away from his home in the buzzing Malasaña district of central Madrid. He loved his family. He missed his children. He felt a sense of foreboding at the thought of not only the shooter still on the loose, but potentially also the CIA in the shadows.

He felt a tightening sensation in his stomach. Pinto had been prescribed beta blockers for anxiety. He feared the worst was yet to come. He had reached out to the Americans, hoping to move the meeting to a tighter, more controlled environment. But those concerns had been brushed aside by the State Department as alarmist.

Pinto was just one of thousands of officers, analysts, and operatives who were trying to figure it out. The sniper was clearly receiving heavy-duty technical support. An operation like this needed inside knowledge. A classified internal briefing memo from the *Centro Nacional de Inteligencia* (CNI) indicated that outside foreign powers might be at work. The CIA almost certainly had connected some of the dots. But he also understood that the CNI had their hands full overseeing the meeting on Mallorca. Palma would be in lockdown. But that wouldn't stop highly trained operatives sent from rogue states trying to crash the event, turning it into a PR disaster for Spain and the West in general.

So why were the Americans, in particular the Secret Service, not being cautious and moving the event to an isolated country estate locked down by special forces? A full lockdown situation like a recent Bilderberg meeting he had attended in Madrid.

Pinto studied the freeze-frame image of Reznick again. The defiance and stoicism were remarkable. This was a man who would die before he gave up the secrets of his shadowy world.

Pinto crushed his cigarette out in the glass ashtray beside his keyboard. He considered all he knew. It was clear that the thread from Muroz was not the priest. But more likely, he should be looking a little closer at the sister, Maria. Maybe, just maybe, the priest was the go-between. The cutout. A close friend of the dead intelligence officer who had lived his final years in Port de Sóller. Which would give the sister, the widow, Maria Garcia, the rumored former lover of Muroz, the role as keeper of the secrets.

Pinto needed to speak to her. And quickly.

Twenty-Two

The yellow light streamed through the wooden blinds of Reznick's hotel room. The excruciating pain in his neck and head roused him from a fitful sleep. He tried to get up from the bed. But a further shooting pain drilled into the side of his head like an electric shock. He reached over and picked up the codeine and swallowed two, washing them down with a glass of tepid water.

The bedsheets were stained red from his seeping wounds. He groaned as he got up and struggled to the bathroom. He checked out his reflection in the mirror. Swollen right eye, cuts and bruises all over his body. He felt nauseous, and was sick again, bent over double.

Waves of pain washed over his body. He took a couple of Dexedrine, hoping that would perk him up. He showered, wincing at the burning pain as the hot water washed off the dried blood. They had really worked him over. He dried himself off with care. It took a few minutes for the drugs to kick in. Slowly the pain began to subside.

Reznick struggled as he pulled on a black T-shirt, jeans, and sneakers. He called room service asking for three croissants, freshly squeezed orange juice, and black coffee.

Ten minutes later, a knock at the door, and the room service guy laid it out on the table on the balcony.

Reznick tipped him twenty dollars.

"Thank you, Señor."

Reznick locked the door and went out onto the balcony amid a humid, balmy southeasterly breeze from the distant Sahara. He sat down and put on his sunglasses, shielding his eyes from the fierce sun. He drank his orange juice, sipped some coffee, and wolfed down the croissants. He felt better with some food in his belly. A lot better. He took two more Dexedrine, gulped down with coffee.

A short while later he was fully alert, sharp, large amounts of amphetamines flowing through his veins. It probably wasn't the best move for his long-term health. His doctor back home in Rockland had advised of the risks to his heart. He had heeded the advice when he wasn't working. But when he was on a mission, needing to stay awake and alert for long periods, he used amphetamines to keep him wired.

His cell phone rang.

"Jon, it's Trevelle."

"Hey, man."

"How you doing?"

"I've been better, let me tell you."

"Jon, you don't need this. This is not what you signed up for. I'm telling you as a friend, you need to go home."

"Trevelle, listen to me. It's part of what I do. If you dish it out, occasionally you've got to be prepared to take some punishment."

"That's not punishment. You were tortured, pure and simple. You could have died. You very nearly died. The doctor said you have to go to the hospital. Get an MRI and a CAT scan."

"I'll survive. Codeine and Dexedrine will keep me in the game."

"Jon, that is not a good idea."

"Listen, thanks again for finding that doctor. Much appreciated."

Trevelle sighed. "I was worried about you, Jon. I'm still worried. Shit, I didn't know if you'd ever wake up again."

"Stop being so dramatic. The magical invigoration formula of codeine and large amounts of amphetamines works wonders. You should try it some time."

Reznick wanted to switch the tone of the conversation away from himself.

"Let's talk business. That townhouse in Sóller I followed the priest to the other night. Anything of note that jumps out at you?"

Trevelle sighed at the change in topic. "A few things. There are a number of highly sophisticated surveillance cameras that cover that townhouse."

"That's interesting in itself. I didn't see any with the naked eye."

"Miniature cameras drilled into the door and the stone walls. What does that tell you?"

"Sounds like someone has something of real value to hide or protect."

"You got it."

"So far, so interesting."

"The priest and his sister, as well as their father, were all prominent Franco supporters. Maria Garcia's husband was killed by a car bomb way back in the 1970s—1975, to be precise."

"This just got a hell of a lot more interesting," said Reznick. "Did you feed this back to Daniel Black?"

"Absolutely. He was stunned. But there's more to it than that. You might want to talk things over with Daniel. Hear his take on it."

"Copy that. You want him to give me a call?"

"I'll handle it. Before I go, Jon, please, I'm talking as a friend, get yourself to hospital. Just as a precaution."

"Duly noted."

"You're a stubborn son of a bitch."

Reznick smiled. He knew what he was. But he also knew what he wasn't. He wasn't a man that was going to walk away. He had been given a specific mission. The mission was critical. A matter of national security. That's all he needed to know. He wasn't going anywhere until the job was done.

"Take care, man," Trevelle said. "I'll get Daniel Black on the line for you in a couple minutes."

Reznick ended the call. And sure enough, two minutes later, his cell phone vibrated. "Jon speaking."

The voice of Daniel Black. "You okay?"

"Felt better."

"Jon, first, I'm real sorry about what happened. I feel sick."

"I'll live."

"I hear they gave you a serious working over."

"I'm still in the game."

"I'm not so sure about that."

"What do you mean?"

"Maybe I should have taken you out as soon as Pinto issued that warning. That's on me. I think we need to get you the hell out of there. It's for the best."

"Daniel, you asked me to come here."

"Things have changed."

"I'm staying. Got it?"

Black sighed. "My protocols are clear. It's time to get you out. I failed you by keeping you in when your cover was blown. But your time there has yielded results. We've made progress. Real progress."

"The job isn't done. Something larger is happening here. I can feel it. I ain't going anywhere."

"Jon, what's the matter with you? It's time to come home, recover, and we can start again."

"That's not how I operate."

"They beat you to within an inch of your life. What don't you understand?"

"When I'm in, I'm in. I don't cut and run. Ever. You need to trust me."

"Jon, I trust you one billion percent. But that doesn't change the fact that this whole thing is fucked. We need to start fresh. New blood."

"You begged me to do this. So, I'm telling you, Dan, I'm fine, I'll work through this. And we'll find this fucker, believe me."

"I don't understand."

"What don't you understand? This is not a fucking drill. More people are going to die if we cut out now. Do you understand?"

"I'm thinking of your health."

"Do you want to come and discuss this with me?"

"No, I fucking don't."

"So, let's get back on track. What do you say?"

"This is irregular. And I'm going to keep this mission and your part in it under review, day-to-day."

"Do what you have to do. I can live with that."

"Listen, for what it's worth, your work has not been in vain. You've gotten us a lot of actionable intelligence."

"What do you mean?"

"Maria Garcia of Sóller. We've been doing a deep dive into who she is and her connections."

"Trevelle told me everything."

"Well, we've done a bit more digging. It gets better. Muroz and Maria were born and raised in Sóller. Childhood friends."

"Has that been verified?"

"Trevelle and some of the top analysts at the State Department have seen intercepted messages. Birth certificates. Whole bunch of documentation."

"Has Trevelle passed on details of the possible ID of the assassin?"

"The photo of the dental imprint in the gum . . . Genius, Jon. So we've been looking into Warren Litt. The name on the Canadian passport."

"The fucker is one of ours."

"I know. Ex-Army language specialist, Frederick Hicks, missing in Mosul years and years ago. I was in Mosul."

"So was I."

"Then you remember what it was like. It was fucking crazy."

Reznick sipped some more coffee, the pain subsiding. He felt more alert by the minute.

The sound of tapping on a keyboard. "I'm just pulling up what Trevelle sent and . . . what we have on this guy. So . . . officially he just disappeared, missing in action. Breakdown most probably. Presumed dead."

"Negative. He's not dead."

"I know."

"So, we've got a problem, Daniel. We've got an American veteran in on this. Trevelle also flagged a suspicious death in Palma."

"We're looking into that. It's an interesting hypothesis. But there's no firm evidence. It's all circumstantial."

"Daniel, gimme a break. Muroz and the politician who died were both former senior intelligence operatives and Francoites. You believe in coincidences?"

Black went quiet for a few moments.

"You still there?"

"I'm still here. It is a pattern, I agree."

"It's more than a pattern. Two assassinations. One killed by a long-range sniper in Port de Sóller. A second made to look like a heart attack in a bar in Palma. Both far-right sympathizers. That's a serious connection."

Black cleared his throat.

Reznick made his point. "Palma, from what Trevelle said, appears to have been a very sophisticated operation by anyone's standards. It was made to look like a heart attack. Classic black-ops. The Port de Sóller death would also have required intense planning and inside knowledge. Frederick Hicks, if it is him, isn't working alone, that's for sure. He has some serious backup. Technical know-how. Intel. State-level. And I don't think he's finished."

"Jon, I still think we should pull you the hell out of there."

"I thought we were going to figure this out day-to-day?"

"We could get an extraction team in place within a few hours. You're clearly not fit for duty."

"Walking away is not an option."

"Well, it's a fucking option to me, Jon. The operation has been compromised."

"Until Frederick Hicks is neutralized, the threat is real. You need to show some fucking backbone. I'm not being extracted. I will find this fucker. You need to trust me."

Silence.

"Do you trust me?" Reznick said.

"Absolutely. I've got a bad feeling about this, Jon. I don't think it'll end well. I'm worried you could be targeted again. We don't know how this ends."

"It'll end when Hicks is neutralized. Until then you need to have faith. Faith in me. Faith in Trevelle. I will find Hicks. And I will deal with him."

"We need the tapes. That's critical. Until we find them, the mission won't be finished."

"Did Trevelle tell you about the cameras at Maria Garcia's townhouse?"

"Yes. We want to covertly access the property very soon."

"Good. Think about it. Pinhole cameras dotted around the entrance of her property. You can't see them. Drilled into the fucking stone walls. And the front door. What reason would an elderly widow have for such advanced, electronic surveillance of her property? Has she got priceless artworks in there?"

"Maybe. But it's a good point. We're working on getting a team on the ground in Sóller and getting into that townhouse."

"You need to get a move on. Get something in place. Maria Garcia could very well be the thread linking Muroz and the priest, and the key to finding the surveillance tapes and recordings that Muroz made."

"Priest as cutout?" Black asked.

"Might be. I'm not a betting man. But if I was, I'd say I need to get in there on whatever pretext. Real fucking quick. Let me handle it."

"Your first job is to find this fucker Hicks. And neutralize him."

"There's something you need to be aware of," Reznick said.

"What?"

"There might be another reason Hicks is on the island. The analysis is pointing in a certain direction. What if the killings in Port de Sóller and Palma might just be a dry run for the main event?"

"What are you talking about?"

"In less than forty-eight hours, Mallorca is playing host to a secret meeting between the leaders of America and Spain. The President will be there. International bigwigs. You see what I'm saying?"

"I think you're reaching, Jon. I'm not buying it."

"Daniel, this is a major red flag. You need to start connecting the dots on this. And fast. Before it's too late."

Twenty-Three

The incessant buzzing from Maria Garcia's video entry system startled her as she woke up from a daytime nap. She got up from her seat and walked over to the videophone screen in her hallway. It had taken her a while to learn the system, but she felt she had it down. The importance had been stressed to her from the moment it was installed. The display showed a man dressed in a navy suit, white shirt, maroon tie. She picked up the handset to speak. "Yes?"

The man showed ID for the *Servicio de Información de la Guardia Civil.* This was no local policeman. This was no Mallorcan Civil Guard officer. This guy was from Madrid.

"Juan Pinto, Señora."

Pinto explained to Maria that he had some questions and would like to come into her house.

Maria's instincts told her to be on guard. She never received visitors unless it was her brother. She occasionally had over a fellow widow from the town, Isabella Avella, who attended the church in Sóller when she could. But apart from those two, Maria spent her time alone.

She contemplated what questions he wanted to ask her.

"Juan Pinto, Señora," he said again. The man was clearly growing exasperated at her lack of response. He wanted entry to the house, maybe as a pretext for a search. But without a court order, she would not let him in.

She considered for a moment if her brother, the priest, had been detained and brought the authorities to her door. But she knew he was strong of character. He would never betray Maria's trust.

Pinto explained that he wanted to ask her questions about issues pertaining to national security. And he needed to speak to her face-to-face.

Maria explained that she was not well and was not receiving visitors.

On the display, Pinto leaned against the wall, frustrated. He explained, slowly, that he believed she could help with an urgent inquiry into the mysterious death of a man at the port. A friend of her brother, the priest.

Maria felt as if she had been hit in the stomach. She realized the connection between the three was already known. She needed to be very careful what she said. This man could not be trusted. No one could be trusted.

Luis Muroz had always talked to her about being circumspect. *Do not give too much away*, he would say. *Saying nothing is invariably the best option. Sometimes feign ignorance.* She understood now what he was referring to.

"Do you speak English, Señora?"

Maria narrowed her eyes at the man on her video display. "Yes, I speak English. Why?"

"Just, Señora, you are not forthcoming. Do you feel more comfortable speaking in English or Spanish? Maybe you are concerned that what you say would be overheard by someone on the street."

Maria was fluent in English. She had studied the language at the University of Barcelona in the early 1960s. She had worked as a translator for publishers for most of the late 1970s and 1980s to make some extra money after her husband's murder. That Pinto knew she spoke fluent English told her that he had read her file. "I don't mean to be rude, Mr. Pinto. But I am a widow. And I am not well. Besides, I don't accept male visitors to my house since my husband died, apart from my brother."

"I fully understand and respect that. But it won't take long. I really need to speak to you face-to-face. This is a vital matter."

"I can see you on my video intercom, thank you. Besides, how do I know that your identification is legal and correct?"

Pinto shrugged, shaking his head. "Señora, please. I need to speak to you."

"Do you have a court order to gain access to my house?"

Pinto bowed his head as if beaten down by her obstinacy. "I would rather not. I assumed you would let me in so I could speak with you about a crucial security matter. It is your duty."

"My duty? My duty is to my faith. To God."

"I respect that."

"So, answer me this. Do you or do you not have a court order?"

"No, I do not."

"Then, you must speak to my lawyer. Maybe he can help you."

"Your lawyer? Why do you need a lawyer?"

"He is a man I trust. Speak to him first."

Pinto pursed his lips. "This is most irregular."

"Do you want his name or not, Señor Pinto?"

"Yes, what is your lawyer's name?"

"His name is Antonio Riego. His firm specializes in family law. He is based in Palma."

Pinto seemed to be keeping himself calm now, projecting quiet authority on the video screen. "I don't understand. I simply want to speak to you about an important matter. The death of a man. You are a good citizen, are you not?"

"Indeed I am. But I do not appreciate your tone or insinuation, Señor Pinto."

"If necessary, I will get a court order to get access. Sadly, if it comes to that, we might have to arrest you if we believe you are hindering a police or Civil Guard investigation."

Maria scoffed at the well-dressed man. "I will be calling Antonio Riego myself. You will be speaking to him from now on. Good day, sir."

Maria ended the conversation and padded back to her drawing room on the second floor. She called her brother and relayed what had happened. He listened intently. But he didn't respond. He said not a word. Just put the phone down.

Twenty-Four

Reznick floated on a sea of thick red blood, gnarly dark sky overhead, drones buzzing the night sky, a flock of ravens swooping low as if in formation. In the distance, gunfire echoed. Blazing choppers crisscrossed the sky after being hit by surface-to-air missiles. The sound of a child's screaming got louder and louder. He felt himself drowning, gulping the warm blood, struggling for breath.

He awoke bolt upright in his hotel bed, soaked in sweat, breathing hard. He took a few moments to figure out that the codeine had knocked him out. It had also given him fevered dreams.

He checked his watch. It was late afternoon, 1703 hrs. He stumbled to the bathroom and took a cool shower, careful as he washed his wounds. It still stung like crazy, but nothing he couldn't handle.

He put on a navy linen shirt, his Levi's jeans, and black Asics sneakers. He picked up his Beretta from the bedside and slid it into his waistband, underneath his shirt.

Reznick put on his sunglasses to conceal the heavy swelling around his eyes. He locked his door, headed downstairs in the elevator, and walked through the hotel's cool, light-filled lobby into the broiling heat.

He mulled over what delights awaited him in Port de Sóller. Juan Pinto and his masked pals from the Civil Guard, or whatever agency they worked for, might want to pay him another visit. But maybe they would think that he would be incapacitated for days or weeks, unable to be of use.

He replayed the conversation with Daniel Black about an upcoming meeting, attended by the President and numerous other important politicians, and how it might be the big one. Was this what Frederick Hicks was being primed for all along? Was this what Hicks had been practicing for? Maybe it was all just a dry run before the main event. Shit, what a mess. And still, Hicks was nowhere to be found.

Reznick feared the worst. He was running out of time. He was on the clock. He struggled to understand how Hicks had such detailed knowledge of the President's secret trip to Mallorca. It pointed to insider knowledge once again.

The timing was worrying. A frightening scenario was emerging. A rogue American veteran was at large, maybe still on the island, perhaps helped by a foreign power reckless enough to spill blood on European soil. Whoever was backing Hicks had the resources, money, and connections to carry out such a coordinated act. Geopolitical ambitions. The purpose? Unsettling Western Europe. But would that foreign power really to try and kill the President on foreign soil? Who would even conceive of such a plan?

He suspected Hicks had been trained for years and years, maybe the last decade or more, to be inserted into a country as a sleeper. And if Hicks succeeded, whichever foreign power had done the training could point the finger at America. *Look*, they would say, *it's one of your own.*

Reznick felt powerless without the intel to get a fix on Hicks. He walked half a dozen blocks down a shaded tree-lined street, toward his favorite local bar. He felt like he was just killing time.

Maybe he was. But he needed a breakthrough within the next few hours. The task of getting a real-time GPS fix on the target was proving more difficult than he had imagined. He just had to hope and pray that Trevelle and Daniel Black could manage it sooner rather later. It was worrying that Hicks was, theoretically at least, still at large on the island.

When he walked into the bar, Peter winced. "You had a fall, my friend?"

"Something like that."

Peter handed Reznick a cold bottle of Estrella Damm. "You look like you need a drink."

Reznick took a mouthful, enjoying the feel of the cold lager in his throat. "Hey Peter," he said, "you ever take a day off?"

"Me?" The sweat was beading on the Chilean's forehead. "Are you kidding? I work all the time. For my family. That's my responsibility, right?"

"Good for you, man."

"I work by the grace of God."

Reznick looked out through the open window at some surly locals eyeing him with suspicion as they sat around the tables outside. He took a fifty-euro bill and handed it to Peter. "Treat those guys to a drink. They look like they need it."

"You sure?"

"Why not?"

Reznick sat down in the corner of the bar, eyes on a Spanish quiz show. He knew that a bit of cash, a drink or two, opened the occasional door. Maybe not immediately. But his experience told him that in certain circumstances flashing a bit of cash, especially in a largely low-paid, tourism-heavy economy, was money well spent. Besides, he had already learned about the cleaner who had witnessed the assassination from her alcoholic brother, and made contact with the local cop, the other brother. People talked. People opened up. But he was running out of time and patience.

Had there been a coverup? For Reznick, that's exactly what it was beginning to look like: the Spanish state neutralizing anyone who would reveal the shocking murders on Spanish soil, which included the cleaner sent to a psychiatric hospital, and cremating the remains of Muroz before a full autopsy could be done.

He sipped his beer.

Reznick's cell phone rang. He didn't recognize the number on the screen.

"Jon, it's Daniel Black. How you feeling?"

"I'll survive . . ."

"Where are you? You resting up?"

"Actually, I'm sitting in a bar, having a cold beer. It's ninety-two degrees in the shade. What's not to like?"

Black laughed. "You're one of a kind, Jon. Listen, we're still piecing together the threads of what you and Trevelle uncovered. Looking into Hicks's past. Working with the Pentagon and the FBI to see what they have on him."

"I know a bit about him already," Reznick said.

"I've got more."

Reznick sipped the beer. "I'm listening."

"The CIA station in the Green Zone at the time sent a classified report back to the Pentagon, but somehow it wasn't included in his file."

"What did the report say?"

"It was talking about intel gleaned from informers among the Shia elders in Baghdad and Mosul. Men we trusted in the community. And that was a treasure trove for us."

Reznick knew that to be true, having operated in both Shia and Sunni areas of the tinderbox cities. The memories of the blazing cauldron of heat, hate, dust, and blood permeated his soul. The smell of death had hung heavy in the rancid alleyways he had patrolled, dogs eating the innards of corpses. Men with their eyes drilled out.

"Bottom line? The work from two prominent informers in Mosul told us that Private Frederick Hicks quietly reached out to a member of the Mahdi Army before he went missing. He spoke Arabic, so the US Army patrol with him couldn't understand what exactly he said."

Reznick saw immediately where this was heading.

"Hicks, in turn, passed on coded messages, sometimes messages written in Arabic, when he was in their neighborhood."

"So, he went over to a Shia militia? Willingly?"

"Damn straight, he went willingly."

Reznick's mind was racing. "So, this has to be Iran, right?"

"Got it! That's what the cables from the station chief say. It also says that a Shia cleric who was a cutout back in Tehran confirmed this under interrogation. Gave Hicks's name, rank, date of birth, blood group. They knew everything about him. The Agency believes that the Quds Force smuggled Hicks out of Iraq via Iranian-backed militias and back to Tehran."

"And he's been out of sight all this time?"

"Until now. This classified report has been buried in the archives of the Pentagon. Misfiled or some such shit."

"Hicks has been activated by Iran?"

"We believe he's been activated for a major operation. That's what the analysis says."

"Fuck." Reznick finished his beer as Peter sent over another cold bottle and a shot of vodka for him. He gave Peter a thumbs up. He waited for the Chilean bartender to clear up the glasses at an adjacent table and go back behind the bar before he spoke.

"You still there?" Black said.

"I'm still here."

"Let me ask you something, Jon. You made this forensic connection that put us on the road that led to Hicks. But we also believe that Maria Garcia is the key to this. She may very well be holding the secrets that had been hoarded and accumulated by Muroz all these years."

"I told you. You need to get in there."

"Jon, there are diplomatic niceties. Besides, I believe the Civil Guard might have visited her house very recently."

"Did they get in?"

"Negative."

"Sounds like they're onto her as well." Reznick knocked back the shot of vodka, feeling the liquor burn his belly. He felt better, the pain subsiding with the booze. "You need to deal with this before it's too late. I think she's crucial. We're behind the curve on everything."

"We're on it, around the clock. Getting back to the death in Palma, Trevelle and a couple of my analysts believe Frederick Hicks was—with an eighty percent degree of certainty—responsible for the death of the far-right Spanish politician in Palma."

"As I thought."

"A bartender remembered seeing a clean-shaven guy with a baseball hat leaving a few minutes before the guy was found."

"No forensics on the guy's glass, or surveillance?"

"Conveniently, all cameras were remotely disabled for one hundred yards in every direction. Hicks is not working alone."

Reznick sipped his beer. "No question. Both jobs were sophisticated, both needed technical backup, intel, the wherewithal. I'd say, taking that all into account, hell yeah. Hicks has done both. Have you informed the Secret Service about Hicks?"

"Affirmative."

"What did they say?"

"They want me, or rather you, to find this fucker and deal with him. Seemed pissed. The Secret Service guy didn't like being told what to do by the Agency."

Reznick was being watched closely by a guy drinking wine outside. "Hicks is expendable. The Iranians obviously wanted to use a white guy to carry out this operation. What if they have set up a couple of warmups to prove his worth? And then the big one."

"The capital, Palma. The city is still not in full lockdown."

"Maybe I should really head on down to Palma then."

"Not so fast. We've also learned that the President and his wife will be attending a party hosted by Rick Francis at a villa in the city."

"Who the hell is Rick Francis?"

"American tech billionaire. AI mastermind apparently. It's not just the party in the city, though. There's another function."

"What else? What's the other function?"

More silence.

"Spit it out, Daniel."

"The itinerary also includes a trip on Francis's megayacht."

"Where's it docked? Palma?"

"I have been informed by a friend of mine within the Secret Service . . . and this has been verified by the Pentagon . . . the yacht will be in northwest Mallorca."

"Latitude, longitude?"

"I don't have that . . . yet. But I've been told that it will be close to . . . you're going to love this, Port de Sóller."

"What?"

"I know."

Reznick took a deep breath. "When's this party?"

"Tomorrow night."

"Holy shit. Are you kidding me? Seriously?"

"Yes, seriously."

Reznick couldn't believe what he was hearing. "How close will the yacht be to shore?"

"Close enough."

Reznick finished his beer as he considered the risks of having the President at sea with a possible American-born Iranian assassin still at large on the island after two kills.

"What are you thinking, Jon?"

"I'm thinking this is not good. Cancel this bullshit yacht trip. That's what I'm thinking. You need to get the plans scrapped. We can't take any risks."

"Too late, Jon."

"What do you mean? It's never too late."

"It is . . . I've already asked for that. I've been told negative; the trip is happening."

"Who says? Who made that call? Who's the guy in charge? Give me a goddamn name!"

"Wendel Cain. Secret Service."

"You get back to Cain."

"And tell him what?"

"Tell him this—a government assassin, sent by the Iranians, is on the loose. He's killed two men already. It's highly probable, maybe even likely, that he is planning to launch a third attack. The Secret Service is not connecting the dots. They're blindsided by protocols."

"Jon, I've reached out to them."

"Well reach out again. What if this time his target is the President of the United States?"

Twenty-Five

Frederick Hicks sat in a café, nursing a glass of red wine. He wore sunglasses and a Panama hat. He was forbidden to drink in the culture and faith he had embraced. But his handler had stressed the need to integrate fully into the customs and culture all around him in Mallorca.

He pondered on that as the smells of cigarette smoke, fresh-cooked seafood, and fries mingled in the humid evening air. The lights from the ornate streetlamps added a soft glow to the square. But towering over everything like a Gothic sentinel was the imposing church, looming large. All around, children laughed and played games like hopscotch as their parents dined and drank.

Hicks's gaze was drawn to the police station adjacent to the church. A cruiser pulled up and the officers inside the vehicle cast their eyes over the diners and drinkers in the square. He wondered if they were looking for him. Then again, he sensed it was just what cops did.

He felt his cell phone vibrate in his pocket. He took out his AirPods from his case, pressed them gently into his ears, connecting wirelessly and seamlessly to his phone.

"How are you feeling?" a familiar voice asked.

"I sense we're reaching the endgame."

"Very true. You have been patient."

"I await my fate."

"*Let those who would sacrifice this life for the Hereafter fight in the cause of Allah. And whoever fights in Allah's cause—whether they achieve martyrdom or victory—we will honor them with a great reward.*"

Hicks smiled as he felt tears behind his eyes. A beautiful quote from the Quran.

"I will not let anyone down."

"We know you won't. You are a humble man."

"Have you got specifics?"

"This is a fluid situation. We've had to draw up new plans for you. All will be revealed at the right time. Rest assured we have this in hand. But for now, we would like you to take a cab up to the marina at Port de Sóller."

"Why?"

"Simply to reacquaint yourself with the town, the promenade, before tomorrow."

Hicks weighed why he was being asked to head back to the port again.

"Acquaint yourself with everything. Do not take notes or photographs. Just observe. Stay no more than one hour tonight. Very casual. Keep your AirPods in at all times. We will be watching you. Then return in the tram to Sóller before midnight."

"Why will you be watching me?"

"We are always watching you."

"You are?"

"Yes, of course. We have our reasons. Is there a problem with that?"

"None at all."

"One final thing. We believe our surveillance expert has located the whereabouts of the tapes and recordings."

"How exciting."

"We will forward you the location when the time is just right."

"Things are shaping up nicely."

"Take care. Not long now."

Hicks ended the call. He finished his glass of wine, left twenty euros to pay for the sandwich and drink. He walked away from the square, then cut down a narrow side street. He walked across to a small taxi stand.

He slid into the back of a taxi. "Port de Sóller marina, Señor."

The cab driver nodded and drove off, past the scented orange and lemon groves surrounding the town.

Hicks wondered if he was going to be sent to Palma tomorrow. He imagined they were planning for him to escape via a boat from the port. But then again, maybe the two other support operatives, both women, would be observing him from afar to make sure he wasn't being followed. It would make sense. A smart countersurveillance move to ensure that Hicks had no tail.

He had been trained extensively in techniques to detect and disrupt surveillance teams or operatives. He needed to be situationally aware. The other two operatives could be surreptitiously photographing people, gathering intelligence to analyze later, making sure he wasn't being tailed. That could be why his handlers were watching him. Then again, maybe they were testing him, keeping him on his toes to make sure he followed orders and hadn't been compromised. Maybe they were making sure he wasn't going to meet up with any third parties.

The cab slowed down as it turned down the scenic side streets of Port de Sóller. Night fell fast.

Hicks asked to be dropped off a block from the promenade. He paid the driver twenty euros before he got out, slipping down a quiet street near the church. Then he walked to the marina. The promenade was buzzing with tourists and locals alike.

He took a left toward the lights of the yachts, bobbing around in the shallow waters of the marina. He walked along the gangway as he perused the owners and friends drinking on deck, some cooking, some chatting. Then he veered off the gangway and back toward the main marina, where the largest yachts were berthed. He passed a lobster boat and a fishing boat. The yachts flew flags from Germany, Britain, Italy, and Spain, among others. Thick cables were plugged into charging stations on the quayside. The smell of diesel and gasoline mixed with the salty air and spicy cooking from some of the yachts.

A few tourists were taking photos of each other on their phones. He walked on, trying to appear aimless, on a stroll.

Hicks spotted what appeared to be the biggest yacht in the marina up ahead, berthed close to the naval base. He gazed across the dark waters and up to the lights of the villas perched high up on the cliffs opposite, overlooking the sea. His eyes wandered from villa to villa. All the lights were on. Apart from the bleak silhouette of the abandoned villa he had visited.

Hicks afforded himself a smile. It had been twelve days since his sniper shot. One shot. One death. His gaze searched the rest of the marina. Crews dressed in crisp white polo shirts and navy shorts mingled as the owner of one impressive yacht sipped champagne with a couple of bikini-clad girls laughing on a sofa, talking into his cell phone. The German flag fluttered on the bridge. He pondered who the man on the phone was. He was dressed in the understated but extremely wealthy way of the modern billionaire. Possibly a tech guru. Maybe the owner of a car manufacturer. Maybe a media company. Or perhaps the guy was a drug dealer from Munich. Who the hell really knew. The guy, whoever he was, was enjoying the close attention of the two scantily dressed women, that was for sure. Living his best life.

Hicks walked on past a yacht with a small Stars and Stripes painted on the hull. It was a medium-sized yacht but it must have cost millions. Maybe tens of millions. He looked around and wondered what the third part of his assignment would be. Maybe a terrorist spectacular here in the port. The more he thought about what lay ahead, the crazier he felt.

Hicks strode purposefully around the marina, occasionally stopping as if to admire the view, but in reality, he was observing the comings and goings in and around the harbor. He saw another American-registered yacht, *Virginia Cloud*. A couple of weather-beaten local fishermen, one with a cigarette sticking out of the corner of his mouth, sat on upturned wooden crates, repairing nets on the quayside.

Hicks moseyed on past the rest of the smaller yachts until he was back on the promenade. Dozens of people were waiting to catch the tram. He checked his watch. He had been in the port for fifty-four minutes. He had been told to leave after an hour. He climbed on near the rear of the tram and sat down on the hard wooden bench.

A few minutes later, the tram lurched forward and pulled away. Hicks gazed over the serene nighttime scene, anticipating what was in store the following night.

Twenty-Six

Reznick was sitting alone at a table outside the fashionable Hotel Espléndido on the promenade. He swallowed two codeine tablets and a Dexedrine with his beer. He checked his watch. It was nearly one in the morning. The promenade was still alive with tourists returning to their hotels or on their way out for a nightcap. He looked toward the eastern headland, at the lighthouse behind the naval base. Across the bay, high up on the cliffs, was the Cap Gros lighthouse, flashing intermittently for sailors approaching or leaving the sheltered harbor of Port de Sóller.

He felt a mixture of fear and trepidation that the events which were unfolding had taken on a life of their own. He knew little of the plans surrounding the secret meeting in Palma. That, by itself, concerned him. He needed to know the itinerary.

He assumed, having worked alongside the Secret Service on several occasions, that there would have been months and months of careful planning for a foreign visit. Everything locked down. Perimeters enforced. Exclusion zones. No-fly zones.

The problem was that Frederick Hicks could still be on the island. And there was likely a second or even third fake identity. If Hicks was no longer Warren Litt; he could be anyone.

Hicks was like a ghost. He might not be Delta-trained, but he remained a real and present danger. A serious threat. And he was very smart. Maybe his intelligence had tipped into arrogance, and the chewed-up gum had shown a casual disregard for taking care of every single detail, something that was second nature for ex-special forces men like Reznick. Reznick had been trained not to leave any trace as he hunkered down in bombed-out houses, forests, ditches, foxholes, camouflaged scrub out in the desert, watching and waiting for a target for days, weeks, or even months at a time.

In the States, the scene would have been examined inch by inch in microscopic detail by the Feds. No stone would be left unturned. Every camera around the villas on the cliffs, every camera overlooking the port, every Ring doorbell, even webcams would have been seized, examined, every avenue pursued. The town would have been searched, maybe even locked down, to stop the assassin escaping. But maybe, just maybe, the shooter had been in and out of the town in minutes before the cops or Civil Guard could mount a response. Maybe he had escaped through the Sóller tunnel and disappeared into the night.

Reznick felt himself going down a hypothetical rabbit hole, exploring not only what had happened and how it been allowed to occur, but also how the Civil Guard hadn't tracked down Hicks yet. Was there complacency in their approach? But then again, maybe any proper investigation would unearth the culpability of the Civil Guard in not protecting Muroz better. By letting Hicks escape, they were more or less covering their own asses. Muroz had been brought to the sanctuary of the naval base.

But, in many ways, all this theorizing was merely academic with hindsight.

Reznick picked up his cell phone and called Trevelle.

"Hey man, do you ever sleep?"

"Not as much as I'd like," said Reznick.

"How you feeling?"

"Some aches and pains."

"You should really go to the hospital. Come on, man, you need to think about your health."

"You sound like my daughter. She's always on me."

Trevelle laughed. "She's not wrong."

"Listen, let's cut the bullshit. I was talking with Daniel Black. He mentioned this goddamn meeting in Palma. But what I'm really concerned about is talk of the President going out on some fancy yacht moored off Port de Sóller? Where the hell is Hicks? Is there a reason why we can't find this guy?"

"I've been scanning numerous CCTV and surveillance databases across Spain, but it hasn't brought up anything on Hicks or Litt or whatever he's calling himself. Not a thing."

"How is that possible?"

"I'm trawling everything."

"How can he evade surveillance? I just don't get it."

"It's not easy in this day and age. But to be fair, the coverage in Mallorca is nothing like what it is in London or New York."

"So what are we talking about?"

"I'll put it out there, Jon. I believe . . . and this is just my opinion . . . Hicks is operating with advanced anti-jamming technology, neutralizing any surveillance or video cameras operated using Wi-Fi security jammers. It's a well-known vulnerability across the world."

"Are we talking military-grade technology?"

"I'd bet on it. If the cameras in towns are Wi-Fi operated, that might offer a rational explanation. Maybe he's using GPS spoofing technology so his exact position is unclear. Also, if we believe that Frederick Hicks is working for a foreign state, I would suggest he might also be getting help from the Leer-3."

"What's that?"

"Russian-made. It suppresses the GSM, the Global System for Mobile Communications. But that would mean an Orlan-10, an unmanned aerial vehicle, would have to be within a thirty-kilometer radius."

"Isn't that more battlefield military operations?"

"It is. But that's exactly how foreign rogue states would prepare for this."

Reznick mused on that point. "I'm assuming the Iranians have capabilities in this field?"

"No question. Not as good as ours, of course. But with the help of Russia, they have some hugely capable and effective GPS jamming devices used across a spectrum of operations. It's not too big a leap to believe they could mask Hicks's movements. I might add, such capabilities can be installed on tankers at sea, for example. Russia has extensive experience of that, jamming signals from sea."

It made sense. But it made things that more urgent. Hicks was dangerous enough if they simply hadn't found him yet, but he became exponentially more dangerous if they couldn't track him, especially if he was still operating on the island.

"One more thing. Daniel Black said there's a yacht. Owned by an American tech guy. It's berthed here in Mallorca."

The sound of a keyboard tapping in the background. "I know the one you mean. *Spirit of Freedom.*"

"Right. At this precise moment, where is it?"

"Two nautical miles south-southwest of Palma."

"So it's out at sea?"

"Copy that."

"But close enough for a chopper to land without much hassle."

"Bingo."

"Do you know if it's anchored?"

"Yeah. I'm looking at the yacht's cloud database. Data says it hasn't moved for twelve hours."

Reznick pictured the scene in his mind's eye. "Is the President on the yacht?"

"Negative. He's at a villa on the outskirts of Port d'Andratx."

"I thought the presidential detail was all going to be locked down in Palma."

"Originally it was planned for him to stay at a former monastery outside Palma. It's all changed, apparently in the last seventy-two hours. The villa in Port d'Andratx is secluded, with an air exclusion zone in force."

"Interesting. Do we have a time for the President to be onboard the yacht?"

"The Secret Service are very reluctant to share anything. But from what I gather, at this moment, the yacht is to set sail at 1700 hours today. So, sixteen hours' time. And they would arrive off Port de Sóller a few hours later, I'd imagine." There was a long pause while Reznick thought through how he would do it, trying to think like Hicks would. "Talk to me, Jon."

"What concerns me is what has always concerned me about this operation. Something doesn't make sense. It's uncanny. It's like he has a sixth sense. And I'm trying to unravel who the leak could be? Who's the mole?"

"Moles within Spanish intelligence? Spies?"

"Maybe. I suspect their cybersecurity systems have been penetrated in some way. They had to have been."

"Do you need anything else to put you in a better strategic position?"

"It would be useful to know the float plan. The full itinerary."

Trevelle groaned. "Secret Service has locked that down."

"Terrific."

"However . . . I just found a circuitous workaround. Cloud vulnerability, backdoor stuff."

Reznick felt himself smile. "I love it when you talk dirty."

Trevelle laughed. "Okay, so we've had three draft float plans so far."

"So far?"

"But the most recent one has been approved by the Secret Service. Signed off on by their top guy, Wendel Cain. He's traveling with the President."

"How long has Wendel been in that job?"

"Eighteen months."

"So he's just in the door?"

"Apparently. He was a policy advisor after getting a PhD in Criminology. Executive Leaders Program Homeland, Defense, and Security."

"What kind of on-the-ground experience does he have?" said Reznick.

"He has experience coordinating significant security operations, according to his résumé."

"That doesn't mean shit."

"He won a marksmanship competition."

"For the love of God. Have you got anything we actually need to know about this guy?"

"He was previously married, three kids. He's a fitness fanatic. But he moved out of the family home into an apartment building in DC popular with government agency employees. He was rumored to be in a relationship with a fellow fitness instructor who was believed to have worked for Homeland Security."

"What's the latest on the President's schedule?"

"The President will be flown by helicopter from the villa outside Port d'Andratx at 1630 hours today. It is estimated to take four minutes to cover the eight miles to the yacht. The President will join the host and guests for a champagne reception on the yacht before they set sail at 1700."

"Is the President going to be brought ashore?"

"That is not on the itinerary. But we can't rule it out. It's a possibility."

Reznick gathered his thoughts. "I don't like it. It needs to be called off. The whole fucking thing."

"What did Daniel Black say?"

Reznick sipped his beer. "He asked, or at least he says he asked, for the same thing. Secret Service vetoed that idea."

"Seriously? Do the Secret Service have access to the intel on the assassination in Port de Sóller? Do they have the name Hicks?"

"They've got that. The CIA has shared everything. So why are plans not being modified?"

"Politics, I'm guessing. Sometimes the advisors to the President don't want any more changes. Big party donors and all that. The tech guy splurges a hundred million on a whim to get access."

"The plans for the President need to be changed. It's reckless."

"I'm not disagreeing, Jon. Listen, I'll talk to Daniel again. I'll pass on these concerns of yours."

Reznick finished his beer. He peered across the dark waters. "I can't put my finger on it . . . I don't fucking get it."

"What don't you get?"

"The optics are wrong. Everything is wrong. The Secret Service aren't thinking straight. And it's gonna get people killed."

Twenty-Seven

Juan Pinto lay prone on the rooftop of a penthouse apartment by Repic Beach, training powerful night-vision binoculars on Jon Reznick. The American was sitting by himself at a table, outside Hotel Espléndido, wearing sunglasses, drinking a beer, talking into his cell phone. Pinto had instructed Spain's intelligence agencies to activate the microphone inside Reznick's phone. A roving bug, the FBI called it. But despite their best efforts, they could not decipher the layers of encryption the phone was wrapped up in.

Pinto had Reznick under close surveillance. He'd pulled together everything they had on the American. He had learned that Reznick worked with an ex-NSA cybersecurity genius, Trevelle Williams, who supplied him with modified cell phones, protected by military-grade encryption. Reznick worked off book. Assassinations, classified intelligence gathering, black ops, whatever was required.

He watched the American closely.

Pinto was in the dark as to the identity of the man who had assassinated Muroz, but he sensed that the CIA and Reznick already knew who it was. That explained why Reznick was still hanging around.

Pinto zoomed in closer with the binoculars. He watched as Reznick carefully took off his sunglasses for a few moments. The American's face was messed up bad, swollen right eye, cut above the other eye. Pinto could make out the swelling around the temple, even the stitches. He had been told the Madrid crew would put *appropriate* pressure on Reznick. He had not expected it to spill over into full-on torture. A lesser mortal could so easily have been killed. But Reznick was still here. Still around.

Pinto wished to God that Reznick had just taken his advice. He had a begrudging admiration for the American, sitting alone, nursing his beer. Reznick hadn't yielded despite being drowned, slashed, and beaten black and blue.

He felt deeply conflicted. Most of his team from Madrid were in and around Palma for the summit. Hundreds of police and Civil Guard were due to descend, not to mention sharpshooters on roofs to protect the politicians. He had seen the President's proposed itinerary. He had been told by his best analysts that any credible attack or threat would arise in or around Palma.

The problem for Pinto was there was one dissenting voice among the Spanish intelligence community. One analyst, a young woman, with a background in military intelligence, suspected a threat was possible in Port d'Andratx.

The analyst had come up with a hypothetical threat scenario that the megayacht to be used by the President and his guests, anchored off coast near the exclusive resort, would be rammed by a speedboat packed with explosives. It was apocalyptic. It was brilliant. He saw how it might happen. But no one, apart from Pinto, had seemed to take the young analyst seriously.

Still, Pinto knew the Secret Service would have tweaked their plans so the yacht would mostly be on the move, cruising around the island. But the Americans had not been forthcoming about the exact float plan for the megayacht. This posed yet more problems for the Civil Guard and the military.

The Secret Service feared someone leaking where the President would be. But Pinto knew American intelligence, including the Secret Service, was not infallible, and this compartmentalization of intel—a reluctance to share intel among US agencies—was a blind spot that could be exploited by the assassin and those backing him.

Pinto surveyed the promenade before he fixed the binoculars back on Reznick's position. He had to assume that Reznick was working on behalf of the CIA and might have advance knowledge of the float plan. And if Reznick *did* have access to the float plan, that would make Reznick's presence in Port de Sóller very interesting.

The American tech billionaire Rick Francis had a huge modernist glass house in Port de Sóller, up in the hills, overlooking the harbor. Pinto gathered the port might be a perfect place for the President to disembark. But, given the terrain, it would be a security planning nightmare.

He wondered if the President was going to be led ashore to the house or maybe helicoptered off the yacht to the house. The sprawling home had a helipad, as did the yacht. But then again, maybe the billionaire just wanted to wine and dine the President at sea, showing off his fabulous yacht cruising around the island.

Pinto watched through the binoculars as a waiter approached Reznick, the man none too subtly checking his watch as if he wanted to clear up and go home.

Reznick never took the hint. He just sat, sunglasses back on, staring out over the water. He knew that during the interrogation Reznick hadn't given up any secrets. Not a thing. But Pinto's twenty years of experience in intelligence operations across Spain, his gut reaction, had led him to believe that Reznick perceived the threat was either in or around the Port de Sóller area. It was as if Reznick, like a lone wolf, was waiting in anticipation of his prey.

But was his prey the man—a ghost—who had killed Muroz? Or was the prey actually the President of the United States? Maybe Pinto had Reznick wrong. Maybe they were being played. Perhaps the Americans wanted Spanish intelligence to believe that a mystery man had killed Muroz. But maybe the truth was that it had been Reznick all along. A classic shadow operation. But if it was Reznick, why was he still here, out in the open? None of it made sense. Was this actually all part of an elaborate, smoke-and-mirrors, clandestine CIA operation to destabilize the government of Spain? Was this a shadow operation to hoodwink the true threat?

Pinto was abreast of political developments between America and Spain. He knew there were underlying, ongoing tensions between Washington and Madrid. He had read three recent classified State Department briefings showing alarm among policymakers, politicians, and power brokers in Washington. It was said that America's economic, political, and governmental elites were alarmed that the Spanish socialist government had moved to deepen links with China. He considered if this was an operation to cause unease in Madrid and even across Europe. Sowing doubts. Sowing fears. Was this classic PsyOps?

The Spanish prime minister had been the first European leader to visit China following a major summit with Russia. Pinto wasn't the only intelligence expert within the European Union to be concerned. The confidential US briefings concluded that in the Chinese visit the CIA saw "serious potential headwinds" and ramifications following the actions of a so-called NATO ally.

A CIA station analyst in Madrid had sent a cable back to DC which had been intercepted by Spanish intelligence. It detailed Chinese intent to open a new car terminal in Barcelona. The terminal would allow direct access to the port's railway, allowing cheap Chinese electric cars to be offloaded to Europe. Billions more in investments had been poured into old or ailing Spanish car plants, taken over by Chinese companies. A smart way to avoid tariffs for the Chinese. There was talk of Spain as a connector country within Europe. The Council on Foreign Relations had even sent a report to the CIA and FBI, warning of the economic and geopolitical fallout with the increasing closeness of the two nations.

Pinto wondered if this was what it was all about. But he had to push those thoughts to one side for now as he focused back on Reznick. Was the man he was watching, casually drinking a beer, in fact overseeing the operation on the ground that had led to the killing of Muroz?

But this was all pure speculation. He just didn't know. And for someone in Pinto's line of work, ignorance was dangerous.

A terrorist attack in Mallorca would be viewed as an intelligence failure. He could not allow that to happen. But with hours to go until the President would be on the yacht, traveling around the waters of Mallorca in peak tourist season, he was still dealing with an intelligence black spot.

Pinto ducked back into the penthouse and took the stairwell down to the street where he got into a waiting car. He pointed the driver toward Reznick and the car pulled away. Across the bridge, a left at the pizza restaurant, then he had the driver pull up opposite the Hotel Espléndido.

He got out of the car and walked across to Reznick.

Pinto sat down and smiled. "Hello, Jon. Mind if I join you?"

Reznick fixed his gaze straight ahead.

"We keep meeting like this," Pinto said.

Reznick finished his glass of beer.

"You keep unusual hours, Jon."

"So do you."

"Which gets me curious . . . why the hell are you still hanging around here after everything that happened?"

Reznick sat in silence as a waiter approached the table.

Pinto ordered two glasses of a favorite Mallorcan red wine. "It's very good," he said. "Very underrated."

"What do you want, Pinto? Why are you here?"

"I was asking myself that. I couldn't sleep, if I'm being honest. Do you have trouble sleeping?"

"Not really."

A short while later the waiter returned with two glasses of Manto Negro. "Gracias, Señor," Pinto said. He picked up his glass and took a small sip. "I'm on duty, I shouldn't really."

Reznick took off his sunglasses and turned to face Pinto, exposing, close-up, a bloodshot right eye, stitches in the gash on his temple, a swollen cheekbone, and a gash on his forehead. "What do you want?"

"Take a drink."

Reznick raised the glass to his mouth, taking a large gulp. "Very nice."

"I was thinking earlier about why you're here in Mallorca. Your résumé is interesting, Jon. Or should I call you William?"

"Is there a point to this conversation?"

"The point is, I still can't figure you out. And that's problematic for me."

"I already told you, I'm here on vacation."

"I'll let you in on a little secret. I'm trying to decide if we're being hoodwinked. Maybe the shooter is you. A covert operation. Is that what this is?"

Reznick gave a lazy grin. "I think you're suffering from sleep deprivation, Pinto."

"Maybe. I don't know."

"What do you really want to know?"

"Who sent you. Nice and simple. Just talk to me, man to man. Who are you working for? What's the plan?"

Reznick's attention meandered off into the distance as if he were distracted.

"I'm a patriot, Jon. To my bones. And I believe you are too. Would that be accurate?"

"Correct."

"You see, men like us know what it takes to keep not only a country, but its people, safe. Keep society safe. I can't remember if it was Churchill or George Orwell who said it best. *People sleep peacefully in their beds only because rough men stand ready to do violence on their behalf.*"

Reznick said nothing.

"You wouldn't allow or countenance a threat to your homeland."

"No, I would not."

"I believe you have been sent to this beautiful island, not as a business traveler or because of a vacation, but because of a mission. Later today, we have an important gathering here in Mallorca. Right here on this beautiful island. Your President is here."

"Sounds like quite a gathering."

"Have you been sent to disrupt this event or embarrass our country in some way? Destabilize Spain? You might know this, but we've already had two deaths on the island. Deaths which I am not at liberty to talk about at length. But I'm guessing you might know something about those already. Are you hiding in plain sight?"

"You've got a very vivid imagination, Pinto."

"No country can have that. No country can allow that. Why? Perception is everything. A country which is rocked by killings is viewed as a risk. We don't want risk. We want tourists. Tens of millions of visitors every year to Mallorca. They bring in billions. The economy employs millions in tourism across Spain. Do you understand what I'm trying to say?"

Reznick put his sunglasses back on, staring straight ahead.

"I believe there are elements at work—and maybe you're party to this, I don't know for sure—who will sow death and destruction. Europe has enjoyed peace since the end of the Second World War."

Reznick looked at his watch and slid a fifty-euro note under his glass on the table. "It's getting late. Are we done with the geopolitical lecture? It's getting to be time for bed."

"I just want you to know that we'll be watching you."

"That's very flattering."

"This is no laughing matter, Jon. We could arrest you here and now if we wished."

Reznick shrugged as he got to his feet, staring down at Pinto. "What's stopping you?"

Pinto finished his drink and leaned back in his seat. "Don't push me on this. Be careful, Jon. Your face seems to have already met with an unfortunate accident. I don't want you getting really hurt."

Twenty-Eight

Reznick walked back along the near-deserted promenade, returning to his hotel, replaying in his mind the surreal conversation with Juan Pinto. He went up to his room and turned on the TV. Every Spanish news channel was covering the President walking around Palma's Old Town the previous evening, surrounded by a phalanx of Secret Service bodyguards.

His cell phone vibrated.

Reznick checked his watch. It was 0243. The middle of the night. He saw he had a message from Daniel Black.

I need your help. Quick. We got a situation here at a farmhouse outside Sóller. Critical.

The text gave Black's location, nearly overlapping Reznick's. Reznick had not known that Daniel Black was so close. He took a note of the farmhouse's address, two and a half miles northeast of Sóller. He texted back, *What's the problem?*

I'll tell you when you get here. Secret Service here too.

Reznick left his room, bounded down the stairwell and out into the suffocating heat of the night. He turned the corner and quickly flagged down a passing cab, relaying the address of the farmhouse.

The guy drove steadily as if on a day outing.

"Do you want to step on it, pal? I'm in a real hurry. It's urgent."

The cab driver nodded as he accelerated along the promenade and out of town. "No problem, Señor. You on holiday, sir?"

Reznick shook his head. "Not exactly. Bit of business."

"What business you in, sir?"

Reznick gazed out of the window. He did not need to get involved in a conversation. "Property rental," he lied.

"Big market, Señor? Everyone love Mallorca. The Germans are huge in this market. I have a property myself."

Reznick nodded, his mind racing as the taxi picked up speed, into the tunnel, lights flashing by, and up a narrow road into the sleepy, beautiful Old Town of Sóller, its streets deserted. He couldn't imagine what Daniel Black would contact him for if not something essential to his mission. Nine times out of ten, a CIA handler would pass on coded, encrypted instructions, but they rarely ever met up with the black-ops guy during an operation. It wasn't something that was done. They always kept black-ops at arm's length.

The cab sped past open fields, farmland. Olive groves, oranges hanging from ancient trees.

The driver took a sharp left, down a winding dirt road, then pulled up sharply in a cloud of dust. The lights were on inside the stone farmhouse, a black SUV parked outside. Reznick paid the driver fifty euros.

"Thank you, very kind," the driver said. "You want me to wait for you, Señor?"

"No. I'll find my own way back."

Reznick got out of the car, slamming the door shut. The driver reversed down the track and sped off into the surrounding countryside. The wooden front door of the house was slightly ajar. He pushed it open. Inside, the smell of wild brambles and spices, as if from cooking. "Daniel, where the hell are you?"

The sound of soft music playing upstairs.

Reznick's senses switched on. He knew something was off right away. He took out his gun as he climbed the stairs. He wondered why there was only one car outside. He couldn't see any Secret Service.

He stood at the top of the stairs and scanned the landing. He slid through a doorway into a bedroom. Beds neatly made. It was a kid's bedroom, bright colors and cartoon characters on the walls. There was a door ahead, shut. He tried the handle. But it was locked from the inside.

The sound of dripping came from behind the door. Reznick rapped on the door with his gun. "Daniel, are you in there?"

No answer.

Reznick took a step back and kicked the door in. His gaze slowly began to process a nightmare scene. Blood splatter across the while tiled walls. Lying in a bath of blood-red water, a man's naked body, savage cut across the throat, the side of the head blown off, eyes still open. It looked like Daniel Black. "Fuck!"

Reznick took a photo of the dead man's face in the bloody bath. He sent the photo in a text message to Trevelle with the word *identify*. A matter of seconds later, his phone vibrated with a text message. *Daniel Black of the Agency. 100%.*

"Shit."

Reznick kneeled down on the floor. He looked closely at the cut across the throat. A half-inch gash. There were powder burns around the entry wound for the bullet hole, indicating the shot had been taken at close range. He sprang back up on his feet, pacing the bathroom. "Motherfucker!" he screamed.

It was a setup. The whole fucking trip to the farmhouse was a setup. His instincts told him this was the twisted work of Hicks. The cutting of the throat indicated to Reznick that Hicks, if he was indeed the killer, wanted to sicken as well as horrify. Classic PsyOps—targeting the mind of the enemy. In this case Reznick.

Just then, Reznick saw something. A cell phone wedged between two hand towels. He could hear his heart beating. The device was meant to be found. *Shit.*

He was about to reach out for it when the phone rang.

He moved aside the towels and picked it up.

"Who am I speaking to?" It was the voice of an American man. Maybe a hint of a Midwest accent.

Reznick felt as if his mind was going to explode with fury. He was holding Black's cell phone, which the killer had carefully left behind. Now his prints were all over the place. He had been played. "Who's this?"

"You know full well who it is. By the way, it's real good to hear your voice, Jonny! I never anticipated I would be given such an opportunity."

Reznick closed his eyes, his grip tightening on the phone.

"You don't mind me calling you Jonny? I feel like I know you. Do you believe in fate, Jon?" A pause, then a chuckle. "Whatever. Listen, man, this is so good that we could finally hook up. Veterans shooting the breeze, right? Long way from home, right?"

Reznick peered out the window in case the police were on their way. In case he was being watched at that moment.

"I've been dying to talk to you. So much to discuss. You see, Jon, I heard from a friend of mine that you might be looking for me. And I've got to say, I was flattered. I take that as quite a compliment that you've come all this way. So, I thought it was rude not to introduce myself. What do you think?"

Reznick checked around the bathroom for any sort of camera, any sort of listening device. He methodically wiped surfaces he might have touched with a hand towel as he went.

"You still there, Jon? You know who this is? I'm assuming you do. I got sloppy, I realize that now. But shit happens, right? I heard from a little birdie that you retrieved a piece of my nicotine gum from the villa in the port. It put you on my tail, but I've got to hand it to you, that's ingenious, man. You found that. And you figured it out."

Reznick took his cell phone out of his pocket with his other hand and texted Trevelle. *Trace guy calling Daniel Black's number at this moment.*

"Jon, are you still there?"

"Yeah, I'm still here. Where are you? Let's talk, man-to-man. We can iron stuff out. Face-to-face, what do you say?"

Hicks laughed. "I love that special forces sense of humor. Delta, right? That's what I heard. I kind of miss that camaraderie and all that tough-guy stuff, don't you? You're one of the real hard cases, right?"

Reznick kneeled back down to study Black—see if he could pick up any other clues before he had to flee.

"The irony of all ironies, Jon."

"What's that?"

"The hunter has become the hunted. How does that feel, Jon? How does that really feel?"

"Frederick Hicks, right?"

"I haven't been called that for a while, Jon. I just want you to know that your handler needs to be far more careful when he's shaving. Am I right or am I right?" The sound of crazed laughter down the line. "He needs a proper razor. Right?"

Reznick seethed. "Let's talk this over. What do you say?"

"I thought that's what we were doing, Jon. Listen, beautiful offer, and I'm sorely tempted, believe me. The problem is I'm really super-busy for the next twenty-four hours. I could maybe fit you in the day after next. How does that sound?" The sound of more jackal-like laughter.

Reznick stared at the dead eyes of Daniel Black, naked and dead in the bath.

"It's only business. After that's done, we can kick back and get to know each other. What do you say?"

"What exactly do you want?"

"I want to be your friend, Jon. When I heard that you were on my tail, I've got to be honest, I was intrigued. The CIA sending one of their granite-hard killers after humble old me. I'll tell you, it made me feel wanted. Do you know what I'm talking about, Jon? The feeling of being wanted. I miss that connection."

"Who are you working for, you piece of shit?"

Hicks sighed. "I've been told you were in Iraq too, Jon. That's what I heard. Baptism by fire or what? You there?"

"I was there alright."

"Where exactly?"

Reznick wanted to keep him talking in the vain hope that he might slip up. It might get Trevelle time to miraculously get a GPS fix on where he was calling from. "You name it, I was there."

"I was in Mosul for quite a while. You ever been to Mosul?"

"Yeah."

"Not good, Jon. Not good at all. I mean, what a mess we made. But that's where it all began for me, Jon. The place where I began to understand. Make sense of it all."

"You ran away, Freddy. You joined the other side."

Hicks laughed. "The other side . . . I like that. Me and you, we're more alike than you realize."

"I don't think so, Hicks."

"Listen, let's cut the crap, Jon."

Reznick's cell phone vibrated. A text message from Trevelle. *Got a fix on where he is. Townhouse in Sóller where Maria Garcia lives. He's there now.* Reznick ran downstairs, saw a set of keys on the kitchen table—presumably for the car Daniel Black had hired. He fled outside.

"Sounds like you're scurrying around, Jon. Let's see if you get here in time. Fingers crossed! See you soon, tough guy!"

The line went dead.

Twenty-Nine

Reznick jumped in the car outside, started up the engine, and sped off, headlights on full. He put his foot to the floor and accelerated down the dusty track toward Sóller, skirting the town's main plaza, down the narrow streets. He sensed he was being lured into a trap. But he was willing to take the risk.

He took a sharp right, then down an alley, onto an upscale street of townhouses in the center of the town. He pulled up outside Maria Garcia's home, took out his gun, braced himself on the top step, and kicked in the mortice lock on the thick wooden door.

Reznick stepped inside the darkened house, Beretta in hand, flicking off the safety as he scoured the first floor, prowling room to room. Tables and chairs overturned, cabinets upended, papers strewn over the floor, as if Hicks had been frantically searching for the tapes. He padded across the mosaic tiled floor. A chink of light from an upstairs window bathed the landing in a ghostly gray hue.

He began to climb the ancient wooden stairs. A dripping sound as if from old water pipes put him on edge. He reached the second floor, eyes down the dark corridor ahead. He moved stealthily in the beautiful, grand, old Mallorcan house. He was watched from the walls by black and white photographs of ancestors.

He raced up to the upper floors, clearing rooms as he went. Wardrobes overturned, chests of drawers ransacked, clothes lying scattered. The house looked to be empty. The likelihood of that chilled Reznick even more.

Reznick bounded down the staircase until he got back down to the first floor. He carefully pushed open the narrow door that led to the kitchen. Pale moonlight bathed the room in an ethereal white glow. A door at the far end of the kitchen. He turned the handle. Locked. The sound of the wall clock ticking echoed around the old stone interior.

He gripped his Beretta tightly as he took a step forward. He was listening for any other sounds. He sensed a presence. He crouched low. He saw a tiny red spot on the flagstone flooring. He looked closer. Blood. Congealed blood.

Reznick kicked open the door, gun drawn. A woman lay in the darkness, nearly motionless, fingers twitching. She was drenched in blood. Gray hair tied up. This had to be Maria Garcia, the sister of the priest. She looked up at Reznick, tears in her eyes.

"Oh my God . . . don't be afraid," he said, holding her hand. "Who did this?"

The old woman's eyes rolled back in her head.

"Señora, who did this?"

"*Americano*," she whispered. "*Americano*."

Reznick took out his cell phone and called 112. "*Emergencia!*" He gave the address in central Sóller. "Hurry! I have an older woman; she is bleeding out. *Lo entiendes?*"

The dispatcher said, "Señor, help is on the way. What is your name, Señor?"

"Just get here!"

Reznick ended the call. He leaned closer and studied the old woman's face. Her left eye was shut, swollen, blackened.

"*El me golpeo! Americano el me golpeo!*"

Reznick spoke the words into the translate function of his phone. *He beat me. American beat me.* "Help is on the way, Señora! I promise you."

The woman shut her eyes, drifting away.

"Stay with me! Don't fall asleep! Stay with me!"

The woman slowly opened her eyes. She leaned closer and pursed her lips, as if she had something to say.

Reznick put his ear to her mouth. "What is it?"

The woman groaned, rasping very shallow. "I did not tell him."

"Tell him what?"

"Where I keep them."

Reznick realized exactly what she was talking about.

"Where is that?"

The woman's breathing was shallow.

"Where are the tapes? The film?"

"*Bodega. Bodega.*"

Reznick knew that meant "cellar."

The woman glanced up at Reznick with rheumy eyes and lifted her bony finger to a door in the hallway. "*Bodega!*"

He felt for her faint pulse. It was slow. He checked his watch. Forty-one beats a minute. Too slow. Bradycardia level. He touched the warm blood on the back of her head. "I am so sorry, Señora."

The woman pointed her finger at the hallway door. "*Bodega!*"

"I understand. I will get people to retrieve what you have."

The woman gasped. "*Padre nuestro, que estás en el cielo, santificado sea tu Nombre.*"

Reznick nodded, recognizing what appeared to him to be the start of the Lord's Prayer in Spanish. "Stay with me, Señora! Don't give up! Help is on the way."

A few moments later, the sound of a siren outside. Two overweight paramedics eventually burst through the door and began attending to the old woman, who was rapidly bleeding out.

Reznick relayed as best as he could how he had found the old woman and that she was bleeding badly. He had no idea if they understood a word he was saying.

"Gracias, Señor," the paramedic said, injecting the old woman with a drug.

Reznick waited until Maria Garcia was placed on a gurney then removed from the house. He touched the back of her hand as she passed. He called Trevelle and relayed what had happened up at the farmhouse and now at the townhouse in Sóller.

"Are you kidding me?"

"Negative. Beaten to a pulp. I don't think she'll make it. Not at her age."

"Hicks?"

Reznick felt like his rage was going to consume him. "I spoke to him."

"What? Hicks called you? Is that why you asked me to trace the call to Black's cell phone?"

"After I found Daniel Black dead, a phone started ringing. It was Black's. I had gotten a text from Daniel to go there immediately. Think about it. What if they wanted to pin his death and the beating of Maria Garcia on me?"

"That is sick as fuck, man," Trevelle said. "He's fucking with us."

"That he is. Listen, she seemed to be telling me the tapes are down in the cellar. A team needs to get in here right fucking now."

"I just got a message a matter of minutes ago. Daniel Black's team is finally en route. Eight men, one woman."

"ETA?"

"They're on the outskirts of Sóller. Six minutes."

"They need to get in and get the fuck out, before this whole thing blows up in our faces. Civil Guard are going to be crawling all over this place."

The minutes dragged. Reznick decided to head down to the cellar. He opened the door Maria Garcia had pointed to and went into a large closet. He looked behind the coats for a panel but found only smooth wall. He then looked down and saw the faint outline of a rectangle in the floorboards. He got his fingers around it and lifted the floor. Stairs led down through a trap door into a sub-basement, where Reznick switched on a light. Then through a dimly lit stone passageway to a door, a numeric keypad outside. He tried the door but it was solid.

Reznick called Trevelle. He took a photo of the numeric keypad. "I need access!"

"Copy that. Hang on, hang on."

The sound of keys tapping frantically. "Try her date of birth. 070237."

Reznick keyed in the numbers. He tried the door. "Red light still showing."

"Fuck. Bear with me . . . Her late husband died in the 1970s."

"Date of death?"

"060775."

Reznick keyed in the numbers and a green light came on. "Bingo!" He pulled open the three-inch-thick wooden door. His gaze wandered around the stone cellar. It appeared to be a hidden, sealed cave. Temperature-controlled, and neatly stacked on wooden shelves, right up to the vaulted ceiling, were hundreds of boxes with reels of old film and audio tapes. There were photos of Franco everywhere he looked. It was a glimpse into the past. A ghostly past. He took a short video on his phone and sent it to Trevelle.

His cell phone rang again.

"This is it," Trevelle said. "This is what Daniel Black was looking for."

Thirty

It was nearly dawn.

Frederick Hicks was driving the RV toward the high cliffs of northwest Mallorca. Headlights illuminated the dark dirt road ahead. Fine dust particles from the bone-dry soil were stirred up by the car and the tires, swirling in the beam. He passed the picture-postcard village of Deià. A few minutes later, he pulled up at a cliff's edge.

Hicks switched off his headlights and turned off the ignition. He looked out across the inky-black sea. He slowly wound down his window and breathed in the sticky night air. The smell of wildflowers and the scent of lemons and oranges mixed in the balmy breeze. Waves crashed onto the rocks far below.

He caught his reflection in the rearview mirror. He was wearing his sunglasses, Las Vegas Raiders baseball cap, polo shirt. The business-casual assassin. He enjoyed the moniker, almost as much as he had enjoyed the little chat with Reznick. Almost as much as he had enjoyed killing Daniel Black. Killing a CIA agent, any CIA agent—that was special.

Hicks felt wired, being in control. He loved it. He craved it. His handler had told him that it was acceptable to needle Reznick. It was a smart psychological mind game. He wanted to live inside

Reznick's head. He wanted to show him who was really in charge. He felt euphoric even thinking about it. But he sensed Reznick's malevolence and cold fury would now be even more focused on finding him.

He checked his watch. The luminous dial said 06:01. A short while later, his cell phone vibrated. His wireless earbuds buzzed softly as they activated a call.

"Good morning," a man's voice said.

"It is indeed a good morning," Hicks replied.

"*And so the day has finally come.*" The code words had been uttered.

Hicks smiled. "It's been an eventful time."

"You've been very busy. A double cause for celebration. Daniel Black and the old lady."

"I also touched base with Reznick."

"I know. We listened in. Masterful performance you gave."

"Thank you."

"But that is behind us now. We need to refocus. Perhaps for the last time."

Hicks sensed it was coming.

"I have some more news."

Hicks closed his eyes. He craved the honor of what lay ahead. The privilege to be picked. To be the one.

"Peace be upon us, and upon the righteous servants of God. I can reveal to you, my friend, because of your wonderful efforts and actions, because of what you have already achieved, that you have been picked for the final leg of the operation later today. You and you alone."

Hicks felt tears spill down his cheeks, flushed with the excitement. "I won't let you down."

"Dawn will soon be upon you. It might be a long day. Cherish every moment."

"I've got all the time in the world."

"I have your instructions."

Hicks felt his stomach tighten in anticipation. He knew it was going to be major. "I await whatever you have."

"May Allah grant you the highest place in Paradise."

Hicks began to weep.

"This is what we want you to do. Are you listening?"

"I am listening."

"We want you to rest up until mid-afternoon. Set your alarm for 1500 hours. We want you sharp. Relaxed. And ready."

Hicks felt drained but happy. A few hours' sleep and some prayers would do him the world of good. "Where is the target?"

"All in good time. We'll keep you informed. Set your alarm. Rest up. It will soon be over."

Hicks ended the call. He wiped his eyes with the back of his hand and got out of the RV. He stretched his legs, which were getting tight. Then he took a piss in the dark against a tree stump.

Afterward, he climbed up onto the roof of the vehicle. He gazed out at the sea. The waves smashed onto the rocks far below, sending spray rising high into the air.

Hicks turned around. In the distance, the streetlights in Deià. He had never visited. But he had read all about it. An artists' colony. He remembered reading a biography of Robert Graves, the English poet and author, in college. The writer had made Deià his home for decades.

Hicks was a prodigious reader, and had been since he was a child. He had been fascinated to read that it was Graves's shocking experiences in the First World War, scarring him for life, which had led to him wanting seclusion. Peace. Isolation.

This resonated strongly with Hicks. He had identified with that same feeling after returning from his first tour of Iraq. He'd just wanted to retreat. Hide away, close his eyes, and never wake up. But he never did find a place of refuge like Deià. Just recurring nightmares.

Hicks had ended up having a nervous breakdown. He found he couldn't speak. He couldn't think. He couldn't get out of bed. He just lay in a fugue state. By the third tour, he couldn't take it anymore. The way he coped was by simply not feeling at all. He grew numb. The smell of death lingered in his nostrils like cold blood in a morgue. He had withdrawn from the camaraderie of his fellow soldiers. He had never really fit in as a recruit. Even in his unit, he had felt out of place. He was the language specialist. The rest of the men only spoke to him when they needed help during interrogations of local people. He grew to loathe what he had become. A witness to torture. A witness to murder. An accomplice. He stopped sleeping. He remembered it all so well. He wanted to curl up and die.

The sound of the morning prayers echoed in the darkest recesses of his mind. A sound he had feared at first when he arrived in the Green Zone in Baghdad. But the more he studied, the more he listened, the more he learned, and as the days became more intense and frightening, the more he started to find the prayers calming. Soothing.

The men who had taught him and protected him in Mosul were elders. Learned men. He talked. They listened.

Hicks had planned his disappearance with their help. He went AWOL three days before his tour of duty was due to end. He made it look like he had disappeared off the face of the earth. His comrades had desperately searched for him.

The sound of the waves hitting the rocky shore below snapped Hicks back to the present. He was alive. He had returned from the dead. His unit had thought he'd been kidnapped and killed in Iraq. He had been told that by his handler. But here he was. All these years later.

He thought once again of Robert Graves, at peace in Deià, after seeing the hell on earth on the battlefields of France and Belgium. The madness. The noise. The explosions. The terror. The deaths.

Hicks couldn't believe he had returned to the same place, perhaps for his final day on earth, to the place of peace where Graves was eventually buried. It was a spiritual connection.

He remembered rereading, under a flashlight, Graves's memoir, *Good-Bye to All That.* He had found a quiet spot at the base in Fallujah. He remembered feeling terrified most of the time, IEDs maiming his fellow soldiers on an almost daily basis. But as he had read the author's words, he no longer felt alone. He felt a kinship. The author recalled the depths of despair as a soldier in the First World War. Poison gas on the Western Front. The suffocation. The bulging eyes of his friends too slow to get their gas masks on properly. Those who did took the masks off as they fogged up, unable to see, gasping their last breath.

Now it felt, to Hicks, as if he had come full circle. It was like it had been preordained. Not by fate. But by Allah.

Dawn was near. A pale light visible in the far-off distance. A few minutes later, a blood-red sun peeked over the horizon, shards of light bathing the waters in a deep-crimson hue. He jumped down from the roof and climbed into the back of the RV. He pulled the curtains shut, locking himself inside the vehicle.

He lay down on the bed, and set the alarm on his watch and cell phone as he had been instructed. Then Hicks closed his eyes as he dreamed an eternal dream.

Thirty-One

Reznick stood guard outside Maria Garcia's townhouse in Sóller as a team of CIA operatives pulled up in a large white van. He was glad to see them.

The lead operator was a soft-spoken Texan, Lance Goruch, a former Ranger. "Hey man, sorry for the delay."

Reznick led Goruch through the house and down to the basement. "What're your orders?"

"We take it all by van to an airstrip and we're out of here within thirty minutes."

"What about the Civil Guard and local police?"

"We'll deal with that."

"What about the body of Daniel Black?"

"Forensics team already up there. His body will be removed on the same flight."

Reznick straightened his spine. He watched as the Agency crew filed past and quickly began to pack up the film and tapes into crates, sealing them shut with rivet guns. Twenty-eight minutes later it was done.

Goruch waited until the last of his men had nailed up the final crate, and taken it upstairs to the van, before he ordered his team to leave.

"What the hell's going on, man?" he asked Reznick once they were alone. "Old woman dead? Daniel Black dead?"

"Long story. Take it up with your bosses at Langley."

"What do I say in my report?"

"Say what you like. Just make sure you get all the boxes and the body of Daniel Black on that plane, Lance. Let me deal with the rest of the shit."

"My guys want to kill the people that deleted Black."

"You deal with your side of things. Classified stuff in the crates. National security. Do not stop until this is loaded onto the plane."

"Got it. You know who did this, Reznick?"

"I can't say any more."

"Can't or won't say?"

"You're on the clock. Get a move on."

Goruch wasn't letting up. "You going after who did this?"

Reznick ignored the question. He thanked Goruch, pulled the splintered front door shut as far as he could, and put the key through the iron-engraved mail slot for relatives to find. He had accomplished one part of the mission. The intelligence Muroz had hoarded over the years was now in US custody.

Reznick watched Goruch get into the driver's seat and speed off down the narrow street, en route to the airport.

He was relieved to be out of the house, the morning sun warm on his skin.

Reznick felt emotionally drained as he walked over to the square, pulled up a chair at a café, and ordered a strong black coffee. He called Trevelle.

"How you feeling, Jon?"

"I've felt better."

"I just spoke to Goruch. The crates are all secured and he knows the drill. They're using Palma de Mallorca Airport, plane-leasing firm from Tennessee. A Gulfstream has touched down after a flight from Virginia. Currently refueling."

"Copy that." Reznick nodded as the waiter returned with his coffee. "Gracias, Señor." He sipped the coffee, enjoying the caffeine jolt to his system. He took a blister pack of Dexedrine out of his pocket and pressed out two pills, as always needing more than just coffee to keep him awake. After swallowing the pills with some coffee, Reznick spat, "This whole thing is a mess. Black is dead."

"I know. But we've got the tapes. A big haul. That's one part of the mission complete."

"True. But we still haven't found Hicks. He's fucking with us."

"I know."

"Why the hell haven't we got a fix on him?"

"I'm working on it."

"Come on, Trevelle, you need to do better."

"It ain't easy, Jon. I won't give up."

"I know you won't. Listen, I want to pick your brain."

"Go ahead. What's on your mind?"

"The megayacht. Talk to me about the float plan. Port d'Andratx departure at five p.m. this afternoon, right?"

Trevelle groaned.

"What is it?"

"That *was* the float plan. Not now."

"What?"

"The third submitted float plan was scrapped."

"Again? Why?"

"I don't know. What I do know is that the yacht has already left the port."

Reznick checked his watch. It was 0739 hours. "When?"

"Sixteen minutes ago, it set sail. The float plan was 1700 hours from Port d'Andratx. But they're obviously mixing it all up."

“Secret Service getting antsy?”

“You better believe it. Comms teams are freaking out. Some of the Secret Service detail want to get the President the hell off the yacht. Some want to get him the hell off the island. But the advice has been overruled.”

“Why is he still on the yacht? That makes no sense.”

“This is politics, Jon.”

“So?”

“Politics means money. Big, big money. This is his top donor’s yacht. And the guy is an old friend of his. The President’s chief of staff said in an email that ‘all things considered’ the trip was fine, the Secret Service were overreacting.”

“Trust me, they’re not overreacting enough. They should have dragged him off the yacht. What happened to Daniel Black, and what happened to Maria Garcia? The bastard is going to do something, maybe to the President. And he’s going to do something today, tonight, even if it kills him in the process. Has this intel been passed on to the Secret Service?”

“Affirmative.”

“Let me get this straight. Because of the close personal relationship, this guy being a super-major donor trumps national security?”

“Money talks loudest.”

“Okay, let’s back up for a moment. So, the yacht just left Port d’Andratx and is destined for where exactly?”

“Still the same spot.”

“Trevelle, tell me you’re joking.”

“The float plan shows they’ll anchor off the coast of Port de Sóller sometime later this afternoon. Roughly five o’clock. Langley has an open line with the boat. CIA are going ballistic, as you can imagine.”

"A state actor is directing Hicks and others. He killed the Spanish intelligence guys. He killed Black. And he left the old woman fighting for her life."

Silence.

"What?"

"Jon, there's been a development on Maria Garcia. She was braindead on arrival. Cranial bleed. Brief coma. She passed away."

Reznick felt numb. "Goddamn. She managed to speak a few words. Enough to let me know where the footage was kept."

"Which brings us back to the question. What exactly is Hicks's endgame?"

"Quite simple. I believe he will try, in some capacity—no idea how—to try and kill the President today."

"Jon, this is fucked up."

"If Hicks is an Iranian asset in some capacity, they'll risk it all to achieve that. They want to sucker America into a full war."

Trevelle sighed.

"Anything else on the float plan?"

"ETA in the waters off Port de Sóller of 1700 hours ahead of a sunset dinner at 2047."

Reznick's brain was churning through ideas and scenarios as if in a fever. "The only way to guarantee to stop this is to cancel the yacht trip."

"Jon, this whole thing is messed up."

Reznick sipped the strong black coffee. "Quick question. How many people are onboard this megayacht at this precise moment?"

"The latest float plan cleared by the Secret Service has forty-five people aboard, including the President and his family. It's divided into, first, presidential staff and family. Second, Secret Service agents. Third, billionaire donor, his friends and family. And last, fourteen-strong crew."

"So all the President's staff, they have Yankee White clearance?"

"Absolutely. And the Secret Service agents assigned to the President."

"What about the crew?"

"The crew have been vetted."

"What does that mean?"

"Single Scope Background Investigation on all of the crew."

"So everyone onboard has been vetted?" said Reznick.

"There is one name, the daughter of the tech billionaire, who went to school with the President's granddaughter. She's onboard. But I can't see any indication of vetting."

"Why not?"

"Her name is Audrey Samantha Fairchild. She was born in New York. American citizen. Close friends with the President's granddaughter. Attended Yale Law School together."

"So why hasn't she received either Yankee White security clearance or a Single Scope Background Investigation?"

"I don't know. I'm assuming they would have done a deep dive into her background."

"Look into that. That's bugging me."

"What else?"

"You need to get me a solid fix on Hicks. I feel like I'm repeating myself over and over again."

"Jon, that's all I've been trying to do. He's a fucking ghost."

"Yeah, well, it's time to find this ghost. Before it's too late."

Thirty-Two

The sound of incessant banging woke Frederick Hicks from a fevered dream. He opened his eyes. Someone was banging on the RV windows. He felt the polymer-framed Glock against his skin, underneath the sheets. He carefully placed the gun into the waistband of his khaki shorts, under his loose-fitting pale blue linen shirt.

A man's voice shouted, "*Polícia! Polícia!*"

Hicks's stomach tightened. "Coming!" He knew that if the cops searched the RV he was fucked. He had fake IDs, guns, ammo, rifles, rangefinders, all hidden from sight. It wouldn't take the cops or the Civil Guard too long to find it all. "Hang on, just making myself decent."

"*Polícia! Polícia!*"

Hicks pulled back the covers and opened the curtain, squinting against the harsh afternoon light. A lone cop, a municipal policeman, pointing to the window. At least it wasn't the Civil Guard. Those were mean fuckers.

"Señor, please step outside!" he shouted. "We need to see ID. Passport."

Hicks nodded vigorously, wanting to show respect, courtesy, and also that he was cooperating. He feigned a yawn. "Excuse me." He smiled. "I just woke up. Too much sun!"

The cop shrugged and took off his sunglasses as if he would rather be enjoying a siesta. "Open the door, Señor!"

Hicks complied. He unlocked the side door of the RV and pulled it open, a blast of hot air blowing in. He handed over his fake Canadian passport.

The cop took the passport, carefully examining it. "Ottawa?"

"Yeah, you got it. That's where I was born. Ottawa, Canada. You ever been there?"

The officer waved him back. "There is no parking here, Señor. This is dangerous to park here."

"Is that right?" Hicks lied. "I did not know that. I was just resting up. The sun is brutal. I was a bit tired from the heat. I'm sure you understand, right?"

The cop took off his sunglasses. "Step outside the van, Señor."

Hicks smiled as his mind raced. He needed to play this cool. He needed to be convivial. A good tourist. But one who didn't fully understand the local laws. He squinted against the sun's glare as he stepped out of the RV, partially shielding his eyes.

The cop's radio crackled to life. A garbled voice in Spanish.

"Everything okay, Officer?" Hicks grinned lazily. "I never realized this was a prohibited area. So beautiful."

"Your name is?" the cop asked, looking at the passport.

"Charles Edgar."

"And you are a Canadian citizen?"

"I am, sir. You know what us Canadians are like, right?"

The cop analyzed the camper van intently. "Where did you pick up this vehicle, Señor Edgar?"

"This RV?"

The cop nodded.

"I bought it from a British guy, I think, in Puerto Pollensa. Real nice dude."

"You bought it? Was it from a dealership run by a British man?"

Hicks smiled. "Not exactly, sir. It was a cash transaction."

"Did you get a receipt?"

"No, I did not. I was in the town and saw an ad in a bike shop that someone was selling a used RV. I checked it out. And I bought it from this guy who lived near the beach. I needed something to get around in. Sleep in, too. It was a good price."

"And you paid cash?"

"Correct?"

"How much?"

"Five hundred euros. I thought it was a fair price. And we shook on it."

The cop nodded. "Have you any companions with you? Inside the camper van?"

"Me? No I don't, Officer. Just me."

"What is the purpose of your visit to Mallorca?"

"I need some time away . . . a death in the family," he said quietly.

"A close member of your family?"

"My sister. We came here as kids on vacation with my parents."

"Do you mind if I look inside the van?"

Hicks stepped aside, feigning a yawn. "Not at all, Officer. Be my guest. It's a bit of a mess."

The cop glanced inside as he held the passport in his hand. "Señor, wait right here."

Hicks nodded, complying with the order like a good tourist would.

"Señor, I am just going to check your identity on my radio, okay?"

"You've seen my passport, right?"

The cop walked toward his car. "Si, Señor. I just want to make sure we have the correct details."

Hicks nodded. The cop was suspicious. He probably didn't buy the story. Hicks reached into his waistband, pulled out the Glock, and walked up to the cop. He aimed it at the back of his head. "On your knees, motherfucker!"

The cop fell to his knees, turned around, eyes wide open, suddenly terrified. "Señor, do not be so crazy!"

"You think I'm crazy? You should see my mother! She's clean fucking gone, let me tell you!"

"Señor, this is a big mistake. Please do not shoot."

Hicks motioned with his finger for the policeman to lie on the ground. "I'll decide if it's a big mistake. Face down!"

The cop complied and began to weep and wail. "Señor, I have a family who I love. A family I care about. I beg you, do you not kill me. I have three beautiful children, a wife I love. And a mother and father who rely on me."

Hicks attached a silencer to the end of the Glock. "Very moving, if I was interested in hearing sad stories."

"I am not a threat to you. Please, I'm begging you, in the name of God."

"Your God ain't gonna help you, my friend. Sorry to be the bearer of bad news."

The cop wept like a child.

Hicks pressed the gun against the back of the man's head. He pulled the trigger two times. The gunshots made a dull *PHUT* sound. A couple of holes drilled into the back of the man's head. Blood and brain matter exposed in the matted black hair. Crows took flight into the azure sky.

He pushed the Glock back into his waistband.

Hicks grabbed the policeman by his black boots and dragged the dead body to the cliff's edge. "Look what you've gone and made me do," he laughed. He kneeled down and shoved the body over the sheer drop. Heard a heavy, dull thud as it landed on rocks and sand hundreds of feet below.

Hicks looked back and questioned if he should do the same with the cop's car. He quickly decided against it. It would attract unwanted attention if it burst into flames. He got back in the RV, started up the engine, turned around, and pulled away. Inside the cruiser, on the police radio, a man was talking fast in Spanish.

Hicks laughed as he headed back down back the dirt road. He drove slowly, carefully, around the narrow streets of Deià, then on toward Port de Sóller. He skirted the port and continued to a location just north.

He ventured off the asphalt road toward an isolated spot farther on—Torre Picada, a seventeenth-century watchtower that had once been a lookout for marauding Moorish invaders. The irony wasn't lost on Hicks.

He drove farther down the dusty, narrow country road and along a single track, past orange groves. He pulled up in front of a wooden fence. He switched off the engine and picked up his large backpack, heading toward the watchtower.

The watchtower, as he had been told, was deserted.

Hicks crouched down. He unzipped a pouch at the front of his huge backpack and pulled out a rangefinder. He directed it across the sparkling blue waters under the heat of the late-afternoon Mallorcan sun.

He needed to know the distance to the target.

Hicks took a few moments to locate the vessel. And then, slowly, he saw it clear as day, on the far horizon. The huge yacht.

The distance calculated automatically. The craft was two thousand, one hundred and thirteen yards due northwest.

Hicks reached into the backpack for his binoculars. He saw people mingling on the yacht's teak deck. It looked like a party, a luncheon for people to sip champagne. And then he saw a man, the center of attention. It looked like the President of the United States. Laughing, arm around a young woman. Hicks watched through the binoculars for a few minutes. He studied the man's features. But it wasn't him.

His cell phone vibrated in his pocket.

Hicks took it out, pressing it tight to his ear.

"Are you in place?"

"Copy that. I can see it!"

"Tell me, can you see the target?"

"Negative. But perfect line of sight."

"Excellent. Listen, what happened back in Deià?"

"I had a problem."

"What kind of problem?"

"Cop woke me up in the camper van."

"That's bad, bad luck. Is he dead?"

"Affirmative. Shot him through the head. Then threw him off the cliff."

The handler groaned. "Even the best-laid plans, I guess. What about his vehicle?"

"I just left it there. Was tempted to push it over too."

"No, you did the right thing. The last thing we need is an explosion on the horizon. Or anywhere."

Hicks watched the guests on the yacht enjoying the hospitality being dished out. "So, I'm ready."

"You are in position?"

"Correct. Listen, I think I can make the shot. I've got this."

"Negative. The target is not in sight, correct?"

"I can't see him. True."

"So, that is why we have a plan. It's calibrated to succeed. Besides, the distance is too troublesome."

Hicks felt frustrated. He wanted to fire off round after round across the deck of the megayacht. He figured he would get lucky. But this wasn't about luck. It was about maximum impact. "I understand."

"But do you, my son?"

"Copy that, I understand the rationale."

"Good. Make your way down the cliffside path. A boat has been left for you, anchored thirty yards from shore behind the rocks."

"Is it quick?"

"Very, very quick."

"I like it."

"You will have to swim out to the boat. You will have a full set of equipment, fresh clothes, ID also on the boat before you set off."

"What do I do with my backpack, the RV?"

"Take the backpack onto the boat. Then get your hunting gear on. Ready?"

"Ready as I'll ever be."

"Let's get ready to make some history."

Thirty-Three

The delivery of the weapons was running late.

Reznick read the text and assumed the whole operation was cursed. He paced his room. He couldn't believe that the equipment Trevelle had promised he would receive was still in transit. It was just the latest in a line of mishaps and missteps, but it could not have come at a worse time.

The megayacht was already off the coast of Port de Sóller. He was running out of time. But most of all, running out of patience.

The decision to allow the President to be within sight of land—and potentially a long-range sniper—was just to appease some wealthy political donor. It was ridiculous and reckless. It defied logic. But whatever the twisted rationale, he could see a bloodbath on the boat if Hicks got the guests in his sights.

Hicks had been one step ahead of him this whole time. And the cold-blooded killing of Daniel Black had taken things to a whole new level. It was personal now. But if all that wasn't enough, the President's advisors, for whatever reason, still seemed oblivious to the critical risk that was presently unfolding. That was inexcusable.

Reznick was running out of time. He needed hard intel on Hicks. And he needed it right now. He figured if Hicks did have an inside track on the movements of the President, the assassin would be preparing to act imminently. And there was nothing Reznick could do without equipment.

If he were Hicks, he would again use a long-range sniper rifle. Just like for the Muroz killing. But he wasn't sure that would be the MO this time. The yacht would be far, far out at sea. Miles and miles. Though not be an impossible shot to take.

Reznick needed to find and neutralize Frederick Hicks. And quick.

Frustrated, he left his hotel and wandered around the marina in Port de Sóller. He spotted three cop cars patrolling the small town's promenade. He looked over at the harbor entrance. It was clear an exclusion zone was in place. A cargo ship had blockaded the entrance, stopping any movements by yachts, boats, or any other craft in or out of the harbor. It was a smart move.

Reznick checked his watch. It showed 1703 hours. He felt like he was wasting his time. He was in the unprecedented position of having no intel on his target or Hicks's movements. But to compound matters, even if he did, he still needed the delayed weapons Trevelle had promised.

The sun was blisteringly hot, burning his neck. Local kids were jumping off the wooden jetty into the shallow waters, families lounged on the beach, enjoying the late-afternoon rays.

His cell phone rang.

"Jon, you okay?"

"No, I'm not okay. You promised a backpack of equipment."

"It's en route."

"I'm going to be too late. Besides, why don't you have a fix on Frederick Hicks? That's all I'm interested in. And I can't seem to catch a break. What the hell is going on?"

"I understand."

"You understand?"

"Jon, things are going wrong, I know. You don't have to tell me. But I'm working on it."

"Tell me about the yacht. Tell me you've got something on Hicks."

"Negative on Hicks. What I can say is that the yacht is now anchored off the coast of Port de Sóller."

Reznick paced the jetty. "Which is not much use if I have no gear."

"Working on it. I should hear about that any minute."

"What's happening out at sea?"

"Spanish naval boats are patrolling, so no one is going to get close."

"That's something, at least. Are you sure?"

"Affirmative. I've seen the naval boat positions. No one can get close at sea."

"I still don't like it."

"I know you don't. But Jon, we're doing the best we can."

"Well, my friend, we are in the eleventh hour, and I'm still none the wiser where that fucker Hicks is. So, you need to scan every fucking intelligence channel, cop channel, coastguard channel on the island. Use AI, use whatever! But I want to know something, anything that gets us a fix on him! Real-time intel! Do you hear me?"

"Loud and clear."

"I'm running blind. We have a potential target on a yacht. But still no sign of Freddy."

"I understand."

"Do you?"

"Jon, stop! It's me you're talking to. I'm doing my best."

"If we don't know where Hicks is, at least tell me any intel on plans for the President."

"So I do have the latest revision on the float plan. The President and the people onboard will be dining in the next two hours onboard the yacht."

Reznick pondered that. "That's something, I guess."

"You think it's safer out there?"

"It should be . . . we just don't know." Reznick felt a gnawing sense of foreboding. It felt like Hicks—radicalized, crazed, dangerous, intelligent, and with blood already on his hands—was being lined up for a spectacular act of terrorism. "I need to get a visual on the yacht. My mind is going crazy with this."

"Let's back up, Jon. Hear me out. What if Hicks, and I'm playing devil's advocate here, has the same intel? Maybe advanced hacking of Secret Service encryption?"

"Maybe more likely Spanish intelligence mole?"

"That's the assumption for me, too. So, if Hicks is still on or around the island, and he's already been used to such devastating effect . . ."

Reznick pondered for a few moments. "They would want to sign him off in style. A big show of an attack, right?"

"Got it! So, if there's a naval blockade around the yacht, that would rule out a possible attack from the sea. I'm going through this, and this is just me thinking out loud . . . what if he tries the same location he used previously?"

"The abandoned villa?"

"Yup."

Reznick shielded his eyes from the glare of the sun as he shot a glance toward the high cliffs. "I considered that. The line of sight from the abandoned villa was perfect for the naval base. Not sure it would be the right line for a yacht that far out at sea. Besides, the distance is problematic for all but the finest long-range sniper."

"You don't think he'll try it again?"

"No guarantees. But I'd be surprised if it was from the same villa."

"Why?"

"I don't know . . . I just don't buy it."

"What if he's up there, watching and waiting?"

Reznick looked at his watch. "Can you do a calculation? Terrace of the abandoned house Hicks used, to the exact GPS of the yacht."

The frantic sound of the tapping of Trevelle's keyboard. "2.09 kilometers, line of sight."

"That's what . . . ?"

"1.12 nautical miles."

"Which would make 1.29 miles, right?"

Trevelle cleared his throat. "Precisely."

"Like I said, if Hicks is planning to do that, that would be one hell of a long-distance shot. Only the best Army shooters would even consider taking that on. And they'd have to have the very best tech. Perfect eye. And luck."

"He's done it before."

"But that was only a third of a mile, give or take, right?"

"I see what you're saying."

"It's three times the distance out to the yacht from the abandoned house. Nearly four times the distance. Over water."

"What if he takes the shot? What if he takes the fucking shot? What then? He's got nothing to lose. Imagine if he pulls it off?" said Trevelle.

"The shorter-range shot that Hicks carried out was brilliant. Devastating. But pulling this off would take someone with a far more specialized skill set. An extreme long-range sniper with years of experience."

"What if he fires off multiple rounds, hoping to hit the President, but also kill or maim anyone around him? That, by itself, would be a statement, wouldn't it?"

"Yes, it would," said Reznick.

"Are you ruling out him trying that again?"

"Never. But the conditions would have to be perfect to even stand an outside chance of success to get a direct hit on the President."

"I hear what you're saying."

"That said, I think I'll head up there, just in case. I'm just wasting time down here."

Trevelle sighed. "It's the waiting. The not knowing."

"It's not easy, I know. But if you can't control it, try not to sweat it. Focus on what you can control."

"Hang on . . . I think that's it here."

"What?"

"Your delivery."

"It's finally here?"

"Correct. UPS Access Point. Parcel pickup for you. Up the street from Bar Albatros. UPS sticker in the window. Tactical backpack with fresh gear for you."

Reznick made a mental note. "Good. Copy that. And do a thorough sweep of police channels, any intelligence naval vessels in and around the port. I just need a nugget of intel, my friend. Something. Anything. It might seem innocuous. But find it."

"Will do."

"You got an update on the billionaire's daughter, Audrey Fairchild? The girl that's on the yacht?"

"Tier 5 investigation came back all clear. Some bullshit Homeland Security delay. She's fine."

"Copy that."

"One more thing, Jon."

"What?"

"Take care, man. I think the bastard is going to resurface soon."

Thirty-Four

Reznick shot straight to the UPS Access Point, up near the old fishermen's quarter, not far from the marina. He needed these military-grade weapons. He also needed to get a visual on the yacht, as one of the scenarios he imagined was an asymmetric attack from the sea. He knew there were naval vessels patrolling an exclusion zone around the megayacht. But he also knew there were ways and means to deal with that. He had participated in a few himself.

He returned to his hotel room, locked the door, and opened the package. Inside was a brand-new tactical backpack. Inside was just what he was looking for. A classic American sniper rifle—the Barrett MRADELR, along with Nightforce scope with TREMOR3 reticle. The ammo was EnABLER 375. This was serious gear. Also included was a pocket-laser rangefinder with a stunning range of up to six thousand meters, a state-of-the-art Kestrel ballistics meter, a high-powered telephoto lens and camera, and a map showing all the dirt trails and paths in and around the port.

Trevelle had done good. He had come through at the eleventh hour.

Reznick inspected the weaponry as he considered that the threat to the yacht might come from elsewhere. The yacht itself might be boobytrapped and detonated by text or call to a cell phone. A series of apocalyptic scenarios raced around his head.

The more he thought about what might unfold, the multiple dangers that might emerge, the more he felt himself flipping back into the zone. A psychological zone where he was comfortable. His mind switched into operation mode. But what he still needed, still craved, more than anything, was for Trevelle to finally get a fix on Hicks.

Hicks had to be receiving no less than high-level state assistance. Almost certainly the Iranians. Maybe with the help of Russian hacking groups. Maybe a hacking group called Fancy Bear, part of Russia's GRU military intelligence service. Reznick suspected the source was the Iranian Cyber Army, aligned with the Tehran regime.

Reznick stripped down the weapon before carefully packing it away into the tactical backpack and zipping it up. He schemed out what he would do if he were in Hicks's shoes. His mind flashed back to the killing of Muroz. Trevelle had mentioned that method as a possibility. But he wasn't so sure that Hicks would return to the location for a second shot. It would be highly challenging long-range shooting. The margin of error, at such a distance, could be made by only the world's finest long-range rifle experts. He knew a few. One, in particular, a soft-spoken guy from Texas, had trained with special forces in the United States, the UK, Germany, and Australia. He could make the shot any day of the week. But could Hicks? That was doubtful unless that was his specialty. But Hicks had achieved the kill shot on Muroz at just over six hundred yards. Tremendous accuracy and skill. Who was to say that Hicks wouldn't try the same tactic again? Maybe he had been trained to do ultra-long-distance kills.

The harbor had been blockaded, so no boats in or out. He figured that a massive, state-of-the-art yacht, especially with the President onboard, would have radio jamming equipment, precluding any approach by drone. At the very least, the Secret Service would be deploying such equipment. Under those circumstances, a long-range shot made perfect sense.

Reznick couldn't shake the feeling that the villa might, just might, provide the bird's-eye view that Hicks would need. Or a different elevation, not far from the abandoned house, perhaps.

Then again, what if the approach was direct, from the sea? He theorized how that scenario might unfold. He began to think of fast boats approaching the megayacht. Then he considered a shoulder-launch Russian RPG-7. A maximum range of seven hundred meters. An Iranian RAAD anti-tank guided missile was effective up to three thousand meters. A blockade wouldn't necessarily be able to stop that; a boat wouldn't even have to be particularly close to fire on the yacht. That might be it. The problem would be getting weaponry like that into Spain without anyone noticing. That said, it couldn't be ruled out. If Hicks had help, there was no telling what resources he might be able to obtain.

Reznick had read classified Shin Bet and CIA briefings about Hezbollah, allies of Iran. The Islamist terror group had used such weaponry in Lebanon, but so had Hamas in Gaza.

He needed to get moving.

He strapped on the backpack as if he were a serious hiker and took the stairwell down to the basement. He left out of a side entrance to the hotel. Reznick walked in the opposite direction from the promenade. He saw a small white van up ahead. He took out a fob sent to him by Trevelle and quietly deactivated the vehicle's alarm and locking system. He climbed in, placing the large backpack on the passenger seat.

Reznick turned on the ignition and pulled away. He took a road off the beaten track before heading back down to the promenade. Then over the wooden bridge, down a side street, and up the winding cliffside road. Higher and higher he drove. A few minutes later he pulled up outside the abandoned house and reversed into the weed-strewn driveway.

He scoured the grounds in his side-view mirror.

Reznick pulled on the handbrake and switched off the engine. Picking up the backpack, he walked up to the side door of the house, out of sight. He took a lockpicking device out of his pocket and gained access within seconds. He quietly shut the door, then pressed his ear to the wall of the kitchen, listening for vibrations. The sound of any movement. Creaks on the floor. But nothing. The property still appeared to be empty.

Reznick scoured the house to make sure it really was empty, going from room to room. Satisfied he was alone, Reznick opened up the French doors of the attic onto the terrace. He took out his binoculars from the backpack, searching the far horizon. Nothing. He took out his rangefinder and checked to see if he could get a fix on the yacht's position, longitude and latitude.

The megayacht should have been visible. It should have been in position out at sea. But all he saw were the deep azure waters of the Mediterranean in the late-afternoon sun.

Reznick sensed a new problem straight away. He called Trevelle. "Check your numbers. The yacht is not in position. I repeat, the yacht is not in position."

"Hold on, Jon."

Reznick strafed back and forth over the horizon to see if he had gotten the wrong location. He wondered what the hell had happened.

"The last position I gave you, that was in the float plan."

"Well, it's not there now."

"Fuck . . . Hang on, hang on . . . shit, the GPS is showing that they moved a quarter of a mile due west of the original position.

That's why it's not visible from the house. The terrace of the house faces northeast, right?"

"Correct. Do we know why it changed? This is bullshit intel. I need the real stuff. Real-time. Come on!"

Trevelle gave the new longitude and latitude. "That's a slight change. But there's nothing I can see confirming why it was done."

"I still can't see a thing. I need to move position for line of sight, if that's even possible, I don't know."

"Try the Cap Gros lighthouse. Beyond the lighthouse there's a hiking trail. It's barely used in summer. Right on the very edge of the cliffs. It's dangerous. But I believe it might give you line of sight to the yacht."

Reznick pulled out the local map from the backpack, scanning the topography and trails. He could see there was a strip of land between the rear of the lighthouse compound and the edge of the cliffs.

He ended the call, got back in the van, reversed out of the driveway, and drove up the winding road toward the lighthouse. He drove on past the chain-link fence that fringed the lighthouse until he got to an isolated dirt road. He drove for another hundred or so yards, pulling up adjacent to what looked like a deserted old shepherd's hut.

Up here the heat felt even more scorching. Cicadas buzzed incessantly in the trees. Reznick squinted against the fierce, sharp glare, despite wearing sunglasses. His wounds were still stinging like crazy.

He slung the backpack over his shoulder, wincing as he jogged down what looked like an old donkey track, northwest across rough, bone-hard ground, rocky outcrops, and dried grass. He continued on for fifteen minutes, the blazing sun burning his neck and arms.

He saw a low stone wall, jumped over it, and made his way toward a rocky outcrop.

Reznick checked his watch for his GPS position. His elevation was one hundred and ten meters, or three hundred and sixty feet—slightly below the Cap Gros lighthouse, which stood one hundred and twenty meters above sea level.

Reznick looked out over the waters to the far horizon. Then he saw something, virtually a speck in the distance. He took out his binoculars. The megayacht came into focus. He saw a crowd of people onboard, drinking. His heart started to race. He turned around in the direction of the lighthouse, less than hundred yards behind him. No one was around. It was only him up here.

The isolated spot had an uninterrupted line of sight to the yacht.

Reznick took out the pocket-laser rangefinder from his backpack as he surveyed the magnificent yacht out at sea. He checked and rechecked. It showed the yacht was two thousand, two hundred, and fifty-three meters from his elevated position, which he worked out as one-point-four miles. Pretty far from the shore. But still within range.

In his mind, the yacht was too close for comfort. The proximity to shore was making Reznick alarmed, again questioning the decision-making of the Secret Service agents in charge.

He switched on the Kestrel ballistics meter, which gave a real-time analysis of atmospheric conditions like wind speed, direction, altitude, air density, and pressure.

Reznick set up the bipod, attached the Barrett rifle, set the scope in place, and locked down the throw lever. He lay down in the prone position and peered through the eyepiece. He carefully adjusted the elevation knob at the top of the scope to account for bullet drop at such a long distance. Then he adjusted the windage knob on the right-hand side of the scope to account for the fifteen miles per hour stiff southeasterly breeze. He aligned the sights one more time and the yacht came into sharp focus in the crosshairs.

Reznick felt sick. He reached over and picked up the binoculars, training them on the yacht. Men in polo shirts and Panama hats, women in pretty summer dresses, waiters in all-whites serving champagne and canapés. He fixed on one man wearing a Marine Corps baseball cap. Laughing freely. A familiar face. He took a few moments to compute that it was really *him*. The President, wearing sunglasses, a white Ralph Lauren shirt, a pair of faded jeans, and boat shoes. The President of the United States of America. In his crosshairs. Fuck.

Reznick felt a blind fury. If he could get a visual on the yacht, what would stop Frederick Hicks?

He was about to call Trevelle. But his earpiece buzzed first.

"You in place, Jon?" Trevelle's voice was a whisper. "You got a visual yet?"

"I've got more than a visual. I've got eyes on the President. Uninterrupted view."

"Seriously?"

Reznick trained the binoculars on a tray being carried by a waiter. "I have him in my sights."

Reznick put down the binoculars and took out the camera from the backpack. It had a high powered, ultra-long, 1,300mm telephoto lens. He zoomed in on the yacht. He switched to a high shutter speed to stop any blurring. He focused tight on the man wearing sunglasses and the Marines baseball cap. He took six or seven quick photos. He wirelessly sent them to Trevelle. "Should be with you . . ."

"Copy that. Holy shit—great quality. And . . . gimme a few moments."

"Face recognition now!" Reznick put away the lens and camera. "Is it him? It goddamn looks like him. But I need to know for sure."

"Gimme a second, Jon . . . I'm running the images. Holy cow! One hundred percent facial recognition hit! It's him! I repeat, it's him. That is our President."

"Are we fucking sure?"

"It's him, Jon. Facial recognition on five separate systems I'm using has pulled up a perfect match."

"This is bullshit! What the fuck are the Secret Service even doing? He's exposed no matter the long odds. Don't they understand?"

"Jon, I'm telling you, everyone and their dog has tried to reason with the President. He won't listen. But I said we had a problem . . ."

"I know we've got a problem. I'm staring at it."

Trevelle sighed. "That's not what I mean. Something else. We've got a situation developing not far away. Right now, I mean."

"I know that!"

"You don't understand. I mean . . . I'm scanning police channels, Civil Guard radios, shortwave frequencies used by several intelligence agencies."

"What've you got?"

"A local Mallorcan cop was just found dead at the bottom of cliffs, near Deià. Cop car still at the top of the cliffs. Blood found on the ground, believed to be from the dead officer."

"Got to be Hicks."

"Spanish haven't mentioned any name they believe is responsible. There's some scuttlebutt the cop jumped to his death."

"Bullshit. Tell me the location."

"Less than a mile from Deià. Not far. As the crow flies, that's approximately six miles away from you."

"And Hicks isn't at that spot now?"

"No. Police are all over it."

"Could he have been planning to use that vantage point to make the kill?"

"Maybe. But he's not there now. Like I said, he's a ghost."

Reznick questioned what method Hicks would use to approach the yacht if his position had been given away. "Here's a question for you. When exactly was the yacht built? By that I mean, is it state-of-the-art, technology wise?"

"You bet. It was built three years ago in Germany. Best in class. Not much change out of five hundred million euros."

"What protections systems onboard?"

"Cool stuff. Anti-drone, underwater diver detection, wall-to-wall surveillance, ultra-high-definition cameras, long-range acoustic devices to drive away intruders, pirates, that kind of stuff."

Reznick wondered if a long-range sniper shot might indeed be what Hicks was contemplating. It was a possibility. But if so, where would Hicks be hunkered down? The probability was that it would be somewhere camouflaged, high up on cliffs, maybe not too far away.

He peered through the eyepiece of the long-range rifle. He slowly went face-to-face on the yacht. "I'm assuming the sights have been zeroed?"

"Affirmative. Anything else?"

"Get me the head Secret Service agent onboard the yacht."

"Now?"

"Right fucking now."

"Jon, that's something that's going to attract attention to you. The Secret Service will get the Spanish Civil Guard to arrest you. And Hicks will still be on the loose."

"Maybe. But get him on his radio channel. Let me talk to him."

"Jon, are you sure? It might jeopardize your operation."

"I'm way past caring about that. I'm worried for the President."

"Give me a minute."

Reznick waited as he squinted through the crosshairs at the most powerful man in the world. A couple of minutes later, his earpiece buzzed to life.

"This is Assistant Special Agent in Charge of the Presidential Protective Division Wendel Cain, who am I speaking to?"

"My name is Reznick, Jon Reznick. You need to listen very carefully, Wendel."

"How did your associate manage to contact me?"

"He used to work at the NSA. Highest-level clearance. I used to work for Delta, the CIA, and the FBI. You've got a problem."

"Excuse me?"

"Are you on the yacht at this moment?"

"Reznick, listen to me . . ."

Reznick saw a middle-aged guy wearing chinos, a red polo shirt, and a linen jacket with a white pocket square, finger pressed to his ear, staring in his direction. He guessed this was Cain.

"No, you listen to me. You have your earpiece in, right? You on the starboard side? Red polo shirt?"

The man on the yacht craned his neck to look around. "Who the fuck are you? This is a secure channel."

"I already told you, Wendel. My name is Jon Reznick and I'm looking straight at you. The President is sitting on a chair on the stern side."

Wendel stared out over the blue waters, looking toward the shore.

"Yeah, I'm watching you alright. In real-time. So that means you've got a problem. The problem is Frederick Hicks. He's on the loose on Mallorca. And before you ask, I have clearance at the very highest level too."

"What do you want?"

"There is a high probability that there will be an attempt to kill the President. Frederick Hicks was an American citizen. But he has been sent, I believe, by a foreign government, to kill the President."

"I'm not at liberty to discuss anything like that. I suggest you send us what you have."

"You're not listening. Hicks disappeared in Iraq. He has been turned. He has gone rogue. He is almost certainly working for Iran. He has already killed two Spanish intelligence operatives. But it's not over. I don't think he's finished. If he pulls it off, it would be a trio of assassinations."

Reznick watched as Cain turned to another agent and picked up a pair of binoculars, searching the horizon.

"I see you. You see me. Are we good?"

"What the fuck?"

"You need to get the President the hell out of there."

"That is not protocol."

"Fuck your protocol."

Wendel put the binoculars back up to his face. "My colleague has confirmed your credentials. You worked for Assistant Director Meyerstein for a few years."

"Correct. Delta. Agency. Here and there. This and that. This is not a drill."

"Why were you sent to Mallorca? Were you brought in to find Hicks?"

"Sort of. A local cop was found at the bottom of cliffs near Deià, just down the coast. Including the cop, five cold-blooded killings in Mallorca in the last week. Two assassinations of former Spanish intelligence agents. An old woman murdered in Sóller. I found her. The cop at Deià. But Hicks also brutally killed a CIA operator. This is all pointing one way."

"I don't know what you think you're trying to prove."

"I'm not trying to prove anything. The guy who did this is Hicks. He is an American. But he's working for Iran."

"I have no intel on that."

"How is that possible? All that was shared with the Secret Service. Listen, I'll get my associate to send over everything he has."

"Copy that. Shit."

"This is a credible threat. My advice, least worst option, turn the yacht and move two miles further north. Out of range. Best option, get the President back on Air Force One and back home."

"You're not calling the shots. We have protocols."

"Your protocols have been compromised. I don't know if someone in your Secret Service detail has been using their personal phone instead of their government device."

"That would be irregular."

"I know that. But we know it happens. Did you not see the Inspector General's report that the private cell phones of groups of Secret Service agents were being spied on three years ago?"

Silence.

"Did you hear what I said?"

"I have work to do. I'm going to end this conversation."

"Not yet. Know this. I believe there may very well have been some sort of penetration of your communication systems."

"You know as well as I do we use only government-approved devices."

"We can have a discussion about that another day. What is not in doubt is that you need to get him out of harm's way. Do you understand?"

Wendel spun around, binoculars staring off in an easterly direction. "What the actual . . ."

Reznick turned his attention to the waters east of the yacht. He saw what looked like a small Tarpon boat. The type of boat he had seen being used in Florida for deep-sea fishing. He checked the deck. It appeared there was nobody onboard. "Wendel, you see what I'm seeing? You checking out the boat?"

"Yeah, damn right. What the hell?"

"I thought the Spanish coastguard was setting up boundaries, exclusion zones?"

"They are."

"So what the hell is this?" Reznick took out the rangefinder. "The boat is less than a mile from your yacht. It's drifting in your direction."

"It must've lost power."

"Wendel, wake the fuck up! Get the yacht the hell away from that location. You're wide open."

"Reznick, don't tell me what to do. I'll send a couple agents out in a boat to tow it away."

"Far easier to move away."

"I can't do that."

Reznick was watching a new drama unfold in real time. He saw the lead Secret Service agent pointing to two of his colleagues. The Tarpon boat was now just fourteen hundred yards away from the yacht, drifting like a ghost ship. "Wendel, will you, for the love of God, get the President away from that location. I've got a bad feeling about this. And where are the Spanish coastguard and naval boats?"

"They're positioned farther out."

Reznick scanned the small Tarpon boat, untethered, rolling in the swell as if in slow motion, yard by yard, toward the megayacht. He turned his binoculars back to the yacht. He watched the two agents get into what looked like a high-powered patrol vessel. It was lowered off the starboard side into the azure Mediterranean waters. It began to maneuver sharply and sped off.

Reznick rechecked the distances with the rangefinder. The craft was drifting closer, seemingly faster, now twelve hundred yards from the yacht.

"Jon, you still on the line?" Wendel.

"Copy that."

"I've just been told about the officer found at the bottom of the cliffs. Shot in the back of the head."

"Wendel . . . first Muroz inside the naval base. Second, his pal, a Spanish politician and former intelligence officer who served with Muroz, killed in a bar in Palma. Franco-era intelligence officers."

"We have no concrete evidence this is Frederick Hicks."

"Have you been told about the dental imprint photo from the gum?"

"What the hell does that mean?"

Reznick relayed what he had found at the abandoned house.

"I don't have that intel."

"My associate, a computer expert, shared this intel with the CIA and also the Secret Service. How do you not know that?"

Wendel picked up his binoculars as he watched his two agents in the fast boat slowly approaching the abandoned craft.

Reznick could only watch. He felt a sense of foreboding wash over him like he hadn't felt in a long, long time.

Thirty-Five

Frederick Hicks paddled hard in the kayak, his breath coming in pulses, as he knifed across the water out to the tiny, uninhabited island of Sa Illeta, just northeast of Port de Sóller. Only noisy cormorants squawking kept him company upon his approach. He got out of the kayak into the shallow water, backpack strapped to his back, pulling the craft behind him up the beach. He walked up a dirt track, shrouded by thick foliage, to a higher elevation. There he kneeled down and unpacked his backpack with care. He set up a tripod and attached his military-grade binoculars. He scanned the horizon for a few moments. Then he saw it.

Hicks thought his heart was going to stop. He zoomed in closer on the Tarpon boat, bringing it into sharp focus. He felt crazy as shit. His technical backup team were geniuses. They had allowed the boat to drift slowly, inexorably, toward the target. It appeared to have lost power, swept by the tides and the balmy southerly winds blowing in from North Africa, guiding the craft toward the megayacht.

Hicks smiled as he searched the deck of the massive yacht to see if he could locate the President. He drew a blank. But he wasn't discouraged. He knew that the President was onboard. Maybe he was relaxing in his cabin. Maybe sitting on the far side of the yacht, away from the long lens. Hicks took out his rangefinder. The yacht was two thousand, three hundred yards from his position. He put down the rangefinder and again trained the binoculars on the small Tarpon boat.

Hicks watched in rapt fascination as two casually dressed guys boarded the drifting craft. The younger of the two agents took out his cell phone as if conveying the situation to his boss on the yacht. And all the while the other tried to restart the engine, which Hick's backup crew had sabotaged less than an hour earlier.

No one knew what was happening. He had known the plan would work. He also knew boats, having worked for the US Coastguard for several years before he joined the Army. He knew engines. He could strip them down, build them back up. He could cannibalize them for spare parts.

He watched the younger agent put his cell phone into his pocket, trying to help his colleague restart the boat.

It was almost comical. He felt omnipotent. He clenched his fists in anticipation of what he was about to unleash.

Hicks reached into his backpack and pulled out a specially modified Android phone. He took a few final seconds to watch the pair sweating in the brutal sun. Feverishly working, crouched around the outboard motor, using wrenches and screwdrivers to find out the problem.

He observed the faces of the men, their linen shirts soaked in sweat and oil.

The Tarpon boat had already been prepped. The bags were hidden from sight under the deck, pager inside, wrapped in wires, stuffed with slabs of nitroglycerine.

Hicks took one last look at the men. He said a silent prayer. Then he texted the number of the pager to begin the three-minute countdown, as he watched from afar.

Thirty-Six

Reznick tracked the Tarpon boat through his binoculars. The two Secret Service agents were both trying to restart the engine without success. But all the time the boat was drifting closer and closer, yard by yard, to the megayacht. Why had the Spanish Navy or Civil Guard patrol boats not towed it away? Why hadn't the megayacht taken evasive action and steered away from the slow-moving craft as a precaution?

He sensed this was no coincidence. This was clearly a deliberate act. Drawing in the Secret Service. Getting their attention.

Reznick conjectured that this low-tech ploy had been set up by Hicks or one of his associates. He figured that the direction of the craft, due west, was at odds with the southerly winds—which would surely have taken the boat, if it had lost power, in a more northerly direction. The other factor was the highly suspicious situation of the boat being unmanned. And this pointed to the Tarpon craft being remotely controlled by a third party in some way. Perhaps a receiver installed in the boat's dashboard.

Shit.

None of this was good. He somehow knew how it would end. But no one could do anything to stop it now.

Reznick's cell phone rang. He swiped to accept the call, expecting Trevelle with an update.

"I was given this number by a close friend of mine in the Secret Service, Jon." The man's voice sounded eerily familiar.

The voice triggered something in Reznick. Ice ran through his veins. He felt sick for the helpless Secret Service agents, desperately trying to restart the outboard motor of the small craft.

"Don't want to chat today, Jon. Why is that?"

"Who's this?" Reznick said, pretending he didn't know.

"I love that special forces humor. I think you know who it is, Jon. You want to hazard a guess?"

Reznick felt a black rage within him, threatening to consume him.

"No? I'm going to be honest, Jon, I'm going to let you in on a little secret. I'm somewhat surprised that the Secret Service communications are so badly compromised. Why would that be? Still trying to figure it out?"

"Who is this?"

"You're killing me, Jon. You know exactly who it is. You're a smart guy. You know who I am. Your fellow countryman. I've got to hand it to you, man. You're the dude who figured it all out. That was clever, I'll give you that. Problem is, it's all in vain."

"What are you talking about?"

"I've been listening in to your conversation with . . ." He took a deep breath. "Assistant Special Agent in Charge of the Presidential Protective Division Wendel Cain. Big title for such an insignificant man."

Reznick knew the Secret Service systems were encrypted to the highest level. But he also knew that individual agents could be vulnerable. He knew some were clock-watchers. He had met a few in his time. Guys who would pull out their personal cell phone, despite being on duty. He made a mental note to check to see if

Trevelle had detected any unauthorized access to the secure Secret Service communications system.

"Are you still there?"

"I'm still here," said Reznick.

"But anyway, enough small talk."

"Listen to me, you crazy fuck, this stops. And this stops now. You have no idea what you're dealing with."

"I love that strident tone in your voice. I get it. A bygone America. Sacrifice. Values. Very old-fashioned. I get all that stuff. Moral compass and all that, huh? Still rooting for the good guys, huh?"

Reznick skimmed the vast blue waters beyond the small boat with the binoculars. He scanned the surrounding coastline. But he couldn't see a soul.

"I don't know exactly where you are, Jon. I'm guessing you or one of your technical pals at Langley has wrapped up your cell phone in some super-tough military-grade encryption, right? The problem is, they should have done the same for the dumbasses in the Secret Service. Pretty pitiful effort by them. It was almost too easy. You know how easy it is to insert malware and all that backdoor shit into a phone? Way easier than even I imagined."

"Let's talk this over."

"Fine, why don't we. I'm assuming you still have no idea where I am."

"You shouldn't work on assumptions, Hicks."

"I want you to do me a favor. Focus on the small craft, the Tarpon. And those brave Secret Service saps, feverishly working in ninety-five-degree heat to restart the engine. I don't think those guys get paid enough, do you?"

Reznick's whole body tensed.

"And think also of their families thousands of miles away at home, none the wiser of what is going to happen in precisely . . . let's see . . . about thirty seconds."

Reznick knew in that instant that his fears had been justified. He felt an overwhelming sense of powerlessness. He put down the cell phone and walked a few yards away. "Wendel, are you there?" he said into the voice-activated earpiece.

"Yeah, I'm here, Reznick."

"Get your guys off that boat right now! Get them to dive off if necessary."

"What the hell are you talking about?"

"Frederick Hicks just called me. He's going to kill your guys remotely. Get them off the boat now! Before it's too late!"

Reznick watched the Tarpon boat, praying the agents got off in time.

He picked up his cell phone.

Hicks said, "Hey Jon, you wouldn't by chance be calling for help in tracing my call? Get a fix on my GPS? You got a drone on the go? Is that it?"

"Hicks, whatever you are planning to do, don't do it. I'm begging you."

"The great American warrior Jon Reznick is begging me! What a time to be alive! The clock is ticking. And ticking. And ticking. Isn't this fun? Us Americans love some fun, right, Jon? You're going to remember this day for a long, long time, Jon."

"Hicks, you need to stand down. You need to stand down now! It's over."

"It's not over, Jon. How can it be over when it hasn't even begun. I'll decide when it's over."

Reznick watched one of the Secret Service agents on the Tarpon pick up his cell phone, looking back at the yacht as he listened. "Don't do this. I'm begging you, do not do this."

"America knows only one way. One day it will get the message. Goodbye, Jon."

Reznick felt as if his heart was going to break. He wanted to look away. But he watched in horror. A colossal explosion ripped through the Tarpon boat. A gigantic fireball, flames licking the sky. Debris blown high into the air, scattering across the water, burning fragments floating in the wind toward the yacht.

Two agents blown to pieces.

The black smoke drifted up, higher and higher, before creeping across the blue sky like a cancer.

Reznick focused the binoculars on the yacht. Panicked Secret Service agents corralled revelers on the yacht who were screaming in terror on the main upper deck. The sky was rapidly darkening with the dense smoke, secondary explosions rocking the peace and calm. The detonation had knocked the President off his feet, bashing his head on the teak deck.

Thirty-Seven

The sound of the blast reverberated as burning, charred debris was flung toward the deck of the megayacht in the choking smoke, little fires breaking out on the upper and lower decks. Special agents and crew ran around, quickly extinguishing the flames.

Reznick was watching all this from the cliff's edge as his earpiece crackled into life. He half expected Frederick Hicks to be on the line. But it wasn't him.

"Jon, it's Trevelle!" His hacker pal was breathing hard. "What the actual fuck?"

"You watching this shitshow?"

"Jon, Wendel Cain. His personal cell phone. It's got an app. A fitness tracker app."

"And?"

"Him and three of his Secret Service buddies have the same app on their personal phones. The app is monitoring every GPS coordinate that the President's bodyguards are located at. Every conversation can be recorded from their phones. Every discussion. Everything. So everything, no matter how secret, can be exploited."

Reznick watched the yacht, stunned at the revelation. "That's crazy."

"That's not all. I've finally got a fix on Frederick Hicks."

"Tell me where he is."

"A tiny, isolated island. Sa Illeta, just a few kilometers north of Port de Sóller."

"Let Wendel Cain know. And the Civil Guard. Actually, don't tell them. Their communications are fucking compromised."

"Copy that. Jon, is the President hurt?"

"No idea. I can't see onto the deck. There are a lot of people around one area. He went down when the explosions happened."

"Oh my God."

Reznick observed the deck of the megayacht as the crew and guests were quickly ushered onto boats. "It looks like an evacuation is underway. I can't see him now." He slowly scanned the upper and lower decks of the massive yacht. "Negative."

"So he must be below deck?"

Reznick watched as a couple of crew members used fire blankets to put out another blaze on the upper deck. "Get me Wendel Cain."

"Now?"

"Affirmative!"

A few moments later, Cain's voice in Reznick's earpiece. "Jon, talk to me!"

"Is the President safe?"

"He's hurt. Hit his head on the deck. He's going to need a helluva lot of stitches."

"You need to get him to a place of safety! Right now!"

"Don't fucking tell me how to do my job."

"I just spoke to Hicks. It was him. And another thing. Your so-called secure communication systems have been penetrated. The personal cell phones of the President's Secret Service close protection team are all running a rogue fitness tracker app. You included. You're being recorded, watched, and monitored remotely, you stupid fuck."

"Who the hell do you think you're talking to?"

"Shut the fuck up! Your personal cell phone is compromised. The one you probably have on board that fucking yacht right now. And all your Secret Service pals onboard. Am I right?"

Cain went quiet.

"Get the President to a place of safety. Off the yacht. Whatever it takes. Right fucking now!"

"We're working on it, Jon."

"This isn't over. The threat is still there. Hicks is out there. Get the President the hell out of there!"

Thirty-Eight

Frederick Hicks climbed down the path on the rocky island. He ambled back into the kayak with his backpack and paddled out of the cave for approximately four hundred yards.

A Civil Guard patrol boat was anchored, a woman watching him through binoculars. He paddled up to the boat, clambered up the ladder with his backpack, and took up position. The woman wore mirrored sunglasses and a Civil Guard uniform. He signaled for her to start up the engine.

Hicks reached into the backpack and pulled out the new high-powered Siyavash rifle as the boat purred into life, gently skimming across the water, toward the target. He lay prone on the deck of the patrol boat and signaled for her to lift anchor. She gave the thumbs-up and slowly maneuvered the boat away from their position.

He checked the compass and GPS as they motored in the direction of the blazing Tarpon boat in the distance.

Hicks looked through the eyepiece of the rifle, gazing through the crosshairs at the burning pieces of the boat scattered across the water, then to the megayacht in the distance. He saw there was an evacuation. He afforded himself a smile.

The Civil Guard patrol boat was slowly closing in. He laid out the bipod, attaching the long-range rifle. He checked the crosshairs. He adjusted the eyepiece. Perfectly in focus.

He watched the wealthy men and women climb into the waiting dinghies. The blue skies were darkening as black smoke billowed and spread across the sky, partially blocking out the sun.

The boat turned slightly, facing away from the megayacht. The anchor was dropped, fixing it into position.

Hicks turned and poked the barrel of his rifle through a specially cut hole on the stern side. It discreetly protruded, pointing in the direction of the megayacht. He was nine hundred and fifty-three yards away. He squinted through the eyepiece of the scoped rifle, lying prone on the deck, making a final alignment of the crosshairs.

He watched as a woman tripped on deck as she scrambled toward the escape dinghies.

Hicks hadn't had so much fun since he was a child. The first part of stage three was complete. But now it was onto the main event.

A few minutes later, his earpiece crackled into life.

"Can you see him?" The gravelly voice of his handler.

"Negative."

"He is there somewhere. Possibly below deck."

Hicks took stock of the faces of those on the dinghy. "I don't see him in the boats."

"He is onboard. We know that."

Hicks took a deep breath, keeping himself calm. He peered through the eyepiece as he fixed his gaze on the panicked figures, looking for one man in particular.

"Our communication specialist says that a chopper extraction is underway."

"Copy that."

His day, his last day on God's earth, was about to come to a glorious end.

Thirty-Nine

Reznick lay hidden in the long grass high up on the cliffs, his binoculars trained on the Civil Guard boat out at sea. He had watched as the female officer steered the boat slowly, pointing it away from the megayacht. He reckoned the Civil Guard patrol boat was eight hundred yards away from the yacht. But what he couldn't understand was why the bow of the boat was facing away, as if it had anchored. Its positioning seemed odd to him.

The Civil Guard officer was talking into a cell phone, staring beyond the burning boat. The black smoke suddenly lifted. There was a glint of light from the stern of the boat. Like from a mirror.

Reznick focused in close with the powerful binoculars, zooming in as best he could. He slowly, methodically moved the lenses across the deck. It was then he saw a figure. A man lying face down on the wooden deck, long rifle pointing through what looked like a hole in the stern, toward the goddamn yacht.

He put down the binoculars.

Reznick got into position. He focused into the eyepiece of the Barrett rifle atop the bipod, through the Nightscope. He had a fix on the man on the patrol boat, spreadeagled, bipod and rifle in place. Reznick adjusted the turret to realign the crosshairs.

He felt his finger tighten on the trigger. He peered through the eyepiece one last time, the sun burning his neck. He took in a deep breath. He squeezed the trigger. The gunshot sounded a few moments later as the rifle recoiled hard.

The man on the boat writhed on the wooden deck. He curled into a ball, face clenched, screaming in agony.

Reznick recognized the man's face, etched in pain. It was Hicks. He'd got him. But Reznick wasn't finished. He aligned the fine lines of the scope's reticule, getting the crosshairs across the top of Hicks's chest. He fired off a second long-range shot, the recoil slamming into his shoulder. The bullet tore into Hicks's throat.

Hicks lay motionless, blood spurting from the gaping neck wound.

"Reznick, who the fuck is shooting?" The voice of Wendel Cain.

Reznick turned his attention to the woman on the patrol boat. He looked through the crosshairs. She had reached for a long rifle. He took careful aim at her torso. He was undertaking a high-risk shot. He couldn't know for sure who she was.

Reznick squeezed the trigger anyway. The shot hit her stomach. She fell to her knees, convulsing, bleeding out. The second shot tore through the side of her head. The sound deafened him, buzzing in his ears. The woman collapsed face down beside Hicks. Both were dead. The threat was over.

"Reznick, who is doing the shooting?" Cain repeated.

"The targets have been neutralized. I repeat, the targets have been neutralized."

"What targets? What the fuck?"

"Frederick Hicks was on a Civil Guard boat with a female pal. The woman is wearing a Civil Guard uniform. Check them out. Both dead."

Cain picked up a pair of binoculars and sought out the Civil Guard patrol boat, through the plumes of black smoke from the

Tarpon patrol boat still drifting in the sky. “Hang on, Reznick, those are . . . Jon, that better not be Civil Guard.”

“Negative. Frederick Hicks was lining up a shot. The woman in the boathouse, she picked up a rifle, aimed in your direction. They’ve been neutralized.”

Forty

Reznick surveyed the scene of carnage. Hicks and his female accomplice lying dead in a pool of blood on the Civil Guard patrol boat. Then he panned around to the luxury yacht. Terrified guests being helped onto dinghies as rescue crafts, fishing boats, closed in. A chopper flew low, descending slowly, landing carefully on the helipad.

The President, wearing a bulletproof vest and flanked by half a dozen Secret Service agents, was frogmarched into the helicopter. Strapped in, two agents climbed in alongside him.

Reznick watched as the chopper took off, banking sharply to the west, before skimming across the water, disappearing into the distance.

The voice of Wendel Cain in his ear. "Reznick? You there?"

"I'm here."

"What the fuck just happened?"

"You had a close call, that's what just happened."

"We're going to be slaughtered in the press."

"We got the bad guys."

"They nearly took out the President. They killed two of my best agents."

"That was Hicks. He remotely detonated a device onboard the boat you thought had lost power."

He watched Cain guiding guests onto the dinghies. "I feel sick."

"We got him."

"At the eleventh hour. Shit."

"No matter what. We got them."

"What a price to pay."

"I know. Line of duty. God bless them."

Cain began to weep. Reznick heard his breath hitch over the phone. "They had families. Both of them had families. Good men. I can see the headlines now, Reznick."

"They made the ultimate sacrifice. Those agents and their families. Be thankful you're still here. Another minute or two, and Hicks would have killed as many as he could on the yacht. And hand over your goddamn cell phone. They've been monitoring not only the location, texts, and emails, but listening in on conversations in its vicinity. Via the tracker app."

"Shit. It was a present."

"What?"

"From a guy who owned an apartment in my building in DC."

"What was his name?"

"He works for Homeland Security. Lawrence Rodriguez. He ran a covert unit he said."

"And he befriended you?"

"Fuck. It was a gift. On my birthday. I swear to God, I thought it was a gift. A brand-new phone. He got us the best tickets for Washington Nationals games. I thought he was legit."

Reznick sensed movement behind him. He spun around, the early-evening sun casting hard shadows.

A four-strong crew of Civil Guard officers approached, guns drawn. "Freeze!"

Reznick complied.

One of the men stepped forward. He smiled and pressed the cold steel of the gun's muzzle against Reznick's forehead. "You're coming with us."

Forty-One

The hours that followed were a surreal blur for Reznick. He was handcuffed and driven in a high-speed three-car convoy away from the northwest of the island down to the Civil Guard headquarters in Palma.

There he was hustled into a windowless interrogation room on the second floor. The AC unit growled and rattled.

A Civil Guard officer pushed Reznick, still handcuffed, down onto a wooden seat on one side of the scuffed table.

Juan Pinto and a colleague came in and sat across from him. High up, in three corners of the room, surveillance cameras covered the space. A third man, balding, was sitting on a chair in front of a mirror, taking notes.

Reznick glared at Pinto.

The Spaniard shifted in his seat as he leafed through official-looking papers in front of him. His colleague introduced himself as Pedro Mendes.

Pinto wrote on a legal pad before he turned on the recording device. "If you're curious as to who the gentleman is sitting behind me, that is Peter Logan, military attaché from the American Embassy in Madrid. He and I have spoken, and he says you are free to discuss the gentleman called Hicks, to the best of your knowledge."

Reznick nodded.

"Quite an eventful vacation you're having, Jon," Pinto said.

Reznick grimaced, handcuffs digging tight into his wrists. "You mind taking these off? It's cutting off my circulation."

Pinto wagged his finger. "No can do, Jon. Not until you explain what you've been doing on the island. Who sent you? And why did they send you?"

Reznick looked across at Logan, who shook his head. "That's off limits, I believe."

"Tell the truth. That's all we ask."

"I feel like we're going in circles again."

"You're a very interesting man, Jon. We've pieced together more information about you. And things have changed after today."

"In what way?"

"When you were arrested, you had line of sight to the yacht that the President of your country was on."

Reznick could see which way the wind was blowing. It seemed like Pinto still had the idea in his head that he was the shooter.

"You were in possession of a long-range military sniper rifle, ammunition, a nine-millimeter Beretta, a rangefinder, military binoculars, and probably enough ammo to wipe out a small town."

Reznick shifted in his seat. He noticed that Logan was scribbling furiously on his legal pad.

"How do you Americans say it . . . *cat caught your tongue?*"

Mendes stopped writing and placed his pen on the table in front of him. "Jon, I grew up in New York," he said in a gravelly accent that spoke of Long Island. "I know how things work in the States. And I know all about the Agency. My father worked for them."

Reznick shrugged.

"Your passport says you're William Nader. But we know, definitively, after checking with our partners overseas, that you are Jon Reznick. American citizen. Former Delta Force operative, CIA Special Activities Center, and then some black-ops programs, before working on highly classified projects for the FBI."

"My passport says William Nader."

"Your passport is a lie! Jon, we want to work with you to understand what just went down. We want you to be honest, up-front, and explain what went on. Was this a shadow operation using Frederick Hicks as cover for your assignment?"

Reznick realized they were deadly serious about this line of questioning. He was in the frame for the whole operation. Logan, for his part, looked around the room as if uninterested. "You've got a vivid imagination, I'll give you that."

"Our forensics people are looking over that Barrett rifle. To hit a target from that distance tells me you're not a businessman on holiday in Mallorca. Unless that businessman is also an expert sniper or hunter."

"Pedro . . . Juan, look . . . I'd appreciate if you could understand. My passport says I'm William Nader."

"Let's leave your identity out of it for now. We need to know what you know about this other American. We've been hearing the name Hicks again and again from various channels. A body was recovered from a Civil Guard patrol boat. Give us something on this."

Reznick was reluctant to give them anything. But he suspected if he gave them the bare bones about Hicks, they might cut him some slack. "I can tell you what I know—not about any operation, but about a man who brought this carnage and death to your island."

Logan nodded as he continued to take notes. "Let's see where that gets us."

"I can live with that," said Pinto.

Reznick cleared his throat. "But you need to let me go when I've given you something. And also, I'm not admitting any culpability. You understand?"

Pinto exchanged a glance with Mendes. "Very well. What can you tell me?"

"Frederick Hicks was, I believe, allowed to operate with impunity, in Mallorca, coming within seconds of killing the President. That's what I know. He managed, with the help of a female accomplice, maybe a few others, to remotely blow up a Tarpon boat, which blew out the windows on the yacht the President was on, starting numerous fires in and around the yacht, leading to the emergency evacuation of the President of the United States. This explosion killed two Secret Service special agents. Frederick Hicks had one final plan. He was lining up to shoot and kill the President as soon as he got perfect uninterrupted line of sight."

Pinto's face was like thunder.

"This happened on your watch. I'm just visiting your island. This is just what I heard."

Mendes leaned back in his seat, his arms folded. "That's an interesting way to look at it, Jon. How do you know this?"

"I'd rather not say. But it was part of a sequence of events that indicate Hicks was getting state-level help."

"What kind of sequence?" Mendes asked.

"The sequence that let up to the attempt on the President today."

Pinto pinched the bridge of his nose as if stressed by the whole unfolding of the disaster in his backyard.

"I believe Frederick Hicks killed Luis Muroz, who had been taken to what should have been the safety of the naval base in Port de Sóller, under the auspices of the Civil Guard."

Pinto rolled his eyes, unwilling to accept that this had happened.

"I'm guessing you tried to cover this up. It doesn't look good. But it happened, all right?"

Pinto's face flushed red. "Who the fuck do you think you are? We're asking the questions here."

"I saved your asses. Can you imagine the fallout if the President had been gunned down in Spanish waters? Seriously? Can you imagine the reaction of the American government? The world? It would have been a firestorm which no one would have escaped."

Mendes cleared his throat. "I was hoping you would show some contrition, maybe. Maybe fill in some of the intelligence black spots."

"That's what I'm doing right now. And I'll tell you something for nothing. I'm guessing that intel was passed to the *Centro Nacional Inteligencia* with whatever the CIA had. And I'm guessing the Civil Guard Information Service would have that too. So I'm wondering, was Hicks under surveillance when he arrived on the island?"

Mendes scribbled furiously on the legal pad, nodding occasionally.

"Did he arrive by boat from North Africa by any chance?"

"We have no proof of that," sad Pinto.

"That's a common entry point for illegals. Was that it? Did he drop off the radar? Was he never on the radar? Did you lose him? Or was there something else at play? Was this a shadow operation being run by the Spanish intelligence services, using Hicks as a useful foil?"

Pinto looked furious. "What the hell does that mean? You've crossed the line."

"That's what I do. I wasn't the guy responsible for allowing Hicks free rein on this island. Someone fucked up. So don't pull that crock of shit with me. And another thing, before I forget. A

CIA officer, Daniel Black, was killed in cold blood at a farmhouse outside Sóller. That was the work of Hicks too."

Pinto shook his head, annoyed at the direction the conversation was taking. "And what about the old lady who was beaten so badly in Sóller . . ."

"The old lady who was killed? Maria Garcia? Who do you think? Hicks. I found her!"

Mendes continued to take notes. "How does she fit into the equation? What does she matter to Hicks?"

Reznick leaned back in his seat, arms folded. He wasn't going to tell anyone about the treasure trove of covert surveillance tapes and recordings that had been amassed by Maria Garcia. He had completed his mission. But the fallout and the ramifications of what had happened on Mallorca would reverberate like shockwaves across the Spanish intelligence community and their NATO partners for years to come.

Pinto loosened his tie. He was just getting started. The interrogation went on for three, maybe four hours. Reznick lost track of time. Backward and forward, crackling tension, angry outbursts. But it was nothing he couldn't handle.

Eventually, once they were satisfied they had as full an explanation of what had happened as Reznick could give, he was escorted back to a six-by-nine-foot cell, bed against the stone wall, and uncuffed.

Reznick laid down in the cot and took in the flaking paint on the ceiling wall, a fan whirring sticky air around his cell, contemplating how long he was going to be kept there.

Forty-Two

The following morning, after a sleepless night, Reznick felt like shit. His mood lifted slightly when he was informed that the US Consul General, Aileen Ash, had arrived to join US military attaché Peter Logan, along with a couple of high-powered lawyers from the State Department.

Reznick followed them down a corridor and into an elevator, then down to an underground parking garage. He got in the back of a black BMW SUV and was driven away at speed to a luxury office building on the other side of Palma. He followed them up in the elevator to a penthouse suite, surveying the long, highly polished mahogany table and leather chairs.

The Consul General sat down, the military attaché at her side. She opened her briefcase and handed him some papers. "How you feeling?"

"Like I could sleep for a week."

"Sign the last page and you're out of here."

Reznick quickly skimmed the legalese in the documents before signing and dating the last page. "And that's it?"

Logan leaned forward, shaking his head. "We didn't want to talk to you in case of eavesdropping by the Civil Guard. Do you understand what I'm saying?"

"Got it."

"Thought this was a better way to deal with it."

"Smart," Reznick said.

"Jon, I'm delighted to say you're free to go," Ash said. "We have been working with the State Department and other agencies to understand your role."

"It's complicated," Reznick said.

Ash smiled. "It always is with you, Jon. Or so I've heard."

Reznick nodded.

"This document is legally binding," Ash said. "You will not face charges or investigation, even with regards to the alleged fake passport in your possession."

"What are the Civil Guard saying about this?"

"Not much. Probably best to try and stay out of trouble for the rest of your stay."

Reznick said nothing.

Logan said. "We have a Cessna ready to take you from Palma direct to New York within the hour if you wish. Choice is yours."

Reznick folded his arms and reflected on that for a few moments. "I'd prefer to hang around until tomorrow."

"You mind me asking why?" Ash said.

"I have my reasons," Reznick said.

"Not a problem," Logan said. "Hell of a couple of weeks you've had."

Reznick nodded, his thoughts turning to the killing of Daniel Black. He also contemplated how close Frederick Hicks had been to pulling off a terrorist bonanza, killing the President. He realized the simple gift of a brand-new phone to Wendel Cain with a popular fitness tracker app on it, by a so-called friend within the Department of Homeland Security, might have allowed the Iranians backdoor access to Cain's world. No wonder Hicks had always seemed to be ahead of the game. For his money, Reznick still believed this had been an elaborate operation run by the Iranians. They had maneuvered and plotted, and Frederick Hicks had come within a whisker of killing the most powerful man in the world.

"Jon, we understand this was highly, highly classified," Logan said. "Even I'm not privy to what went on. We get it. We just wanted you to know that we're grateful for what you did, for what it's worth. We're only just beginning to put this all together—get to the bottom of what happened."

"Kind of a shitshow, actually."

Logan leaned back in his seat. "It was. It was a PR disaster for America. For the Secret Service. Think about it. A boat with explosives detonating less than a mile from the President? But also, a simple tracker app being used to hack the personal phone of a Secret Service agent. A simple gift?"

"Ridiculous situation. I think Cain was played. You might want to check out what else turns up. Maybe other gifts. I don't understand how he could have been so naïve."

"Cain is in debt. He has an ex-wife and four kids. I'm guessing a new thousand-dollar phone from some guy who claimed to be from Homeland Security was welcome."

"He should be in jail."

"Heads will roll. Lessons will be learned."

"In the Secret Service?"

Ash nodded. "They have some serious questions to answer."

"What I can't understand is why there wasn't a simple five-mile exclusion zone in place around the yacht."

Logan sighed. "From what I'm hearing from the State Department, who are going apeshit on this, the Secret Service, after a review, thought a one-mile exclusion was sufficient."

Reznick groaned. "Wrong fucking call. They should've locked it down."

"They had an air exclusion zone in place. But they seemed not to have considered any simple asymmetric attack from the water."

"From an Iranian proxy." Reznick tested that theory. Logan kept a straight face.

"We'll take that under advisement in our inquiry," he finally replied.

Reznick remained silent.

Ash checked the signed document. "This all appears in order. So, you staying in Mallorca for a while longer? Not too long, I hope."

"I'll head out tomorrow."

"Is that a promise?"

Reznick nodded.

"Plane can wait until midnight tomorrow before it leaves from Palma. Can I let them know you'll be on it?"

"I'll be on it."

"Make sure you are."

Forty-Three

In the morning, Reznick's taxi pulled up outside the small boutique hotel. He walked into reception. He was surprised to see Juan Pinto sitting on a leather armchair, talking into his cell phone. He looked up, ended the call, and got to his feet.

"I thought we were done."

"We are. I just wanted to talk, man-to-man."

Reznick wanted to shower and enjoy some sleep, maybe rest up before his midnight flight back to the States the following day. "Fine."

Pinto cocked his head and Reznick followed him out of the electronic glass door to the street. They walked without saying anything until they got to Hotel Espléndido.

Pinto sat down at a sidewalk table outside and Reznick did likewise. "I like it here. What can I get you? My treat."

"Black coffee, fresh orange juice, and two poached eggs on rye toast."

Pinto ordered an omelet and a black coffee. They sat in an icy silence, gazing out over the burnt orange waters as dawn broke over the Mallorcan port. The Civil Guard intelligence officer stared off farther down the promenade toward Repic Beach, where a handful of television news crews had assembled beside the marina. He pointed in their direction. "It's making worldwide news," he said.

Reznick waited until the two breakfasts were served and the waiter out of earshot before he spoke. "I'm not surprised. But you need to learn some hard lessons."

"And so do you guys."

"Point taken."

"There's going to be a far-ranging, independent inquiry. This was not only an intelligence failure on multiple levels, perhaps due to not sharing intel between agencies, perhaps other reasons from the past. We like to think of ourselves as more progressive, forward-looking. But we did not deal with the assassination of Luis Muroz in the proper manner," Pinto acknowledged.

Reznick drank his orange juice and then sipped some hot coffee. "Is that why you set those goons on me?"

"I can't talk about that. What I can say, in all honesty, is I am not responsible for them or what happened to you. I was operating without the full picture. I believe they were from a paramilitary unit attached to Defense. I do not condone what they did. I'm sorry, for what it's worth."

"Whatever. The big takeaway is that hard lessons need to be learned on both sides. Better cooperation. Better sharing of intel. How did Hicks get entry into Spain? Someone or some agency fucked up bad. How can it be that easy?"

"That's a fair point," Pinto said, spearing a piece of omelet. "Failures with our coast guard and yes, Civil Guard . . . we all deserve to get our asses kicked. Luckily, we will get our asses kicked."

"For what it's worth also, I love this island. I love the people."

"You do?"

"Don't worry . . . if I'm back, it'll be for a real vacation."

Pinto gave a wry smile as he wolfed down his omelet. "A real vacation? I'll believe it when I see it."

Reznick didn't answer. He ate the sumptuous breakfast, and finished his first coffee of the morning before it was refilled. He glanced over the sparkling blue waters of the bay, thinking back to the crazy events of the previous evening.

"I'm sorry about you getting roughed up. Really. I had no idea what was being planned for you. I hope you believe me."

Reznick shrugged. He didn't know what to believe anymore.

"Nothing personal, Jon. I thought they might interrogate you for ten or twelve hours, psychological pressure. I swear."

"Shit happens."

"I also wanted to express my condolences on the loss of Daniel Black. Was he the one who initiated your appearance here?"

Reznick smiled, realizing Pinto was still fishing for intel. "I think this talk is over, don't you?"

Pinto showed his hands as if he wouldn't pursue the point. He gestured vaguely toward the harbor entrance. "It's hard to believe what happened out there yesterday. Surreal."

Reznick nodded as he sipped his coffee.

"I wish you well, Jon. Until next time."

"Let's hope there isn't a next time."

Forty-Four

After Pinto left, Reznick hung around at the café outside the hotel. He had another strong coffee, enjoying the caffeine in his system as the crazy events of the last couple of weeks raced through his head. He took a couple of Dexedrine, washed them down with some orange juice. He paid the bill and walked along the promenade as the old tram rumbled past, already packed with eager tourists.

He headed up the narrow street that led to the bar run by the burly Chilean, Peter. He passed a neon sign on a pharmacy. The sign showed it was already a blistering thirty-eight degrees Celsius. More than one hundred degrees in the shade. And the sun had only just come up.

The bar was already open.

Peter was sweating through a white Levi's T-shirt, putting out chairs in front of the bar. He spotted Reznick through the window hatch.

"Hey, Mr. American, how are you?"

"I'm good, Peter."

"Coffee? Maybe something stronger? Estrella Damm?"

Reznick smiled. "Beer sounds good."

"You got it."

Peter went inside and reached under the counter to the refrigerator. He pulled out a cold bottle of Spanish beer, expertly removing the top, and handed the bottle to Reznick. "You starting early today, my friend?"

"Yeah, kind of. Just wanted to have a couple beers for the road. I'm headed home tonight."

"Long flight home, man. You looking forward to seeing your family?"

Reznick smiled, unable to go into the intricacies of his estranged wife who he had thought was dead but was now living in Connecticut, or his daughter Lauren in the CIA. "Something like that. What about you? When's the next time you get home?"

"This is my new home. My wife and kids live in Port de Sóller. We love it. And we are grateful every day to have this as our home."

"Your kids like it, I'd imagine—with the beach and sea."

"Love it. It's paradise."

Reznick sipped the cold beer, quenching his thirst. "It's going to be a hot one today."

"It's a hot one every day here. At least in the summer months."

Reznick finished his first beer of the day as Peter moved to the fridge to get another. "Get one for yourself."

Peter wiped the sweat away from his brow with a handkerchief. "Don't mind if I do." He pulled out two cold beers, handing one to Reznick. He lifted up his own bottle. "Safe journey home, my friend. And I hope to see you back here next summer."

Reznick clinked his bottle against Peter's as the air-conditioning blasted ice-cold air into the bar. He thought of Daniel Black. "To absent friends."

Peter closed his eyes, crossed himself, before he proceeded to knock back the beer from the bottle in three large mouthfuls. He put down the bottle. "I need to get myself a fucking hobby!"

Reznick laughed and toasted Peter again before ordering them two more beers. "I was thinking the same thing myself."

Epilogue

Three months later, Reznick was back home in Maine under leaden skies, walking on the beach, wrapped up in multiple layers against the biting November chill. According to the forecast, wintry snow showers would be blowing in from Canada. He stopped and stared out across the icy, dark waters of Penobscot Bay, waves crashing onto the rocky shore.

His cell phone rang.

Reznick took his phone out of his puffer jacket and checked the caller ID. He didn't recognize the number. But he answered the call anyway.

"Jon, it's Trevelle. You okay to talk?"

"Yeah sure. How's Florida?"

"Steambath hot."

"Lucky you. Freezing up here."

"Jon, there's someone who wants to talk to you. He called on a secure line."

"A secure line? Who is it?"

"A guy in the West Wing. Chief of Staff. And before you ask, I checked and verified. It's legitimate."

"Seriously?"

"Absolutely. He'll call you in five minutes. Do you want to take the call?"

"Sure. I'll be here."

Trevelle ended the conversation abruptly.

Reznick walked on. He pondered what the White House Chief of Staff wanted. He figured it had to do with the classified operation that had turned into a shitshow in Mallorca in August.

A few minutes later, his phone rang. He picked up on the third ring.

"Jon Reznick?" A man's voice spoke.

"Who's this?"

"Matt Steiner, President's Chief of Staff. You got a moment?"

"Sure. What's going on?"

"The President is on the other line as we speak. He wants a few words."

Reznick's heart nearly skipped a beat. "The President? Wants a few words with me?"

"If you're not too busy."

Reznick braced himself for a moment, thinking that this was an elaborate prank. "Put him through."

A few moments later, the President's familiar voice boomed down the line. "Am I speaking to Jon Reznick of Rockland, Maine?"

"Yes, Mr. President."

"Nice to speak to you at last. I've been briefed by Matt Steiner and my national security team over the last few months on what happened over in Mallorca. I believe I have you to thank for saving my life."

"Mr. President, I'm not at liberty to talk about anything classified, I hope you understand."

"I understand. What you did neutralized the threat. I've read your file. And I've read countless briefings from the CIA on what transpired. There will be an inevitable shakeup in the Secret

Service, which you'll be reading about in the papers tomorrow. But that aside, for your actions, your tenacity, I'm eternally grateful. I would very much like to know more about you. Meet you face-to-face and say thank you."

Reznick closed his eyes for a moment. He was not comfortable being in the public eye.

"This would be private, just me and you in the White House. That is, if you have no further operations lined up. But if that doesn't suit you, I'd be delighted to head on up to your place in Maine. Just me and you."

"That would suit me better, Mr. President."

"Limelight isn't all it's cracked up to be, let me tell you."

"I bet."

"So I just wanted to say I salute you. The country salutes you."

Reznick's eyes settled over the gray waters, mind flashing back to the explosion on the clear blue waters of Port de Sóller.

He thought of his father at that moment. A man who had survived Vietnam and returned to his hometown and built the house on the outskirts of Rockland where Reznick lived to this day.

"I've thought long and hard about what you did. And I would like to also say, and am proud to reveal, that you will be presented with a Medal of Honor up there in Rockland."

Reznick's mind went into freefall, disbelieving his own ears. "Mr. President?"

"I've reviewed your work for this country. This is overdue. You have officially retired. But I believe you never stood down. You are a man of honor. And it's my privilege, my real privilege, to present you with this."

"Mr. President, I don't know what to say."

"What also impressed me, Jon, was your ability to help the United States recover a treasure trove of intelligence. Between the tapes and correspondence, all going back decades . . ." He trailed off for a moment. Then returned. "The Director of the CIA described it as a *monumental haul of covert intelligence gold.* His words, not mine."

"Just doing my job, Mr. President."

"*Sine pari.*"

Reznick recognized the Latin motto of the US Army's Special Operations Command. It meant "without equal."

"I look forward to seeing you up in Rockland. My Chief of Staff will be in touch nearer the time."

Reznick inhaled the cold sea air. "Thank you, Mr. President."

Acknowledgements

I would like to thank my editor, Maisie Lawrence, and everyone at Amazon Publishing for their unstinting enthusiasm, hard work, and belief in the bestselling Jon Reznick action thriller series.

Special mention and thanks to Todd Hodnett, long-range shooting expert, founder of Accuracy 1st, who has trained military groups around the world for the past twenty years.

Thanks also to Faith Black Ross for her work on this book, and Randall Klein, who looked over an early draft.

Special thanks to my literary agent, Mitch Hoffman, of the Aaron M. Priest Literary Agency, New York.

Last but by no means least, my family and friends for their encouragement and support. None more so than my wife, Susan.

If your heart was pounding and you couldn't stop turning the pages as Reznick raced to find the killer, then you'll absolutely love *Hard Road* by J. B. Turner. Don't miss the place where it all began for Reznick . . .

When you work outside the law, the only person who can protect you—is you.

Jon Reznick is a "ghost": a black-ops specialist who takes his orders from shadowy handlers, and his salary from the US government. Still mourning the loss of his beloved wife on 9/11, he's dispatched to carry out a high-level hit. Reznick knows only that it must look like suicide. It's textbook. But the target is not the man Reznick expected. The whole setup is wrong.

When Reznick's young daughter becomes a pawn in the game, he has to use more than his military training to stay one step ahead of those responsible. Meanwhile, he is the only person who knows the true extent of the threat to national security—and has the stealth and determination to stop it.

An utterly gripping action thriller that will have your pulse racing as you fly through the pages! Available now or keep reading for an exclusive extract . . .

One

The call came from a man he knew only as Maddox.

Jon Reznick was sitting on his freezing deck as darkness fell over Maine, nursing a bottle of beer, staring out over the ocean. He let his cell phone ring a few times, knowing what lay ahead.

It had been ten long weeks. He pulled his jacket tight and watched his breath turn to vapor. He sighed long and hard before he picked up the phone.

"We got a delivery problem in Washington," Maddox said.

Down below in the cove, the Atlantic breakers crashed with a deafening roar, sending salt water into the winter air. The silhouettes of the tall oaks and maples shorn of their leaves—trees his late father had planted in the garden when he was a boy—bent and creaked in the wind. Away in the distance, out in Penobscot Bay, Reznick could see the lights of the lobster boats as they headed back to Rockland with the day's catch.

Maddox finally broke the silence. "They want to know if you can ensure the safe transfer of a consignment."

"When?"

"You must leave tonight."

Reznick said nothing.

"Is this inconvenient for you?"

"Kinda short notice."

"Are you available?"

"Tell me, how's the weather where you are?"

A long pause. "It's wet."

The word "wet" said it all.

"Someone must want this delivery real bad."

"Will you do it?"

Reznick was silent again.

"This has got to happen. This is an important customer."

He let out a long sigh. "Tell them I'm in."

"Smart move, Reznick. Pick up your tickets at the airport."

"Where am I going?"

"You'll see."

The line went dead.

Reznick's plane landed at Dulles just before midnight. He wore a black leather jacket, a gray T-shirt, dark blue Levi jeans, and scuffed cowboy boots. He slung his overnight bag over his shoulder and headed over to the Avis lot. There he picked up a black Chevy Camaro. In the trunk was an envelope with a fake credit card and two thousand dollars in cash alongside a reservation receipt for three nights at the Omni Shoreham Hotel in northwest Washington.

Reznick knew the city well. He headed onto the airport toll road and drove due east on Interstate 66, over the Roosevelt Bridge, then exited onto Constitution Avenue. The traffic was still heavy, despite the late hour. His mind flashed back to the time he first visited the city with his father. It had been the winter of 1982, the first of many trips to see the Vietnam Veterans Memorial. He remembered his father in the rental car, cursing the snarled-up traffic. But most of all he remembered what his father wore: a dark suit, white shirt, Marine Corps tie, and black shoes polished to a glassy shine. On every visit, without fail, his father had touched the names of the young men carved into the black granite wall the moment he arrived. Reznick would stand in silence, arms by his side, as his father fought back the tears.

The blaring siren of a fire truck in the distance snapped him out of his reverie as he drove over the historic Taft Bridge, past the imposing concrete lions guarding each side. He took a left onto Calvert Street, the hotel up ahead. He pulled up outside the traditional, eight-story building and tipped the valet ten dollars.

Reznick walked through the grand, sprawling lobby. Marble floor, ornate columns, chandeliers. A young man at the front desk took his details as he signed in under a false name: Ron Dixon.

"Three nights. Good to have you with us, Mr. Dixon. Do you mind me asking if you're in town for business or pleasure, sir?"

Reznick managed a smile. "A bit of both."

"Excellent. Can we help you with any bags?"

"No, you're OK, thanks."

His fake credit card was swiped and he took the elevator to the sixth floor.

Reznick used the keycard to open his door and flicked on the lights. He hung a "Do Not Disturb" sign outside before locking the room.

It was too warm, but it was spacious. A huge TV was on one wall, a welcome message on the screen. The decor was the "classic" look—green, floral-patterned carpet, and a king-size bed with a couple of rosewood dressers. The drapes matched the carpet.

Reznick peered out the window over the upscale Woodley Park neighborhood: a good base, well away from downtown. He turned down the climate control switch to "Cool," showered, and wrapped himself in a white terry bathrobe. Then he lay down on the bed and stared at the ceiling, waiting for the phone to ring.

The next morning, Reznick ordered a freshly squeezed orange juice and a black coffee from room service, before getting changed into his jogging gear—navy T-shirt and sweatpants with well-worn Nike running shoes. He walked over to Rock Creek Park under the flawless winter sky for his daily run. When he arrived at the water-powered Peirce Mill near the entrance, he did some stretching and warm-up moves, the temperature in the low thirties. A handful of runners were already pounding the snowy trails.

He switched on his iPod, blocking out the outside world, helping him focus on the task at hand. The thunderous riffs and beats of a Led Zeppelin song got his blood flowing. Reznick checked his watch: 8:48 a.m. precisely. He headed north on the Western Ridge Trail, a smell of pine trees in the mid-December air.

After about a mile, he passed a young woman sitting on the curb of a parking lot near Broad Branch Road. She grimaced as she rubbed her knee.

Reznick ran on by. No need to engage in unnecessary conversation with a stranger. Being anonymous was best. He knew the rules—the list was endless. Do not wear loud clothes, talk too much, appear distracted or lost; in fact anything that meant you were no longer blending in. Appearance is crucial: grays, navy tracksuits, and business suits are good; black shoes, also. But you have to fit in to the surrounding environment.

The way you speak, the way you carry yourself, your accent, dialect—they all give off signals. The moment a concierge thinks your luggage looks too flashy or too beaten-up, it all paints a picture. If you're in a top-end hotel, wear top-end clothes and carry smart cases.

The small things matter. Be attentive. Logos are easy to remember—better without them. The trick is to be anonymous. But don't try too hard. Don't shun eye contact. That in itself will attract attention. *What has he got to hide?*

The senses have to work overtime. And tactics have to be changed, depending on the circumstances. Move to another hotel, change into new clothes, ditch the car and get a different model.

He headed along Beach Drive as he ran through the park. Heart rate steady. Deeper and deeper into this verdant urban sanctuary in America's capital city.

Reznick's mind began to feel clearer. Slowly, he felt his senses sharpen as the sun flickered through the branches of the leafless trees. On and on he ran.

Up a hill and down a ravine, and back onto the main trail, passing a small stone police substation in the center of the park, two officers leaning against a cruiser, drinking coffee. He gave a polite nod and they nodded back.

Heart pumping harder as his head cleared. This was his routine ahead of every job and it passed the time. Kept him focused.

Up in the northern section of the park, he passed Rolling Meadow Bridge and doubled back along a trail by the public golf course. On past the amphitheater and across Bluff Bridge to where he'd started.

He checked his pulse. Only slightly raised.

Ten minutes later, Reznick was doing some cool-down stretching exercises against a park bench when the cell phone in his pocket vibrated. He switched off his iPod and saw the familiar caller ID.

"How you feeling today?" It was Maddox.

"I'm fine."

"So, any questions?"

Reznick wiped some sweat off his brow with the back of his hand. "You got a name?"

A beat. "All I know is that he's an American. OK?"

"On home soil? How come?"

A long pause. "Look, they wanted to keep it in-house. That's all I can say. This is a sensitive one."

"Tell me, where's the subject now?"

"Walking the National Mall with his son."

"What kind of monitoring?"

"Electronic. Far safer."

Reznick stayed quiet, knowing Maddox was right.

"How about we speak later today?"

"When?"

"I don't know. But stay close to your hotel."

Reznick shielded his eyes against the sun. "Why?"

"Why what?"

"Why stay close to the hotel?"

Maddox sighed. "Look, I've not had any confirmation, but I've heard from someone higher up the chain that we might have to move very quickly on this particular delivery."

"Timescale?"

"Sooner rather than later. Bear that in mind."

The rest of the morning dragged as Reznick waited for Maddox to call.

It could be a matter of hours. He dialed "12" and ordered a brunch of scrambled eggs, black coffee, buttered toast, and more freshly squeezed orange juice. After a warm shower, he channel hopped between CNN, Fox News, and the Weather Channel. Bombings across Kabul and Helmand province, as the Taliban launched a coordinated series of attacks to destabilize the Afghan government and instill fear in the population. He could see the way the wind was blowing there and it was all bad.

Early evening, he ordered a club sandwich and a Coke from room service. Afterward, he went for a walk, keeping within six blocks of the hotel. He returned to his room, lay down on the bed, and fell into a fitful sleep.

When he woke, he checked the time. It was 8:09 p.m., and still Maddox hadn't called. Had there been a delay? Perhaps a last-minute change of plan?

The thought of delays depressed him. He'd been asked to do a job; he wanted to get it over with. Then move on. He couldn't abide the drawn-out ones.

Feeling groggy, Reznick headed down to reception, bought a pair of swimming shorts, and swam forty lengths of the empty pool, leaving his phone on his towel on top of a lounger.

He headed back upstairs and changed into a fresh T-shirt and jeans. He paced the room, stopping occasionally to do push-ups and sit-ups, trying to keep sharp, not knowing when the call would come—if it would come at any moment.

Eventually, he slumped in the room's easy chair and turned on an old black-and-white Jimmy Cagney film with the sound down.

His cell phone vibrated in the chest pocket of his T-shirt.

"You're on the move." The voice of Maddox.

"Where?"

"Go to the Park America garage, one three zero one K Street Northwest, and leave your car on Level Two."

Reznick made a mental note.

"Proceed to Level Five, where you'll find a black BMW convertible. Your key fob can electronically open it. Proceed to the St. Regis hotel, and book in under the name Lionel Fairchild. New ID and documents are in the glove compartment, and a brown Louis Vuitton travel bag with overnight essentials is in the trunk."

"What's in the bag?"

"The usual kit. Laptop, delivery equipment—it's all there. After you check in, head straight to your room, which has already been allocated, and await final instructions."

Reznick did exactly as he was told.

First, he checked out of the Omni, taking time to thank them for such a pleasant stay but he was sorry, he had to cut short his visit for family reasons. He picked up his car from the valet and drove to the nearby parking garage as instructed. He left the vehicle on Level 2 and climbed the stairs. A rather smart BMW with tinted windows was parked at the far end of Level 5. He popped open the trunk—the monogrammed men's travel bag was inside. He picked it up, got into the car, and clicked the fob to centrally lock the doors before he unzipped the bag.

Inside was a thirteen-inch metallic MacBook Pro, a specially modified cell phone, a pair of night-vision binoculars, a 9mm Beretta handgun and sufficient ammo to kill a small town, a high-tech fob that opened all cars and jammed any surveillance, a sleeping drug in a nasal spray, a military-issue Taser, a powerful muscle relaxant in a syringe disguised as a ballpoint pen, and five thousand dollars in cash.

Reznick zipped up the bag and slid it under the passenger seat. Then he drove straight to the deluxe hotel in downtown Washington to await final instructions.

Two

The St. Regis on 16th Street was known as one of Washington's smartest hotels. Two blocks north of the White House, its impressive limestone facade was festooned with Christmas lights, only hinting at the grandeur inside.

Reznick pulled up shortly after 10 p.m. and handed his keys over to the valet, careful to take the Louis Vuitton bag.

A concierge opened the door and he strode into the lobby. It was like some Italian Renaissance dream—chandeliers hanging from coffered ceilings, gilt-framed paintings, oriental rugs on the marble floor, dark wood furniture.

Reznick handed over the new fake driver's license and credit card to a young woman behind the desk. "Good evening," she said. "Nice to have you at the St. Regis, sir." She brought up his details on the computer. "Is this your first time with us?"

"Yeah."

"Well, we hope you enjoy your stay." She handed over a swipe card as a smiling, uniformed bellhop approached. "This is Andy. You need anything, don't hesitate to ask."

Reznick smiled and was escorted to the sixth floor by Andy, tipping him twenty dollars. "I'll get it from here."

"Are you sure, sir?"

"Absolutely."

The bellhop gave a polite nod and headed back to the elevator. Reznick waited until the guy was out of sight before he carefully swiped the keycard. Inside, the large room was decidedly upscale. A king-size bed, large flat-screen TV, an antique-style writing desk, chair and sofa, and a minibar stuffed with Krug and Rolling Rock beer. Original artwork on the walls and chandeliers set the scene. The bathroom featured brass fittings and earth-toned mosaic tiles, a large mirror that doubled as a fifteen-inch "intelligent" TV, two marble sinks, and a fluffy white St. Regis bathrobe hanging behind the door.

The first thing he did after looking around was hang a "Do Not Disturb" sign outside his room and lock the door. Satisfied he wasn't going to be interrupted, he unzipped the Louis Vuitton bag and placed the pre-configured MacBook on the desk. He opened it, and within a matter of seconds it was up and running.

Reznick sat down, punched in his allotted password—*coldbracelet1*—and brought up his inbox. A soft beep, and there was one encrypted message with an attachment.

He clicked on "Decrypt Message" to view the file and was prompted to confirm two unique passwords. He keyed in *OfwaihhbTn,* initials from the first line of the Lord's Prayer, followed by *DNalKcOr*, his hometown spelled backward. Then three personal questions: his grandmother on his father's side's maiden name—Levitz; his father's birthplace—Bangor; his blood group—Rh negative.

He typed in the answers and the email displayed on the screen. He clicked on the "Reply" button and the attachment was downloaded securely.

A two-page dossier and six black-and-white photos appeared before his eyes. The man he'd been sent to kill.

Reznick's stomach knotted as he scanned the screen. Tom Powell, aged fifty-nine, described as an "imminent security risk." Powell lived with his second wife and their two school-age children in a quiet cul-de-sac in Frederick, Maryland; his oldest son was away at university. According to the file, he had checked into the St. Regis the previous evening—room 674, three doors down. It didn't say exactly why he should be neutralized.

Reznick pondered on that. Usually when he did a hit, the reason was made quite clear. It could be spying, terrorism, or one of a whole host of threats to the country. Invariably, they had an explanation.

So why not now?

Reznick read on. The file said Powell had to be a "suicide." No other options.

This was the first time that Reznick had been asked to kill an American citizen on American soil. He knew that it would have been impossible if he were still a part of Delta Force because of the Posse Comitatus Act, which under federal law prohibited the military being used in operations within the United States. But he was no longer constrained.

In the past he'd taken out a Saudi military attaché in New York, a billionaire banker in London who was funding Hezbollah, a Russian spy in Vienna, a host of jihadists across the Middle East, and a smattering of Islamic fundamentalists living and working in America.

It was business. Realpolitik. The stone-cold reality of politics based on facts and material needs.

He studied the pictures of the man—including one of him playing football in a local park in Frederick with his eldest son, John, a law student at George Washington University. The son was a good-looking kid: clean-cut, short hair, preppy clothes.

He looked at the photos of Powell until he could remember the smallest details. The dime-sized mole on his left cheek, the graying sideburns, the bushy eyebrows, and the small scar above his right eyebrow caused, according to the file, by a schoolyard fight.

Reznick's training at "The Farm" in Virginia, all those years ago, had stressed the importance of knowing the subject inside out. This enabled an appropriate plan to be drawn up and executed.

Maddox and his team would have explored Powell's lifestyle and habits. His sleeping patterns and any health problems. The file noted that he was a keen golfer, not on prescription medication, and led a clean life—a glass or two of expensive French red wine at dinner on a Friday or Saturday evening was his only vice.

Reznick finished reading the dossier, shut down the computer, and waited for Maddox to call. The waiting was always the worst part of the job. Endless hours spent hanging around motels, hotels, safe houses, halfway houses, flophouses, apartments—a myriad of places—before the final phase.

The endgame.

Reznick was not the judge. Nor the jury. He was the executioner. Except he didn't sit in on the trial, because there was no trial. This was summary justice, as practiced by every government in the world. Sometimes the dirty work was subcontracted to a foreign intelligence agency or their associates. But this was in-house.

Just after midnight, Reznick's cell phone vibrated in his pocket. He switched on the TV, which was showing highlights of a Redskins game, to drown out his voice.

"Are you in place?" Maddox asked.

"Yes."

"This is a wet delivery. Do you understand?"

"Absolutely."

"OK, run-through time. Our guy is a creature of habit. He's in his room, fast asleep."

"How do you know?"

"GPS on his BlackBerry and a bug in his room's smoke detector. Hold back until five minutes *after* zero two hundred hours, when the video camera in the corridor will be remotely switched off until zero three hundred and the lights dimmed. You have a copy of his swipe card. Assume you have fifty-five minutes to make this delivery."

It was enough time.

"Do good," Maddox said.

"Count on it."

"Your room will be cleaned as soon as this delivery has been made. A maintenance uniform is hanging in your closet." A long pause elapsed. "Sit tight. Then it's just you and him."

With less than one hour to go, Reznick was sitting in his darkened hotel room, primed to carry out the delivery. He had changed into a pale blue, short-sleeved work shirt and black pants, gold wire-rimmed glasses, and shiny black shoes. There was a metallic nametag on his lapel—*Alex Goddard, Service Engineer*—and a bag at his feet. He pushed a tiny audio device into his right ear for communication; the nametag concealed a hidden microphone.

Everything in place. No diversions. No TV, radio, music, magazines, or newspapers to sidetrack him. The way he always worked during the crucial last hour.

The LCD display on his digital watch showed 01:21. *Not long now.*

Reznick's earpiece buzzed and he tensed up.

"Reznick, do you copy?" Maddox's voice was a whisper. "Reznick?"

"What?"

A small sigh. "OK, we have two room-service types—a guy and a woman—one dropping newspapers outside doors, the other pushing a trolley with food and drinks. They're in the elevator, and they're heading your way."

Reznick could hear his heart beating.

"OK," Maddox whispered, "now they're on the sixth."

On cue, the ding of the elevator doors opening and dull footsteps padding down the carpeted corridor. The faint tinkling of metal against glass, accompanied by a low male voice. Thuds as the papers were left outside each room. The sound of a door opening.

Three long minutes later, they were gone.

"OK, buddy, sorry about that. You all set?"

"How's our guy?"

"Sleeping like a baby. Slam dunk, Reznick. You've got a clear run."

The line went dead at 1:23 a.m.

When it hit 02:05, he peered out of the peephole. No movement or sound. He lay flat down on the floor and pressed his left ear—the one without the earpiece—to the carpet, listening for elevator vibrations, footsteps, sudden noises . . . anything.

He heard the faint sound of water pipes creaking. Perhaps the merest hint of laughter somewhere below.

Apart from that, all quiet.

Reznick got up and stood, picking up the bag. He took half a dozen slow, deep breaths.

Just breathe.

His breathing even, he was ready.

Slowly he turned the handle, stuck his head out of the door, and peered down the dimly lit hallway.

Not a soul.

Slow is smooth, smooth is fast.

The military dictum of the Marines kicked in. It meant moving fast or rushing in was reckless, and could get you killed. If you move slowly, you are less likely to put yourself at risk.

He edged out and closed the door as softly as he could. The metallic locking system sounded to him like a rifle reloading.

Reznick looked around and took the short walk to Powell's door. Carefully, he swiped the card, the metallic clicking noticeably softer. He cracked the door. The sound of deep snoring.

He kept the door ajar for a few moments as his eyes adjusted to the semi-darkness. The room smelled of stale sweat and old shoes. Underneath the window, the crumpled silhouette of the man lying in bed, facing the wall, duvet on. Reznick shut the door softly, and it barely made a noise as it clicked into place.

He crept toward the sleeping man. Closer and closer, careful not to trip on any objects lying around.

Standing over him, Reznick saw the dime-sized mole on his left cheek. Suddenly the man groaned and turned over onto his back. The springs of the bed creaked.

Reznick froze, not daring to breathe. A deep silence opened up for a few moments as he wondered if the man was really awake. He stood still and waited.

One beat. Two beats. Three beats.

Eventually, on the fourth beat, the snoring continued as before, rhythmic and deep. Reznick exhaled slowly. Then he reached into his pants pocket and pulled out a lipstick-sized Taser. He leaned over and pressed the metal device hard against the man's temple. Electric currents provoked convulsions for three long seconds. Powell's eyes rolled back in his head. The sound of gurgling and groaning. Then nothing.

Unconscious.

A standard first-step procedure. Eight minutes, maybe ten, before the man came to.

Reznick rummaged in the bag and produced the auto-injecting syringe disguised as a ballpoint pen, containing succinylcholine chloride, which he knew as "Sux." The drug was a skeletal-muscle relaxant used as an adjunct to surgical anesthesia and had been employed as a paralyzing agent for executions by lethal injection. A twist of the nib and a quick stab into the man's skin would deliver seven milligrams of the drug. But only five milligrams was necessary for death.

The victim would be paralyzed within thirty seconds. The muscles, including the diaphragm, would shut down, with the exception of the heart. He would be unable to speak or move, although his brain would still be working. Then he had three minutes until his breathing ceased, unable to scream out for help.

The beauty of the drug for assassinations was that enzymes in the body begin to break down the drug almost immediately, making it virtually impossible to detect.

Powell was to be injected in the buttocks, as—in the absence of evidence of foul play—most medical examiners would suspect a heart attack as the natural cause of death.

Reznick pulled back the duvet and switched on his penlight, examining the paunchy, unconscious man lying before him. He wore pale blue pajamas with a white tank top underneath. He had on a cheap watch with a frayed, brown leather strap. The last moments in his life, and the poor bastard didn't know anything about it. Reznick never usually felt anything when he had to kill a foreign terrorist or one of the billionaires who bankrolled them. But in this case it did feel strange, knowing that this was an American.

The penlight picked out something around the man's neck, tucked inside his tank. Reznick looked closer, and thought it looked like an aluminum dog tag. He held it in his hand, turned it over, and saw an inscription in Hebrew—the name Benjamin Luntz—and a seven-digit identification number.

Israeli Defense Forces.

He stared at the dog tag for a few moments.

Why the fuck had Tom Powell got the dog tag of an Israeli soldier around his neck? It didn't make any sense.

The doubts began to set in. He needed certainty.

He had to wait more than eight minutes before Powell came to with a low groan. Reznick pressed the Beretta to the guy's forehead. Powell gazed up, confused and scared.

"Shut up and listen," Reznick snarled, hand covering his mouth.

The man nodded.

"Any sound, and you die. Got it?"

He nodded again.

Reznick removed his hand. "All right," he said in a low voice. "Gimme your name, and date and place of birth. Right now."

The man gulped hard. "Please, take whatever you want."

Reznick pressed the gun tighter to his skin, making a small indentation as the guy began to tremble. "This is the second time I'll ask. I don't ask a third time. Now, give me your name, date and place of birth. Failure to comply will result in the maids cleaning your brains off this wall in six hours' time. Got it?"

"My name is Frank Luntz, born New York City, October twelve, 1953."

Reznick's mind went into free fall for a split second. The target's name was Powell. Something was badly wrong.

"Tell me about the dog tag around your neck."

"It's my son's."

"What's his name?"

"Benjamin Luntz."

Reznick wondered whether to believe the man or not. Something wasn't adding up. Was he being played?

"Are you Israeli?"

"No. My son emigrated. He had joint citizenship."

"What do you mean *had*?"

"He was . . . he was blown up by a suicide bomber at a checkpoint in the West Bank three years ago."

The man made a sudden movement and Reznick pushed him back down into the pillow. "Don't even think about it."

"I want to prove it to you."

He reached under his pillow and pulled out a silver photo pendant. A faded color picture of a young man in combat fatigues, rifle slung over his shoulder, sitting atop a Merkava tank.

The man pointed to the bedside cabinet. "The top drawer. Check my wallet if you don't believe me."

Reznick reached over and opened the top drawer. Empty. No driver's license or credit cards to establish the man's true identity. "There's nothing there, you lying bastard."

"That's impossible. Perhaps Connelly has it next door."

Reznick was tempted to kill the fucker there and then. "Who's Connelly?"

The man began to cry.

"Answer me. Who's Connelly?"

"He's a Fed. He's in the adjoining room. He's looking after me."

Reznick's stomach knotted. "What the hell are you talking about?"

"He has the adjoining room to this." The guy pointed a shaking finger in the direction of a door next to the dresser.

"Are you lying to me—because if you are, you die, here and now."

He began sobbing. Reznick placed a huge hand over his mouth to muffle the sound.

"One more peep out of you and I'll rip out your wiring. Do you understand?"

The man nodded, tears spilling down his cheeks.

"Hands on your head."

He complied. Reznick pulled a sock out of the dresser and stuffed it into his mouth, before tearing up strips of the bedsheet and tying it around his head to secure the sock. Then he tied the man's wrists and ankles to the four corners of the wooden bed, crucifixion style.

Reznick shone the penlight directly into his eyes. "Don't even think about fucking moving."

He nodded quickly. Reznick walked across to the door and pressed his ear up against it, listening for several seconds for any sounds. Creaks. Groans. But he heard nothing.

Slowly, he turned the handle and opened the door. His eyes scanned the room. The bed was made, the wooden blinds and curtains shut, as if awaiting the next hotel guest. Perfect order. Empty.

Or so it seemed. The hint of sandalwood in the air told another story. The room had been occupied.

Reznick sensed something was wrong. He shone the penlight toward the bathroom and opened the door. Opulent white marble sinks, bath, and floor. White towels neatly stacked on a metal rack above the bath. A slight smell of damp pervaded the air, as if from a recent shower.

Again, that didn't add up to an unoccupied room.

Reznick went back into the bedroom as the penlight raked the high-quality carpet beside the huge closet. His gaze wandered around the room, past a small flaxen sofa, until he fixed on a white louver door. He saw it wasn't shut properly. Perhaps half an inch ajar.

He moved closer. Kneeling down, he shone the light through the slatted openings. Inside, he saw what looked like tousled blond hair.

He held his breath. Then he reached out and felt the wooden handle, before yanking open the door.

Reznick's heart jolted as the penlight picked out the crumpled, semi-naked body of a blond-haired man. Telltale purple bruises around the neck and throat, hemorrhaging around the dead eyes. Reznick had seen this sort of thing before. Many times. The man had been manually strangled.

This was so fucked up it wasn't real.

His mind was racing when he returned to the first room. He leaned down beside the man strapped and gagged to the bed. The guy stared up at Reznick like a terrified child, afraid of his fate.

Reznick untied the strips of bedsheet around the man's mouth and pulled out the sock. Then he pressed his face right up against the other man's, smelling the sweat and fear. "Who the fuck are you?"

"I already told you."

"Why do people want you dead? Who do you work for?"

"I work for the government. Look, please tell me who you are. What've you done to Connelly?"

"Forget about him. Forget about me. What about you? What exactly do you do?"

"I told you, I work for the government."

"Doing what?"

The man closed his eyes and shook his head.

"Answer me."

"I'm a government scientist."

Reznick stuffed the sock back into the guy's mouth. He walked over to the window and buzzed Maddox on his lapel microphone, giving him the lowdown. The discovery of the murdered man's body—perhaps a Fed—and the possibility that they had the wrong guy.

Maddox listened in silence before he said, "Gimme two minutes and I'll get back to you."

In less than a minute, the earpiece buzzed into life.

"The subject is to be protected and brought in. Make your way with the subject to a motel, the Clarence Suites, six blocks away on N Street Northwest, due northeast, and sit tight. Room seven eight seven. You're booked in under Ronald D Withers. He's your brother, Simon Withers. Clear?"

"Then what?"

"We're sending two of our guys, Bowman and Price. They'll take him off your hands."

About the Author

Photo © Robbie Bald 2024

J. B. Turner is a former journalist and the author of the Jon Reznick series of political thrillers (*Hard Road, Hard Kill, Hard Wired, Hard Way, Hard Fall, Hard Hit, Hard Shot, Hard Target, Hard Vengeance, Hard Fire, Hard Exit, Hard Power, Hard Duty, Hard Lights*, and *Hard Sun*), the American Ghost series of black-ops thrillers (*Rogue, Reckoning, and Requiem*), the Jack McNeal Thriller series (*No Way Back and Long Way Home*), and the Deborah Jones crime thrillers (*Miami Requiem and Dark Waters*). He has a keen interest in geopolitics. He lives in Edinburgh, Scotland, with his wife and two sons.

Follow the Author on Amazon

If you enjoyed this book, follow J. B. Turner on Amazon to be notified when the author releases a new book!
To do this, please follow these instructions:

Desktop:

1) Search for the author's name on Amazon or in the Amazon App.
2) Click on the author's name to arrive on their Amazon page.
3) Click the 'Follow' button.

Mobile and Tablet:

1) Search for the author's name on Amazon or in the Amazon App.
2) Click on one of the author's books.
3) Click on the author's name to arrive on their Amazon page.
4) Click the "Follow" button.

Kindle eReader and Kindle App:

If you enjoyed this book on a Kindle eReader or in the Kindle App, you will find the author 'Follow' button after the last page.